I0565316

The Black Bull

By

H. Bedford-Jones

G. P. Putnam's Sons
New York — London
The Knickerbocker Press
1927

Copyright, 1927
by
H. Bedford-Jones

Made in the United States of America

CONTENTS

CHAPTER   PAGE

I.—QUEEN, SOLDIER, SCULLION . . . 3

II.—TWO MEN CAN BECOME THREE . . 31

III.—THREE CAN BECOME ONE . . . 57

IV.—FINDING IS NOT KEEPING . . . 81

V.—ONE VOICE IN A TREE, ANOTHER IN A
      FOG 104

VI.—FOG CANNOT HINDER A RESURRECTION 127

VII.—CERTAIN CONVERSATIONS . . . 148

VIII.—ARAB, QUEEN AND CARNIVAL . . 168

IX.—ONE CITY—TWO DUKES . . . 190

X.—SMALL MEN PROPOSE, GREAT MEN DIS-
      POSE 210

XI.—THE ROAD TO CORTHIA 233

CONTENTS

CHAPTER   PAGE

XII.—How the Black Bull Was Taken . 253

XIII.—Modena Sends to Corthia . . . 274

XIV.—A Red Feast in Corthia . . . 295

XV.—Fair Exchange No Robbery . . 314

XVI.—Some Men Cannot Be Killed . . 330

XVII.—The Gate of Lucca 340

THE BLACK BULL

THE BLACK BULL

CHAPTER I

QUEEN, SOLDIER, SCULLION

A COACH, headed for Pisa, had broken down at the very fork of the highway. A signboard showed that the other road, less traveled, left the post-road here for Corthia, a league distant, hidden by hills between. The traveler who came riding along on the magnificent white Arab was apparently headed for Pisa likewise.

As he came, he saw this was no simple breakdown. One of the coach-horses had been shot. One of the two mounted cavaliers was having an arm bandaged, and the other was holding a damaged head in both hands. The postilions and a man who seemed to be a valet were busy, and were being lustily cursed for cowards by the owner of the coach —a woman who held the hilt of a broken sword in

3

her hand. She was the only one of the party who knew what she was about; her oaths, in half a dozen different languages, would have astounded anyone ignorant that she had learned them from her father, Gustavus Adolphus. They fairly made the air smoke, on this crisp day of early February, in the year 1658.

The traveler reined in the white Arab to listen appreciatively. He saw the woman was dressed more as man than woman; her features were powerful, masculine, domineering. Suddenly she observed the glances of her men, whirled, saw the traveler, and flung away her swordhilt. She strode directly at him, her heavy-lidded eyes fastened on him in amazement.

"Ten thousand devils—what a horse!" she exclaimed. "Alone? Where from!"

The traveler uncovered. "Vienna, madame. Can I be of service to you?"

"Yes, if you'll catch that damned blackmailer who has robbed me, and put your sword through him!" she returned explosively. The valet came hurrying up.

"Your Majesty, Your Majesty," he panted. "Be careful—"

4

"Go to the devil, fool," she retorted and slapped his mouth and sent him reeling. "Oh, to be cursed with fools for servants!"

"Ah! You should have a king for a servant, Your Majesty," said the traveler, smiling a little. "All Irishmen are kings in their own right—"

"You jest with me?" she snapped angrily. "I am Christina of Sweden, fool!"

The traveler bowed in his saddle. He had heard of Queen Christina—all Europe had heard of her great learning, her mad escapades, her wild journeys between Rome and the Sweden whose crown she had given up, and Paris. In this year of 1658 it was rumored she was to marry the exiled Charles II of England. No one knew what she might do next.

"I am Brian O'Neill, Colonel of Dragoons, Count of Albujaras in Spain," he said quietly. "My offer holds good. Tell me who this robber is who has robbed you—"

She flung a hand toward the Corthian road.

"Raymond of Corthia, blast him!" she exploded. "So-called duke, actual blackmailer of better folk, thief, robber! Go put your sword through him, then come to me in Rome and ask what reward

5

you wish—and bring with you the ebony casket he took from me!"

The traveler stared down at her for a long moment.

"Raymond of Corthia!" he said, and drew a deep breath. At the sudden icy change in his eyes, the woman stepped back a pace. Then he laughed, quite without mirth, and bowed again. "Very well, Your Majesty. I'll bring you the ebony cabinet."

And without further words he turned the white Arab and headed down the hill road to Corthia. Her mouth open, Queen Christina of Sweden stared after him, a quick warm glow in her face—then turned and strode back to her men with another storm of curses.

"A queer meeting!" thought O'Neill as he rode, and glanced at the sun. It was barely past noon. "So I just missed running into Raymond himself, eh? Yet the signal was out that the way was clear— and there are no fresh hoof-prints in the road, so he must have gone back to Corthia by some other way. If this Carbajal still has the shirt in the window, well and good; if not, I'd best watch myself! For all I know, the whole affair may be a trap. So that was the mad Queen of Sweden, eh?

At least, she can curse better than my own troopers
—"

Riding on, he came presently to a rather sharp descent along a hillside above a brook. At the bottom, lying so close against the hillside as to be part of it, was the Black Bull tavern. Corthia itself was over the next ridge, half a league distant. At the top of the hill the traveler dismounted, left the white stallion, and went ahead on foot for cautious sight of the building below. Then, from the roadside, he studied it, not for the first time.

Once the Black Bull had been a castle, but this was in the dim ages; nothing of the castle remained but the lower part, a massive thing of gray stone running along the hillside by the road, merging into the hill itself. Two stories in height, square and abrupt, the side toward O'Neill ended in a walled courtyard apparently carved out of the hillside, from which a great oak sprouted up with wide arms; the back of this courtyard was a stone retaining wall. The whole place looked grim, had an indefinite air of menace, of dark and deep secrets, of harsh defiance.

O'Neill saw a white shirt in an upper window, as he had seen it that same morning from his watch-

ing place on the opposite hillside. He had gone for
his horse, and was now come again. The time was
ripe—unless a trap had been set for him. And he
could see no sign of any trap.

"Must risk it," he thought. "After all, the letter
from Carbajal seemed honest; and I've waited too
long for his signal to hold back now. No more
sitting out on the hillside watching!"

He worked back to his horse, mounted, and rode
down to the inn, and turned into the courtyard
whose rear wall was the mountain-flank itself. Here
was other business awaiting him than a search for
ebony caskets! At thought of Christina, he smiled
to himself, then put away all but what lay to his
hand, and smiled no more. He called, and none
answered, so he led the Arab toward the stables
on the left of the court. He had just put up the
horse when the inn-keeper appeared. This was a
heavy, rubicund fellow, aproned and yawning as
though wakened from slumber.

"All away, signor!" he fumbled out apologies to
O'Neill. "A fiesta in the city—these lazy rogues
of servants are no good, I can tell you! Not like
twenty years ago—will your excellency enter?
Wine and a capon, perhaps—"

8

QUEEN, SOLDIER, SCULLION

No trap after all, then, reflected O'Neill, and touched the pistols in his sash.

"Enter?" he said. "That's what I'm here for. Brrh! It's a crisp day. A stoup of wine, some cheese, and fresh bread if you have it. A fire?"

"There in the hearth, nobilissimo," and the red-faced host bowed him into the great single lower room of the inn, where a log smoked in the twelve-foot fireplace.

As he entered, the traveler changed color, glanced around, seemed to hesitate. Then he went on to a chair and table near the wide hearth, threw back his cloak, and settled down. The host brought him bread and cheese and wine, and he tried to eat, but could down little of it; the food choked him, knowing what had passed in this place. At length he shoved it away and gulped the wine, which was good enough.

"You come from Avignon, signor?" asked the rubicund host, with that air of jovial negligence which had deceived so many unfortunate men. He stood in his niche behind a counter, where wine-kegs were on tap.

"Not at all," said the tall traveler. He leaned back in his chair, looking about the ancient place with keen interest, and his gaze came to rest upon the inn-keeper with a certain singular fixity. "I am from Vienna."

"So? A long journey this winter weather—it's been a cold January," observed the other. Unobtrusively, he cocked the pistolet close to his hand, scraping his foot across the sanded floor to hide the click. "I see you must be a courier; that white stallion's an Arab, by head and saddle."

The traveler set down the tankard and wiped his yellow mustache.

"True, host. You might set his muzzle in that pint pot—true sign of Arab blood! Yet he can course at top speed hour after hour. A fine horse."

"Aye, fine," said the other. "No, you're no courier, excellency! A soldier?"

"Perhaps. You've a great place, here."

The alert, piercing eyes of the traveler swept about the inn-room, missing nothing. They were steely gray eyes, obviously used to commanding others. His cloak and heavy broadcloth garments were also of gray and trimmed with gray fur, as were his heavy riding-boots. From gray hat to boots his clothes had an air of newness; the set of his shoulders and head indicated he had been more at home in uniform.

"Oh, a neat enough place," said the host. "So you're a soldier, eh? Should have a sword in your belt. You're for Corthia?"

The traveler showed white teeth under his mustache.

"For a certain part of Corthia, you fat rogue," he said, yet in the whimsical epithet lay a driving earnestness, drawing the quick eyes of the host. "The English and French are at the end of the Spanish war. Cromwell has more power than any king, and more curses to boot. I'm no longer a soldier but a pilgrim—so there's my news for you. You'll not live long enough to care about it."

The other stared at him, and evidently thought him rambling.

"England? England's a name, Corthia's a city."

O'Neill laughed, yet there was no merriment in his eyes.

"A name? Well, Ireland's a name, too, but some Irishmen have gone far. Come, my good host, my honest host of the Black Bull, you'd like to know who I am?"

The host caught the undertone of menace. "Not I, excellency!"

"You lie," said the traveler coolly. "Ah, you

murderous rogue, I'll quench your curiosity and fatten it all at once! I'm no excellency, but a king, an earl, a count, a poor devil of a wanderer, a queen's messenger! Being a king, however, I always keep my word. I intend to kill you within a very few minutes, and as I have money, you can't buy me off with the fifty thousand gold crowns buried under your hearth yonder."

A pistol jumped from his belt, and with it, the speaker indicated the twelve-foot fireplace to one side. He then primed and cocked the pistol, put away his powder-flask, and left the weapon balanced with nicety against the high rim of his pewter plate.

At this significant action, at these astonishing words, delivered with absolute sangfroid and deliberation, the innkeeper stared blankly. A slow pallor grew in his heavy red countenance. Finding the traveler absorbed in the wine and once more indifferent to him, his gaze lifted and slipped furtively along the walls of massive stone, toward the arch enclosing the kitchen door. It passed on out to the white sunlit courtyard, whose old worn cobbles had felt the tread of popes and emperors, where Charlemagne had laid a stone in mortar with his own hand. The stone was still in the massive retaining wall against the hillside, just past the widespreading oak, with a cross chiseled in it to show the royal touch.

The stone was there, the courtyard and kitchen were there, the huge smoked walls and their ancient secrets; but no help was anywhere today. The fat host glanced again at this ominous stranger, who seemed to know all things, and crossed himself. The traveler looked at him and smiled.

"No, my murderous host, I'm not the devil in person—surely the devil does not go to Rome! You wonder how I knew of your secrets? Well, come out of that niche, where your pistol will avail you nothing, and I'll tell you. Too late now to send to Corthia, nor any use! So come out. I've a message for you from a dead man."

At these further proofs of omiscience, the rubicund host trembled, and a mortal fear came upon him; not without reason, since those cold gray eyes held a deadly intention. He slid out from his shelter and plumped down upon his knees.

"Monsiegneur, do not harm me, upon whom depends a large family—"

"Consisting of a wench or two in Corthia," said

13

the traveler, "and lean Friar Dominic. Well, I hope to kill that false friar soon, so talk not of your family."

"But, nobilissimo, we are strangers!" wailed the host, clasping his hands before his breast and crying out most piteously. "I haven't harmed you— there's no reason to speak ill of me, or to talk of killing."

"I'm going to tell you the reason. Stay as you are; it's an excellent posture for death!"

The traveler pushed away his wine-flagon, drew forth a pipe and a box of tobacco, and stuffed the pipe carefully. He was unhurried, quite careless and negligent in air. The ruddy host, watching with alert and waiting gaze, kept his clasped hands at his bosom.

"The reason," and O'Neill puffed his pipe alight when he had obtained spark and fire, "is not ancient, but it is sufficient. Perhaps you recall a young boy, a girl, and an old soldier with one ear who stopped here late at night, some few weeks ago? The girl was notable because of her beauty; the boy, because of his proud eyes and a certain sword he carried; the man, because of his fidelity. You recall them?"

"Ah, excellency, how well I remember them,

paragons of beauty!" exclaimed the host. "Before she departed in the morning, the maid blessed me sweetly, and the boy gave me a crucifix he had brought from Spain, and the old soldier gave me a strange coin with a hole in it. He said it carried the power of curing all pain in the legs, having been so endowed by the blessed Saint Patricio."

At these words, the face of O'Neill became very pale and cold, his gray eyes icy.

"Have you still this coin?" he asked in a low voice.

"Would I part with so holy a relic? In my pocket, excellency, this very instant!"

Hurriedly, eagerly, the host fumbled through jerkin and doublet, and produced a large coin. He inched forward on his knees, but the traveler put hand to pistol.

"Back! Toss the coin on the floor in front of me."

The host threw the coin, a pierced copper token, out on the stones. It fell so that the worn man's face upon it lay upward. O'Neill leaned forward.

"Ah! You did not know this coined face had been given the power of speech? Well, it is so—I'll prove it. Here, you there upon the floor, you copper image of King Brian of Ireland, I call upon you to speak! Did your owner, the old soldier named Teague, depart from this place alive and sound?"

The inn-keeper stared from traveler to coin, jaw fallen—then he started violently and sweat came out on his ruddy face, and his eyes were distended. For a voice came from the coin on the floor, a thin and distorted little voice like the voice of a fairy.

"He did not!"

"If you know who I am, speak my name," said the traveler, puffing away at his pipe.

"You are called Brian Buidh, or Yellow Brian in Italian."

"But my name!"

"O'Neill," said the coin. "Born in Spain of John O'Neill, Earl of Tyrown, The O'Neill!"

At all this, great terror had seized upon the inn-keeper; his wide eyes were horrible to see, and the sweat trickled down his heavy jowl. Yet the traveler remained calm as though the scene were unimportant, and now asked another question.

"Who were these three people, here at the Black Bull?"

"One was your old and faithful servant," said the

little thin voice of the coin. "One was a distant cousin. One was your younger brother Hugh."

"And what happened to them?"

"Ah, stop, stop!" The host found voice, and cried out in agonized utterance. "Highness, excellency, this is magic—sorcery, rank sorcery! I cannot listen to it!'

"You have only a short while to listen to it, or to anything," said O'Neill, and his hand fell on his pistol. "Speak, coin! What happened to these three?"

"Two men slew my owner, Teague," said the coin. "One of them was this fat host, who thrust a knife under his arm from behind. The boy was wakened from sleep and was slain in fair fight by Raymond, who wanted the sword of him and took it so. The girl was drugged and was sold into the bagnios of Rome. Ask me no more, Yellow Brian."

Now there fell long silence, the calm and unhurried eyes of O'Neill watching the host. This rubicund man, perceiving death close beside him with hand outstretched, began to tremble violently and to babble empty mouthings. He was so utterly terrified by the revelations of the copper coin that he could not even attempt denials.

"I have heard of this tavern," said the traveler

reflectively. "It is a strange and dreadful place, with every stone bloodstained. You are the host, yet the tavern is not yours nor are its secrets yours. You merely serve—"

"Corthia!" broke out the host. "You forget, Highness, you forget Corthia!"

"Corthia!" O'Neill's voice was rich, deep, musing. "My honest murderer, I am going to Corthia on a queen's errand. There is much talk of Corthia in the world; however, all this talk is wasted upon you, since you are no grammarian. Of, to and from Corthia means very little to you, and soon will mean even less—"

The host was no grammarian, true, but he was a keen and alert scoundrel. He perceived that O'Neill was preoccupied with his discourse, and was busily tamping the tobacco into his pipe. His own hand being at his neck, he seized the instant of opportunity, flicked out the knife from under his jerkin, threw it swiftly and accurately.

The throw was excellent, quick as light, quite beyond any parry or evasion. The point of the razor-keen stiletto drove under the arm of O'Neill and struck squarely over the heart—struck, hung in the fold of gray broadcloth, dangled there limply.

QUEEN, SOLDIER, SCULLION

The dumbfounded host stared all amaze, his jaw fallen, his very brain reeling at this inability of cold steel to pierce hot flesh. O'Neill smiled and lifted his pistol.

"Well and handily done—but you forget that a wise traveler wears a mailcoat when he comes to the Black Bull."

The kneeling man stared up, saw the cocked pistol, saw a cold and merciless light in the gray eyes above it. His face became a horrible ghastly gray, and he cried out sharply.

"No, no—stop! Wait—you must not—it is murder—"

"What of the boy you slew, the old man you murdered, the girl you sold? Too late now to cry halt—"

Panic seized upon the host, a mad access of terror. Wild frenzy shook him as he knelt and stared at O'Neill from bulging eyes. The hammer fell, the flint sparked; to the flash and roar of the pistol, to the billowing white plumes of powder-smoke curling along the rafters, to the reverberating echo dying upon the muffling stone walls, the inn-keeper rocked upon his knees and put one hand to his breast. Foam broke upon his lips, red foam.

"Death!" he cried, but less sharply this time. "Death—Rome—ride Romeward—" He paused, flung out one hand, shook it at O'Neill; his eyes were bright and large, distended abnormally. "Rome— a queen awaits you—the fate of Rome—in your hands—fool, fool, fool to slay me—fate of Rome— Here, not there—here—the Black Bull—"

The man fell forward upon his hands and lay there, rubicund no more, in the attitude of a man at prayer. But he was not at prayer.

Silence settled anew upon the room. The traveler laid down his pistol, sucked at his pipe, stared frowningly at the outstretched figure before him.

"Queer!" he muttered. "The rascal was fey in the grip of death—I've seen others that way. What did he say about a queen, about the fate of Rome? Babblings!"

His pipe sucked empty. He thrust it into a pocket, produced a short rod and cleaned his pistol, then reloaded it and stuck it into his sash-holder again. He leaned over and picked the coin from the floor, and remained staring at it with haunted eyes, a long while. Mournful words came to his lips.

"Teague's luck-penny—ah, Teague, faithful old

friend! They got you in the back, or there'd have been more dead men here than you. And Hugh, poor golden-haired Hugh, to be murdered when life was just opening before him—the high blood of the O'Neills to be strewn on the cobbles of a mountain inn! And Mary, sweet little rose, sold into hell—"

His voice died, and tears sparkled out upon his brown cheeks. Then, suddenly, he lifted his face, put the coin in his pocket, and turned, as a thinly mocking voice came to him.

"There are just so many kings in the world— which of them, then, are you?"

The kitchen door, under the high stone arch, stood ajar. O'Neill nodded.

"Every Irishman is a king by descent," he said. "So here's the unknown Carbajal, eh? Come out and show yourself, my letter-writer, and bring more of this excellent wine."

The door under the arch opened more widely. Into the huge main room of the Black Bull emerged a slender figure, with the dull clank of iron fetters. Carbajal approached the table, bearing a wicker-covered flagon, and halted to deliver a kick at the body of the host.

"Ill done," said the traveler. "A true dog does not spurn a dead lion."

"Bah! The lion spurns the dead dog."

"Well said!" O'Neill smiled, poured himself wine, and drank. The two men looked at each other deliberately, slowly, appraisingly.

This scullion whose letter had called O'Neill hither, was a man of medium stature with seamed features, clad in sooty rags. He wore about his ankles iron fetters with a chain between, so that his walk was hampered. The right eye was clean gone from the face, leaving a red and repulsive socket; the remaining eye was livid blue, a stark and blazing dot of color against a bitterly sardonic background. His left hand stuck out awkwardly, showing how the arm had been broken and ill-set or untended. This Carbajal had suffered. Yet, for all his maimed and fettered and half-blind state, for all his rags and unkempt long hair and unwashen body, a spark of vital energy leaped and flamed in the man.

"It was you who wrote me that letter?" asked the traveler.

"As the girl bade me," said Carbajal. "She told where to send it and gave me gold. With the gold

I bribed a road-mender to send the letter—they do not watch me so closely of late. Lucky you did not come yesterday; many men were here."

"I've been on the hillsides for two days, awaiting your signal," said O'Neill. "I saw it today, went back and got my horse, and came. It was well done, Carbajal."

"Aye, a great deed!" jeered the other sourly. "Your brother dead, your servant dead, your cousin gone to Roman bagnios—and you sit drinking wine! When I signaled the coast was clear, any fool could walk in here and pistol this jackal. Well done indeed! You take it calmly enough."

The traveler regarded him impassively. "Why lash the stallion because the mare is stolen?"

"Philosopher! What do you mean to do?"

"First of all comes the girl."

"Then you must go to Rome, on a useless quest."

"I'll return to Corthia."

"Bah!" spat Carbajal. "No one man can overcome Raymond—he's not one man, but a hundred men! He goes everywhere, is everything, knows all things. Blackmailer! He holds half the northern families of Italy in his grip, and the other half fear him. A Medici himself, he bit Tuscany in the

side until the fat bull in Florence bellowed and
paid his price. And you—save the mark! I know
about you, for the girl told me. You are an earl
without an earldom, a man without a country, a
man who sells his sword, a wanderer on the face of
earth without family, friends or followers."

"Such a man may prove dangerous," said O'Neill,
and smiled a little. "And who are you? You
wrote of what had happened here, said to come;
I am here. Who are you?"

"Raymond's slave." Carbajal laughed, showing
white strong teeth. "Do you know who this Raymond is, this Raymond of Corthia? No. He is
one man here, another—"

"I'm asking who you are."

"Bah! A galley slave, become a scullion."

"Then come to Rome with me. Who are you?"

"Your servant."

"Nay, my friend!"

"Agreed. We're comrades." Carbajal showed
his teeth in a snarl. He was not a nice man to
look upon, but there was granite in him, bitter
granite too. "Hm! You're no small man, and we
shall get on together. That remains to be seen."

"You trust no one?"

"Trusting lost me much. Lack of trust never lost me anything."

"Acid tongue and iron heart, my Carbajal." O'Neill rose, stretched his long arms. "Well, get hammer and chisel and we'll rid you of these fetters and take the money from under the hearth, which you mentioned. It'll come in useful."

"Wait—more than money here, comrade." Carbajal eyed him a moment. "Raymond, so-called Duke of Corthia, rules the Black Bull. Stay about here and probe into his secrets; they'll repay probing. I can promise you."

"I've business in Rome," said O'Neill coldly.

"Bah! You can't help the girl now; she's changed hands a dozen times, done for long ere this. And you heard what this inn-keeper said as death was on him? There was second sight in it, but also knowledge. Raymond was drunk yesterday and talking. These rooms go in under the hill, to caverns—secrets are there, comrade! Politics. No use gallivanting over the roads—"

"I go to Rome. Do you come or not?"

"Hm! Raymond goes also—he said so. If you want vengeance, stay here and it'll be ripe to your hand. He had prisoners in Corthia; they'll be brought here later—men like me, but more useful to him, hence more fortunate. Your vengeance waits here, I tell you."

O'Neill dismissed it all with a wave of his hand. The passion for vengeance was hot within him, he wanted the old sword again for which Raymond had killed his brother, he had a mad longing to root out this place to the last stone; but more than all, the fate of Mary O'Neill burned at his very heart and soul, a consuming flame. Until he had found her, for well or ill, he meant to step cunningly, preserve himself against all hazard, and hold all other desires in check.

"Wait here," urged Carbajal, his one eye gleaming feverishly, "and the course of history itself—"

"Devil take history! Go for a chisel—I ride Romeward."

With a shrug Carbajal was gone, presently returning with tools. He perched on the table and O'Neill fell to work at the fetters. From the many old scars he found upon his legs and thighs, tokens of gyves and torturings, he knew Carbajal had suffered deeply. At last the task was done, and O'Neill reached for the wine.

"You're a deft man," said Carbajal, rubbing his ankles.

"Adversity teaches."

"I warn you again—we must go through Corthia and must see Raymond—all travelers of birth come before him or await his return if he's gone. He's no real duke, but some day he'll be more than duke, I think."

"No matter. Get the money and let's be moving."

Carbajal fell to work, asking no aid. O'Neill watched him get the heavy hearth-stone lifted and upheld by a stake at one end, but was not thinking of treasure; his thoughts lay with the road ahead and behind. Raymond must never guess his identity, if he wanted to win through to Rome. Then he remembered the Queen of Sweden, and laughed suddenly—he had found the ruse he sought, the cloak he needed to mask his real self and his errand.

From beneath the stone Carbajal produced two heavy bags. One he kept, the other he handed O'Neill, who ripped it open and filled his pockets with the golden coins.

"Be getting your horse," said Carbajal. "I'll find clothes, get ready, and join you in the courtyard."

He was as good as his word. Out in the huge

courtyard O'Neill was still saddling his white Arab, when the scullion appeared. Now he wore a flapping, wide-brimmed pilgrim's hat, and rusty black garments; over his lost eye was a huge black patch, his hair was raggedly chopped away, and he had scraped some of the stubble from his lean cheeks. He led a mule from the stables, to saddle for himself.

"We're pilgrims together," he said, and grinned. "Men will die of this pilgrimage!"

"I hope so," said O'Neill, watching him. "In your letter, you mentioned a false friar. Didn't he help Mary?"

"The girl? As wolf helps lamb. Friar Dominic cajoled her with promises of help, gave her a drug to drink, and handed her over to a trader. Raymond wanted her gone, for he did the whole work in order to get that sword. The girl's in a cardinal's palace by this time."

O'Neill bit at his lip. "I must see this Friar Dominic," he said.

"You will, never fear. Now hearken!" Carbajal gestured in quick appeal. "Once more—consider! I warn you there's big work ahead here. If you want vengeance, the best way is to remain close by— we can strike a hard blow—"

28

"No," O'Neill shook his head, wondering at the man's persistence. "I've taken up the trail here, and freed you; my first work is to find the girl, do what I can for her, and then work back along the road, taking vengeance on the way."

"Has this affair turned your heart and soul into stone?" demanded Carbajal.

"It's done worse," and O'Neill laughed bitterly.

"Hm! Well, you can't help the girl now! be a philosopher, comrade! If we stay here, we'd have a hand in Rome's fate, I tell you. Raymond plans great things! I'm none too certain of his schemes, but I know what's inside there," and Carbajal's hand motioned toward the hillside. "If I breathed what I know in Rome, they'd call me a madman. Stay here, if you want to wreak vengeance on Raymond."

"I want to find that girl—nothing else now," said O'Neill, eyeing this companion. "As for Rome's fate, it's nothing to me. How can it concern Raymond?"

"Raymond's a great man, Rome's a dissolute and degenerate state," and Carbajal shrugged.

"Stay here, then, if you like."

"I go with you. Ready?"

O'Neill nodded. Hand on saddle, he paused to cast one last glance over the great courtyard half set in the hillside, and the rising ground behind with its stubby winter vines and its chestnut trees, and the gray stones of the long building.

"If there's work for us here, it'll come to our hands," he said. "Where are they buried?"

"I don't know," said Carbajal. "I know only what passed inside."

A trace of feeling drew the harsh features of O'Neill into more tender lines.

"Farewell, brother!" he said. "Some day, I promise you, the Red Hand of Ulster shall efface memory of the Black Bull—when I return here, not one stone shall be left on another!"

"An easy oath," bit out Carbajal's voice. "This place has secrets!"

O'Neill did not reply, but drew back, vaulted into the saddle, found his stirrups. Carbajal thumped the mule's belly and led the way. Ahead of them the white road, brown-green hillsides and long mountain peaks showed empty, for Corthia lay on the ridge beyond the next valley.

CHAPTER II

"THERE'S Corthia ahead," observed Carbajal. "Better let me do the talking—I know the place."

"You don't know my mind, though. Not knowing the place, I shan't weigh possibilities; in those scales lies ruin."

"You're not such a fool—I've learned the same lesson," and Carbajal laughed. "So you're determined to have vengeance?"

"No," said O'Neill thoughtfully. "Or I'd try and kill Raymond now. My first task is to find Mary— all bends to that. If I met Friar Dominic, I might risk wringing his neck, otherwise it's on to Rome at all costs! Hm! Corthia's a tiny place—hardly more than castle!"

"It's not the town, but the man."

O'Neill nodded as they rode on; he liked this comrade he had found, and scented in him something

31

more than mere galley-slave or scullion. On the ridge ahead lay Corthia, dominating the hill-road. Men said its thick walls had been built by the Lombards and repaired by Duke Annibal in the fourteenth century; within their compass the tiny town was overbuilt, houses even running along the walls themselves, so the place looked one huge building.

"The Black Bull!" said Carbajal, pointing to a standard. "Perhaps that gonfalon will wave over Rome or Florence one of these days!"

O'Neill gave him a curious glance. "The Pope rules Rome."

"The old Pope did—not the new one. He stays in the country most of the time and Rome rules herself. What a man Raymond would be there! He has no weakness, leaves women alone, has brains. He's wasted here. This is a hamlet of serfs, vile slaves."

"Whose ruler is a murderer in wayside taverns," said O'Neill.

"Well," and Carbajal pulled down his wide hat, "he's the best man in Italy of hands or brain, now that Carlo Donato the Venetian captain is dead. You'll never get through to Rome, and if you do, you'll never find the girl there."

"Then the Pope will. He'll help me."

"From what I hear, he's the only good man in Rome, therefore can't help you," and Carbajal chuckled. Then he struck off at an apparent tangent. "Do you know how Ferrara was absorbed in the Papal territory. Do you know what happened to the grandson of the last duke of Ferrara?"

"No," said O'Neill, to whom the house of Este meant nothing.

"You're a fool! To come into Italy, thus hidebound in ignorance!"

"Fools die hard."

"Look to it when you stand before Raymond, then. He keeps crossbow-men hidden, and if any visitor draws weapon or seems to threaten—that man dies swiftly."

"Hm!" said O'Neill. "Thanks! That's the first useful thing you've said in all your babbling."

Now and again, Carbajal sent swift glances at this man with yellow hair and mustache as though weighing his implacable nature, piercing to the worth of this absolute and impenetrable poise. An automaton, cold to any human emotion—and unnatural. Carbajal nodded sagely. A brother murdered, an old

33

servitor knifed, a girl sold into commerce; well, the man had reason to be bitter and inhuman!

They came to the gate, where country folk were bringing out some empty wains. Inside this north gate lay the piazza and the palace. Duke Feria built it here instead of in the center of town, in order to make a fortalice inside the one vulnerable approach. It was a square-fronted building of stone, dark and forbidding, giving no hint of the pleasant gardens inside, and was cut off from the little town around by a disused moat, and by streets.

The afternoon was little more than half gone. The guard halted them, asking names and business, demanding their *bulletino* or bill of health—without which no traveler could enter an Italian city, for the plague was feared.

"Pilgrims," said O'Neill, showing the papers he carried.

"Pilgrims have names," said the captain of the guard, an ox-like fellow. "And there's mention here of only one pilgrim."

"Bah! I'm the Count of Albujaras in Spain, Aide to Don Juan of Austria, now a pilgrim, and this is my servant," said O'Neill, and slipped some gold pieces into his hand.

34

TWO MEN CAN BECOME THREE

The captain countersigned the *bulletino* for two men, and sent one of his guard to bear tidings to the palace. Its gray front rose on the other side of the piazza, which was like a courtyard inside the gate, and before the building waved a gonfalon bearing the black bull on a golden ground, arms of Corthia.

"It is the rule," said the officer placatingly, "that all travelers of birth must be received by Duke Raymond. You're lucky—he rode in an hour ago and is in the gardens now. He'll bid you to stop a day or two."

"I accept no hospitality this side Rome—it's a vow," said O'Neill. "What street leads to the Leghorn road?"

They were walking across the piazza, the guard-captain at O'Neill's stirrup.

"Yonder to the right," and he pointed, "the Street of Three Doves. I go to the Leghorn gate even now, to take over the command there until sunset, and may see you again."

The Street of Three Doves went out of the square by the right side, along the corner of the palace, then shot off among houses. The captain had traveled in his day, and said it looked like the street lead-

35

ing to the right of the old Stadthaus in Bruges.
O'Neill said this was true, and they fell into talk of
the Low Countries until the messenger came out to
bid O'Neill follow him into the palace. This snatch
of talk, and the gold, served O'Neill well before a
great while.

Carbajal remained mounted, took the reins of the
white Arab, and sat muffled in hat and cloak, beside
the gilded pole of the gonfalon. O'Neill glanced at
the guards and strode into the palace, his guide leading him through the gray building. Duke Raymond
did not keep any great state, but his corridors were
cool and deep, and when they had passed through
into the gardens, it was like another world. Fountains played, even now in winter, and orange trees
scented the air, for there was no frost in Corthia.

A lute-player idled amid a circle of women to one
side. Beside a marble pool in the sunlight lay the
duke, reading some letters, a small flat black casket
beside him on the silken rug of Samarcand, glittering
yellow and orange-red in the afternoon glow.

O'Neill forced the anger from his eyes. Here was
the murderer of his brother—and he must keep silence. It was all-important to get clear of Corthia,
to reach Rome and do what he could for Mary

TWO MEN CAN BECOME THREE

O'Neill; this sad and bitter errand overshadowed all else.

Duke he might not be in right, but Raymond was able enough—one glance told as much. He was not large, being lean and wiry; his face was high-boned, alert, his dark eyes very piercing. His countenance held a certain vicious cruelty, but no weakness; it was stamped with energy, decision, keen force of character. This man had personality, as he should have, coming from Medici of the left hand. Perhaps some of the ancient greatness of Cosimo had budded anew in him, to lend the air of leaping eagerness that distinguished him from other men. He rose with lithe and springing grace to meet his approaching visitor.

"Welcome, noble pilgrim—and as a soldier, thrice welcome! You'll spend a week or a day with me!"

"I will not," said O'Neill, "having vowed to spend no night beneath a proffered roof until I come to Rome. And I don't like your people."

The dark eyes steadied on him. "Eh? Discourteously spoken. Why don't you like them?"

"I stopped at a tavern outside the city, and the inn-keeper tried to knife me."

"Then that fat rogue shall be traced up and lashed—"

"Don't bother," said O'Neill drily. "He's dead."

There was a moment of silence, eye to eye. A smile grew on the thin lips of Raymond.

"I suppose I should be angry," he said slowly, "but what's one serf more or less? You're a pilgrim, noble, a soldier, though you do not show true Spanish courtesy. Yet I don't like to have my people killed. People have value, you see."

"You speak as though you owned them," said O'Neill amusedly.

"I do," and Raymond was serious. "There are no free men in Corthia except my men-at-arms, so I have a right to my own. Well, I pardon you the killing. So sit down and talk, and tell me what you seek in Rome."

"What I seek here is more to the point," said O'Neill. "I want the ebony box you took from Christina of Sweden."

Raymond stared at him, a flicker of astonished incredulity in the dark eyes, then glanced down at the letters and box which lay on the rug of Samarcand. He looked up again and met the gaze of O'Neill.

"Name of the devil—you're a dangerously blunt man, my lord count!" he said. An abrupt laugh broke from him, though in his eyes lay no laughter. "You weren't with her. How do you know about it?"

"I met her on the road, she said you had taken the box, I promised to regain it for her," said O'Neill. "As any gentleman would do. So I came to get it. That's all!"

The face of Duke Raymond was a study in conflicting emotions, but his anger gradually died, and when he laughed again, it was with unaffected amusement. He attempted no evasions, denials, excuses, as though such things were far beneath him.

"Upon my soul, I like your way of doing business!" he exclaimed. "You and I would get on together."

"We might not," said O'Neill, fighting down the hatred that rose in him.

"Bah! Spanish stiffness will always down. Do you know, I thought that madwoman was up to plotting—I heard she had been making treaties in Milan and other places. And what did I get for my pains? Love-letters—from her pet cardinal! Love-letters!"

Raymond chuckled, as he said this.

"Well, give them to me and I'll return them," said O'Neill.

"What if I refuse?"

O'Neill glanced about at the trees within the high walls.

"For love-letters, it wouldn't be worth playing," he said gravely, "but I promised the lady, so I'd have to tempt a bolt from one of your arbalestriers. Whether he could down me before I had pistoled you, would depend on the priming in the pistol."

Duke Raymond broke into a roar of laughter, and stooped, craming letters into the flat black case. He thrust them at O'Neill.

"For the love of the saints, take them with my blessing! Will you stop overnight with me?"

"I must get on, if I may have your permission. And I give you thanks."

Raymond looked him over, grunted, and reached to his belt. He took pen from ink-horn and scrawled on a bit of paper, while O'Neill thrust the flat case into a side pocket.

"Here's your permission, my good don—heaven speed your road! And when you see Christina, tell her I hope to crack a bottle with her in Rome before long. If you have need of a friend there, come to me. I like your methods."

O'Neill inclined his head slightly, turned, and strode away. It was quite possible he would get a shaft in the back—but none came.

He was halfway across the garden when he was aware of a dark-gowned, saturnine figure approaching. This must be Friar Dominic—no true brother of any order, according to Carbajal. O'Neill halted and saluted him gravely.

"Are you, by any chance, Friar Dominic?"

"I am, my son," said the false friar, his deep eyes boring into the stranger.

"I have word for you from a man whom I met on the road hither," and as he spoke, O'Neill turned the golden coins in his pocket, so that they made the peculiar dull clink which comes of gold. "A message, and money, but I would not deliver it in public—"

The lean friar, knowing this palace all too well, did not care for any public delivery of gold either. His eyes drove about, and he turned.

"Come with me—we can speak privately in a room off the corridor, here."

The two passed from the garden into the gray

stone building. O'Neill strode after the dark slippery figure, and from the corridor where guards stood about, followed into a passage and on into a cool deep room. O'Neill closed the door, and took a handful of gold from his pocket, and put it into the hand of the lean friar.

"Here is the money," he said. "The message was from the inn-keeper at the Black Bull. He said to tell you that a man was coming who knew all your dealings with that Irish girl—how you cajoled and tricked her, and gave her a drug to drink, and sold her."

Holding the gold in his hand, the false brother straightened up; his eyes dilated, and his lips parted, until he licked them.

"What!" he whispered. "A man—who knows? Who is he? Where is he?"

"Here," said O'Neill. "I am the man."

Meantime, out in the pleasant sunny garden, a man came hurriedly to the marble bath, saluted Duke Raymond, and stood with eagerness suppressed.

"Well?" asked Raymond. "What about him?"

"Little; he has one companion, the lay brother of some order, who appears dumb," said the man, then broke forth quickly. "But the horse, highness—the

horse! There is not another like him in all Italy—
the Grand Duke himself has not such a horse! Of
purest Arab blood, and with every point of perfection, and an eye like that of a woman! One to stand
the strain, to run his very heart out—if you seek a
horse to take to Rome for the Carnival races, here's
the noblest of all—"

Though he laughed at the man's excitement, the
duke's eyes glittered avidly.

"Take half a dozen men and kill them both, midway the Street of Three Doves," he said. "I gave
the Spaniard permission to leave—look to it. He's a
soldier and I think wears mail, so put an arrow into
him first. Mind you don't hurt the horse!"

"My life on it, highness!" exclaimed the man, and
departed running.

Presently O'Neill came out of the palace, unhurried, showed his permission to the guards, and came
to where Carbajal waited with horse and mule. A
number of the duke's men were admiring the Arab.
When O'Neill put hand to saddle and vaulted lightly
into his place, they shot swift glances one at another,
for the ease of the action was eloquent of the man.
When the two animals were heading into the Street
of Three Doves, Carbajal spoke.

"You saw Friar Dominic? You look pleased."

"I saw him privately," and O'Neill smiled a little. "I gave him a handful of money, told him who I was, and so left him."

"Eh?" came the eager word. "With steel in him?"

"Good steel to such a dog?" O'Neill looked down at his hands. "No. I strangled him."

"Ah!" The word was a short, choked cry. "Fool that you are—fool!" said Carbajal in bitter accents. "That fiend will never die of strangling! He's one of those men who must be killed thrice to be sure he reaches hell. There are such men."

"So?" O'Neill gave him a slow look, frowned slightly, nodded assent. "You yourself are such a man, eh? Perhaps you're right—I should have made sure. Still, I'm sure enough—"

"So am I," and Carbajal laughed curtly. "You saw the duke?"

"I have his permission to leave."

"And his spies looked over your horse and me, saw our fat saddle-pockets, and ran to get their men placed. That means we're to be killed in the street ahead, here."

TWO MEN CAN BECOME THREE

O'Neill looked at him in open astonishment. "You're not in earnest?"

" Oh, innocent! Don't I know the ways of Corthia? Many a traveler is slain in a street brawl here, so the town has a bad name. And Raymond will go far for any rare thing—a horse, perhaps, or a sword."

O'Neill's face went hard and dark. "Yes? If I thought he meant to kill us—"

"Fool!" said Carbajal. "Look ahead, there—see that archer slinking from sight in a doorway? His bow is strung."

O'Neill bent his gaze upon the street ahead, alert, perceiving they were trapped.

It was a street of deep doorways and latticed balconies, crazily built. The old wooden houses leaned one upon another, and just ahead was an elbow-bend in the narrow way. Most of the shops were closed, for the afternoon was late. Against a house was the smoking stove of a chestnut vendor, crying his wares lustily, for the chestnuts of Massa made good bread and better roasting, so were well sought after.

Close to this vendor, at the curve of the street, was a huge wain of hay blocking all the narrow street. A wheel had come off, and men were gathered about the half-tipped wain with curses, being folk who had hoped to deliver their hay and be off out of town before the gates closed at sunset. O'Neill's gray eyes swept from side to side, instantly seizing on the possibilities.

He saw no archer, but he did see five men-at-arms standing beside the broken wain, talking with the peasant. He slowed his pace and called to them to make way, that he might pass. As he called, Carbajal cried out sharply, and something came flitting through the air.

An arbalest would have done the business, since at this short distance a bolt must have broken mail-coat and bones within, while an arrow had little chance to pierce Milan links. The shaft drove into O'Neill's side, shattering, hanging broken in the gray cloak. Even so, the shock of it was enough to bend him far over in the saddle, sharp pain stabbing through him, so that all who looked on, deemed him finished.

The soldiers shouted, whipped forth sword and poniard, and came leaping. They were too late to save the archer; Carbajal had whirled his mule upon the doorway, and the kitchen-knife of the Black Bull

46

sank into the man's throat as he was notching another shaft on string.

"Poor workman," said Carbajal. "Blood pays for failure—ah! Now for it—"

A soldier leaped at him. The others were about the bowed figure of O'Neill—who straightened unexpectedly. Pistols leaped from his sash, and roared, and now it was another matter for these assassins. With the bellow and the white powder-smoke, the Arab stallion plunged and drove a hoof into one man's face; Carbajal knifed his assailant, and was upon the others in the rear. Of them all, one alone fled away back toward the palace, the rest lying scarlet on the cobble-stones. The street was now clear, the peasants having fled at the first clash of steel.

O'Neill dismounted slowly, pain gripping at him, blood running down his right leg. He went to the stove of the chestnut vendor and opened it, in silence. Taking forth the pot of charcoal by its handle, he whirled it twice about his head and let fly—and the blazing stuff went all scattered into the loose-piled hay of the wain. Then he came back to the stallion and caught at the saddle, and climbed up with an effort.

47

"Ride!" he said to Carbajal, and got out his powder-flask to reload a pistol.

The two of them drew past the stricken men and the hay-wain where flame was already flitting up the sides of the pile. From the piazza behind came the thin shrilling of a trumpet; and, almost at once, the crowded houses of the little burg gave vent to a multitudinous buzz of voices like the humming of a great beehive, though no folk appeared.

A scant hundred yards from the bend of the narrow street, lay the wall and the Leghorn gate. As he looked, O'Neill saw the gates closed, and men came running toward him. He glanced backward, to see a sudden spout of red-streaked smoke shooting forth from the wain, filling and blocking all the street; and now a sharp screaming welled from all the houses roundabout, whence the folk began to pour like frightened rats. The acrid smell of burning hay drifted on the breeze.

"So much for wooden houses," said Carbajal, his cynical voice half-heard amid the mounting uproar. "If these peasants hadn't brought in hay for the duke's stables today, history might have been changed—"

Horse and mule went on. To meet them came the

men from the gate—the guards, headed by that same officer who had been in the Low Countries. This latter saluted O'Neill and came to a halt.

"Is it fire?" he panted out, though he could well see the blaze.

"Blood and fire," said O'Neill. "Here's my permission to leave. The gate's shut?"

"Aye. Here, Antonio! Take the keys and open for the pilgrims. God be with you, noble signor! I must hurry—hell's let loose here—"

One of the soldiers remained, to trot back to the gates and work at them. By this time the whole narrow street was in yelling tumult as folk vomited from the houses, and the black smoke turned into scarlet fire, the column of it licking upon the houses to either hand. Since this mounting flame, not to mention the masses of frightened folk, effectually barred all pursuit, there was no great hurry.

Sitting before the gates, which were heavy and slow to open, O'Neill finished loading his pistol. Through all the din, he could hear a lusty voice roaring forth on the other side of the gates—someone was there, shouting for entry to the city. But now this was forgotten, and at a wild oath from Carbajal, O'Neill turned and looked.

49

A nearly naked man came plunging at him, running. His wrists were bleeding and ridged with marks of cord and gyve, and upon his breast and side was blood, but not his own. He leaped, caught the Arab's stirrup-leather, and hung there panting—a dark, eager man with eyes of fire, and thinly beaked nose over a wide and firm mouth. He looked up at O'Neill, the swift straight gaze of an eagle.

"Aid, soldier!" he sobbed out, less in entreaty than proud demand. "No slave—a soldier like you—I broke clear of them—"

"Silence!" said O'Neill, and cocked his pistol. He saw that the man had escaped from some prison amid the tumult, but for the moment other things held him.

The gates had slowly drawn open, to reveal a single cavalier outside—a burly, red-cloaked ruffian who still shouted for entry. Across his leather jerkin showed the brass pommel of a large sword, and a brass-studded leather baldric. At sight of this O'Neill trembled a little and turned pale, for he knew it well, had played with it as a child, had seen it a thousand times across the wide chest of Teague the faithful. Now, of a sudden, he found Carbajal leaning toward him, speaking.

50

"There is one of the slayers—"

"I know it already," and O'Neill laughed, swinging up his pistol.

As the gates swung open, the burly cavalier pressed in his horse, cursing the single man trying to get the barriers open. He looked at O'Neill and saw the pistol, but this was his last sight on earth; to the shot he fell backward and dragged in the stirrup, his horse plunging.

Now O'Neill leaned over, put down his hand, touched the half-naked man beside him.

"Take horse and clothes," he shouted. "Bring me the sword and baldric. Follow!"

There was need of haste. Behind, the townfolk were flooding for the gate. Ahead, the soldier who had opened the barriers stood aghast at sight of the half-naked man; then he gave a wild cry and plunged for the prisoner, poniard flickering out. Carbajal heaved up his kitchen knife and flung it; the blade went into the soldier's throat.

Touched by spurs, the Arab shot into the air, leaped above the falling soldier, drove between the gates, and plunged down the steep descending slope of the road outside.

"On, Achmet—ride!"

THE BLACK BULL

As arrow from bow leaped the stallion, breaking into full stride, skimming down that steep slope where few beasts had dared to trot, leaving Carbajal's mule far behind in an instant. White was the stallion, with not a dingy nor a gray hair in him, all a rich and deep white as of snow new-fallen; for very coloring alone he was a marvel, and when men added shape and deep lungs, rare saddle and wide nostrils, they might well wonder. But now the white flank was spattered with thin red drops, from O'Neill's right leg.

A Zaporogian Cossack had taken the horse in some Crimean raid, bringing him to Vienna for sale. There, ignorant folk thought the horse a man bewitched, because of his intelligence, and were burning him at the stake when O'Neill heard of it and intervened. After this, Achmet rode at the head of the dragoons.

In this wild flight from Corthia was reason, as there was reason why O'Neill did not pause to get the baldric and sword worn these twenty years by old Teague. Faster flew the white horse, faster and ever faster as he came to the level valley road below, until Corthia was lost to sight behind, and ahead lay only hills and farms, wintry chestnuts and olives girding the road. Then they came upon a roadside shrine, and beside it a fountain.

"Enough, Achmet!" panted O'Neill. "Halt!"

Achmet slowed, stepping carefully, and stopped beside the fountain. O'Neill drooped in the saddle, straightened, and tried to dismount. His face was very gray; only a clutch at the snowy mane kept him from falling as he came to earth; he clung there, until with an effort he stood erect, and laughed shakily.

"Now for it, Achmet—"

When Carbajal rode up, thumping his mule, he found O'Neill stripped to the shirt of fine steel links that covered his body to the hips. Carbajal flung to earth, aided him, got at the blackened spot in his side.

"No bones broken, comrade—"

"But blood's been shed. Lower!"

The gray breeches came down, darkly stained, and a long stiletto-gash in the thigh showed itself; not a bad cut, but badly torn by riding. Carbajal fell to work upon it, while O'Neill sat down, weak with loss of blood, and with worse hurts that showed not.

Presently came the pounding gallop of a horse. It was the dark man, wearing scarlet coat and leather jerkin, beating his horse with the long sword and

53

baldric. He dismounted, laid the sword at O'Neill's feet, and looked down at the wound.

"Who are you?" asked O'Neill in a low voice.

"Your comrade," and the other broke into a quick laugh.

"Agreed. Your name?"

"Donato. You know it?"

O'Neill shook his head, though Carbajal turned and darted one look at the speaker.

"No easy road—with me," said O'Neill, a trifle thickly. Again a laugh broke on the red lips and fiery eyes.

"So much the better! I'm in your debt. You might have worse debtors than Carlo Donato of Venice, comrade—"

O'Neill put out a hand and spoke hurriedly.

"Enough—help me dress—somehow the life's gone out of me—"

On the word he toppled sideways, and would have fallen senseless but that Donato caught and let him sink back against the fountain. Straightening, Donato found the one wild blue eye of Carbajal fastened upon him.

"Carlo Donato, eh? I thought you dead long ago in Candia."

Donato stared at him. "Eh? So does all the world think—so my wealth and wife might go to cousin Angelo! And Raymond, blast his evil heart—"

Carbajal began to laugh. "Raymond, Raymond!" he mocked. "You were part of the game too, eh? Carlo Donato, first captain of Venice—oh, he's a crafty scoundrel, this Raymond! Kept you prisoner too, eh? Well, all three of us to Rome; there's a new Pope now," he added, with certain zestful energy.

"The main thing's freedom." Donato stretched out his arm. "With Carlo Donato free, I promise you a dance! But who are you, one-eyed comrade, who seem to know the dead Donato?"

"You should know me," said Carbajal in sardonic humor. "I, too, am a dead man."

"Hm!" Donato stared at him in perplexity. "But here, look to our comrade—"

"He's all right—his worse hurt comes from within. Never saw me before, eh?" Carbajal uttered his curt, savage laugh. "No wonder—look at this face, this twisted body! But one night we sat in a palace room over a treaty we were making, you for Venice, I for myself—"

Donato started back. His jaw sagged for an instant. Then;

55

"You! That man—and alive? It can't be—"

"Keep my name to yourself—this man knows it not," snapped Carbajal, then pointed to the wave of dark smoke rising from the hills behind. "Our Raymond is a magician who brings the dead to life— but Corthia burns! We three to Rome; all Italy will be there for the Carnival, it's our safest hiding-place. This devil Raymond will be hot after us! We're comrades, we have money, one of us is hurt. We must go by Leghorn, take the hill road to Siena, and so evade pursuit. Time enough for talk later on. Agreed?"

"Agreed."

When Carbajal turned his back, the Venetian crossed himself. Wonder, and a stricken hurt look, deepened in his face, as though sight of this man with twisted body and one eye had wakened in him grieved respect and awe. And this was strange, because the Venetian was a hard man, as one might easily perceive, slow to show heart to the sufferings of others.

In this fashion two men became three, and took up the Leghorn road, with O'Neill sagging in his saddle, while the smoke of burning Corthia mounted into the windless bluish sky of twilight.

CHAPTER III

THE governor of Leghorn, like his master Grand Duke Ferdinand in Florence, was a quiet fellow wishing only peace in his city —one of the most singular places in Europe. Like his master, too, he was niggardly, so when the great Venetian merchant-prince arrived with his wife, he turned over to them the Palazzo Borghi on the great square and let them spend of their wealth freely in gaiety and feasting. No one objected, least of all the English merchants with whom the Venetian had business.

This famed port of Tuscany, a little city lying in an open seaside plain, had its unpleasant features, liberty being here carried to license. Free to all men without distinction of race or creed, settled by invitation of the wise Medici to the oppressed of all countries, Leghorn had risen into a great commercial

center where Moor and Christian, Jew and Pro-
testant and Catholic all met on common ground—and
the Medici prospered. In its harbor lay galleys of
Algiers and Spanish galleons, Dutch traders, English
ships, with the duke's galleys to keep the peace. Here
was sanctuary for all; even a criminal, gaining Leghorn, was a free man and welcome.

Angelo Donato and his lady Beatrice were accounted the handsomest couple in Italy, and the gay-
est, and the wealthiest to boot, since in the slim
Venetian's hands was gathered all the trade of the
Donato family. They were en route to Rome, and
naturally had much business in Leghorn; most of
the trade here lay in English hands, and with them
Donato had agreements to sign respecting the nearer
seaways and the Levant trade. These commercial
treaties were best made over wine and music, for
amid such surroundings Angelo Donato never lost
his sleek head, while other men sometimes did.

Lady Beatrice nestled amid silken rugs in the
sunny patio of her borrowed palace, and avidly inquired after news from one and another; she was
ever very eager to hear of strange customs and men
and things. Meanwhile, in an upper room, Angelo
sat in talk with one Clarkson. This dour and heavy

THREE CAN BECOME ONE

English merchant was a crafty man and had no scruples in his dealings.

"I have need," said Angelo, after some beating around the bush, "to win the goodwill of a certain Roman, once a prince cardinal, but now a prince and not a cardinal."

"Oh!" grunted Clarkson, pawing his beard. "Don Camillo, who resigned his hat and kept his title?"

Angelo smiled; he was often smiling, being that sort of man. Being beyond the sumptuary laws of Venice here, he was perfumed, jeweled, wearing the richest Genoa velvet. A tiny mustache showed against the sleek dark oval of his face—not a strong face, nor kind nor even generous, but arrogant, and filled with a slow, sly balancing of thought and word. It was always thought and word with Angelo, seldom deed; his deeds came by the hands of others.

"Yes," he responded, voice evenly modulated. "To win his goodwill, I need a gift for him. And they say a gift of a certain sort is always acceptable with Don Camillo."

Clarkson chuckled, and his eyes glistened under shaggy brows. He had the scent now.

"Hm! An old roué, they say—resigned his hat to marry a rich widow. Painted like a doll, wears

59

Spanish clothes, has a good deal of influence in Florence; and his country villa is a regular harem, by all accounts."

"Now we approach the point," purred Angelo. "It's been hinted to me that in Leghorn I might find a slave-girl to make his mouth water—a gift unique."

"Hm!" said Clarkson, eyeing him craftily. "Why talk to me about it!"

Angelo disliked blunt questions, but here perceived he must give references.

"I have certain—er—affairs in hand with Raymond of Corthia," he said. "I had a letter from him while I was in Florence, answering one from me. He referred me to you—said nothing definite, of course—hinted delicately—"

"Raymond, eh?" Clarkson grunted again. "Well, Messer Donato, rumor might have said true, but rumor might also underestimate. Supposing?"

"One does not set a price on what one buys," said Angelo gently.

"But if the price ran high?"

"Much would depend on birth, breeding, past history," suggested Angelo.

Clarkson pawed his beard. "Well, to it, then. A

neat bird, caught on the way to common Roman uses and held for such high purposes as yours. Snared and netted not so far from here, and detained with fair words and promises."

"Snared not so far from here?" Angelo smiled. "I see! Raymond knew something—and you're pretty thick with him, too. I rather hoped to meet him here."

Clarkson frowned, a glimmer of anxiety, unrest, coming into his eyes.

"Something's happened at Corthia, no telling what," he said. "I have pigeons there, and Raymond has pigeons here; a swift letter often comes in handy. Well, yesterday morning all my birds came home together, without a message of any sort. We'll have news by courier in another day. Hm! As to price, it would be five thousand ducats and that balas ruby on your hand, unless you love it too well to part with it."

Angelo loved nothing too well to make use of it, except possibly his wife He twisted the big ruby on his thumb and smiled.

"One does not buy in the dark."

"True. Come with me now. You'll be a gentleman who'll escort her to Rome, where she's known to the

Spanish ambassador—rather, your wife will escort her."

Angelo whistled softly, his eyes narrowing in calculation.

"Steady! I have Spanish connections," he demurred. "I cannot hurt business—"

"Bah!" said Clarkson. "She's no Spaniard, but · from Ireland—one of the exiled families settled in Spain. She would have plenty of relatives and friends in Rome, naturally; but that is a matter for Don Camillo to worry over. She's worth the worry, I can tell you."

"Oh, very well!" Angelo rose. "Then, by all means, let us meet the tender dove. I shall, of course, give her every assurance of protection; and when it comes to the point of presenting the gift to Don Camillo—well, Lady Beatrice is rather versed in the use of drugs."

"So I've heard," said Clarkson drily.

The two men went forth together into the surging, noisy piazza, a place unique in all Italy, perhaps in all the world. Angelo was followed from the doorway by his two bravos—men very skilled in all manner of arms, who stood close to his elbow and watched narrowly any who approached him.

THREE CAN BECOME ONE

In the sun-warmed patio, meanwhile, the Lady Beatrice and her two Moorish slave-girls were buying some pretty trinkets from a Jewish merchant and listening to his patter of general news. She was bored, and showed it, and the merchant began putting his things together.

"Fine horses do not interest the beautiful lady?" he said. "Eh, now, but I saw a horse this day! And a man—the handsomest man who ever came into Italy, though as nothing beside the fine Venetian lord upstairs. This man is big, and he has yellow hair and mustache, and is a great foreign lord, and there is not the like of his horse this side Syria! Had the man been in his right mind, he would have made a brave show, but he is ill with a festering wound. His servant is a one-eyed devil out of hell, though calls himself a pilgrim. There was another fine lord with them, but he scattered gold and took the Siena road with a new horse. All bound for Rome and the carnival, most like."

"A German, this foreign lord?" asked Lady Beatrice, her long fingers playing with the chain of greenish-yellow amber beads about her neck, those beads which matched her lovely eyes for color.

"Not he!" asserted the Jewish merchant. "Spanish, I think; it is only the great lords of Spain who have yellow hair and gray eyes, not to mention such an Arab. The servant is an Italian—I heard him talking at the Angel tavern, where they took rooms, and he had the accent of Ferrara or Venice. He wore a strange ring upon his little finger—a ring of gold set with a bit of gray stone, common gray stone, carven in the shape of a cross of Malta. Why would anyone wear a gold ring set with a gray stone?"

When she heard these words, Lady Beatrice became pale as death.

"Take him away and have him paid," she said to one of the Moorish girls, and it was done.

Alone with the other slave, Lady Beatrice sat without motion, save the play of her long fingers with the amber beads, while her yellow eyes looked at the playing fountain without seeing it, and her lovely face was set in pallid rigidity as though some awful fear had gripped and held her very heart. The Moorish girl, seeing those thin, set, beautiful lips, kept very quiet and looked afraid. After a little, Lady Beatrice rose and turned to her.

"Zobeide! Go and bring to my room my lord's costume of silver velvet with ermine; bring his gray

64

boots and his large Mantuan hat, and tell Ceccio to attend me."

The slave-girl hurried away, and Lady Beatrice ascended to her own room, wither the girl brought Angelo's costume. Beatrice was famed for her woman's beauty; she was delicately slim and slender, with small breasts and hips, rich gold-shot reddish hair, a head well set, and calm unwinking amber eyes. Dressed in her lord's garments as she sometimes was, she looked less effeminate than Angelo himself, since the maculine attire brought out a certain hardness about her mouth and chin, unobserved when one looked upon her as a woman.

Ceccio came, a wrinkled old servitor of the Donato family, showing no surprise at seeing her thus arrayed.

"You know the Angel tavern, Ceccio?" she said. "I must find a certain man there, who wears upon his little finger a gold ring set with a Maltese cross of common stone. You can come and do the inquiring."

Old Ceccio started, and crossed himself swiftly. Alarm and fear leaped in his eyes.

"Impossible!" he said. "Or no—the ring might have reached another man—"

"I must see him, before any word of it comes to Messer Angelo," she said. He bowed assent and held open the door for her passing, and followed her out as a servitor his young master; Beatrice in man's attire could swagger with any blade of them all, the ample cloak hiding her figure well.

They came out upon the great square above the sea, and found it well thronged. Leghorn was low-built, the streets crossing at right angles, and the houses around the square were gay with frescoes, most of these picturing victories gained by Tuscan galleys over the Moors.

Here was the general meeting-place and bourse of the Leghorn merchants, and English was chief among the babel of tongues filling the whole piazza; merchants, goods, slaves by the dozen—buying, selling, eating, drinking, sleeping, fighting, what they would. Many of the slaves were in chains. To one side was a tent where any man who wished might gamble against the state, liberty staked against good hard coin, and even as Lady Beatrice passed by, a string of six hapless losers were being haled forth to the galleys amid the jeers of the crowd.

Dicing, gaming, booths for eating and drinking— the whole place seemed to have no order, and confu-

66

sion reigned supreme. There were harpies enough, too, of all descriptions, and one had to keep his wits about him to travel untouched through this assembly. Lady Beatrice was half across the square when a lady of the port district came up to her, with eager voice and eye for this brave young gallant— only to look into those amber eyes and suddenly shrink aside with grayed features, though what she saw there were hard to say.

The Angel tavern was a very good inn, standing in a side street off the square, and upon turning into the courtyard, Beatrice beheld a little crowd of men surrounding a white stallion with open admiration. Though she knew little of horses, she caught her breath at the sheer beauty of the Arab before her, his exquisite perfection of line and color; then she saw a man grooming him, and touched the arm of Ceccio.

"There is our man, grooming the horse. Bring him in to speak with me."

She turned into the inn, almost deserted at this hour, took the empty corner settle by the fireplace, and ordered wine. The tapster served her, and she spoke to him.

"Where is the owner of that white horse?"

"In the best room—a Spanish don, he is, and sick. He'll be sicker soon."

"Why so?"

"Because the fool of a barber they've sent for knows nothing about wounds," said the tapster disgustedly. "He's killed three men in the past week."

Beatrice laid down a ducat. "Give this to him when he comes, and dismiss him. I've some skill with wounds, and will see the sick man myself."

The tapster departed swiftly, to split the coin ere the barber appeared. Ceccio came into the room, and at his elbow was Carbajal. Beatrice looked searchingly at the one-eyed man; vast relief swept into her face, and was replaced by a slight puzzled frown.

"I know something of wounds and will see your master," she said, as Carbajal bowed low to her. "Who are you and where from!"

"I am Carbajal, signor," said he, with wooden and vacant face. "From Spain."

"Your tongue came from Ferrara first," she said. "And I think I have seen your face somewhere; such eyes are rare, though you have but one left."

"I was born in Ferrara," said Carbajal, "and I have been in Venice—I was servant to Messer Nicolo Mocenigo before I went to the galleys."

68

THREE CAN BECOME ONE

"Whence came that ring on your finger?" she said. "I'll buy it at your own price."

Carbajal looked down at the ring. It was of massy gold, a heavy thing, and in the gold was set a Maltese cross of plain unpolished stone.

"Alas, signor, I cannot sell it," he replied. "It is my master's—I wear it lest it be stolen for he is sick and unconscious."

Beatrice pushed away her untasted wine, and rose. "Take me to him. Come, Ceccio."

Carbajal bowed, and led the way back to the courtyard, and there mounted the outside staircase reaching the inn rooms above. He threw back the first door, to disclose a large sunny chamber where O'Neill lay outstretched on the billowy feather-bed, half-dressed, his thigh freshly bandaged.

"He fell from his horse as we reached here, and has been unconscious since," said Carbajal. "The wound seems festering, and he has lost blood—"

"Bare it," said Beatrice, and after a long look at O'Neill turned to Ceccio. "Go fetch my green leather case, with the amethyst flask of ointment. I'll wait here."

"But—alone?" faltered Ceccio.

"No, with these two men. Go!"

Ceccio went.

Beatrice came to the bedside and looked down at the exposed wound, while the one vivid blue eye of Carbajal rested upon her face narrowly.

"It is not bad," she said. "In three days he will be sitting his horse. Ten minutes' work and I can fix this leg."

Carbajal threw the coverlet over O'Neill and stood up, facing her. His slightly grizzled hair was cut by now, and even in his pilgrim's garb there was something in the man to command a second glance. Beatrice looked at him fixedly.

"You are no servant," she said.

"You are no man," said Carbajal, with his dry, curt laugh. At sound of it she started, and the amber eyes flickered.

"Who are you?" she cried out.

"An escaped galley slave," said Carbajal. "You are bound for Rome?"

"Yes."

"Then bring him with you," and Carbajal motioned to the bed. "He is in danger of his life— these wounds are from assassins who followed him from Genoa. He goes to visit the Spanish ambassador at Rome. I dare not wait here, even a day, lest I be seen and taken; I must go on my way, swiftly. I'll tell the ambassador that you are bringing him. What say you?"

The amber eyes dwelt upon him searchingly. "Why should I thus cumber myself?"

Carbajal's lips curved thinly. "You might gain by it, Venetian. In his saddle-bags, yonder by the window, are twenty-five thousand crowns."

"I have no need of money."

"But of other things. Perhaps you know of Cardinal Ludovici?"

She regarded him a moment, scorn and yet a certain appraisal in her look.

"What does a galley-slave know of the most powerful man in Rome?"

Carbajal's dry bitter laugh rang upon the room.

"Enough, so that at my request he will damn or pardon, give aid or withhold it. Help me now, in helping this man, and you may make what demand you like in the name of Carbajal, and Ludovici will grant it. Worth while?"

"If true. How should I trust the word of a galley-slave?"

"He trusts yours. Not because he values your

word, but because you'll be afraid to break it. Understand?"

Here was challenge, defiance, menace; the amber eyes glowed luminous before them.

"Slave—you dare threaten me?" When Beatrice laughed as she did now, few men would have faced her squarely; but Carbajal did. "Threaten me! And with what, dog?"

The sapphire eye glittered sardonically upon her, and Carbajal twisted his lips into his bitter dry grin.

"Threaten you—threaten Beatrice Donato?" he said mockingly, yet the undertone in his voice drove alarm into her gaze. "Nay, beauteous lady! How could I threaten you—my tiny incidents are nothing to you! Perhaps with word of a toy lapdog dead of the worms, perhaps with news of a galley lost on Istrian reefs, perhaps with a gray ring carven from the stone of the Holy Sepulchre—eh? What's the matter?"

She shrank suddenly from his jeer. "You mean—what do you mean?" she exclaimed.

"That you had best keep faith with me!" Carbajal's jeer turned to a wolfish, pitiless snarl of fury. He thrust his bent arm at her savagely, so that the ring came before her eyes again. "Shall I bring another Lazarus from his grave—a Lazarus drugged by his own wife and given to the assassins? Keep this man safe, deliver him safe! It's no longer a request but a command—murderess! Fail, and you'll be thrown into the gutters of Venice like any common adulteress—you who murdered Carlo Donato!"

A mortal pallor had crept across her face at these words.

"Then—he lives?" she whispered.

"You'll know when you come to Rome, or before," snapped Carbajal. "I'll tell you his fate, or I'll see that you know the truth; that's my price now. You wouldn't accept the better price I offered—so accept this! You understand, murderess?"

Silence of horror gripped her, and sheer terror—she understood well enough.

Then sudden intervention—the quick scrape of feet on the stone steps outside, the panting of Ceccio on his way to them. Swift as light, Carbajal doffed his snarling, savage air, became again the humble servitor; she, no less swift, turned as the door swung and held out her hand to Ceccio for the little vial and the large green leather case he carried.

Silent, she turned to the man on the bed, and Cec-

73

cio lent her deft assistance. The leg was bared and she worked over the wound, cleansing it of dirt and ferment, anointing it, bandaging it anew with fine linen from her case. It was no nice task, yet she accomplished it with delicate nicety, then closed the leather case and straightened up.

"He'll be in his right mind again when he wakens," she said. "Ceccio, we're to take this man on to Rome with us. Have him moved to our house within the hour; he'll sit in the coach when we leave on Saturday—can ride if he must. Have all his belongings brought." She looked at Carbajal. "Do you accompany us or not?"

"Not I," said Carbajal. "I'll take his horse and you'll find me in Rome. Bring him to the Villa Ludovici if you don't hear from me."

"Very well," she said quietly, and so departed, Ceccio bearing the leather case.

When they had left, Carbajal closed the door, barred it, and then darted to the bedside. He got water and bathed O'Neill's face, giving him to drink as well, and after a little the gray eyes opened. O'Neill looked up at him and gripped his fingers.

"Carbajal! What's happened?"

"Much. Lie quiet and let me talk."

74

THREE CAN BECOME ONE

Carbajal settled himself on the bed, twisted the ring from his finger, and slipped it on that of the wondering O'Neill.

"This is from our Comrade Donato; it's made from the Holy Sepulchre and is more precious to him than life, but he lent it to us. He had to skip out of Leghorn on the instant—folk are here who know him, and he dared not pause an hour. Be careful you don't breathe his name to a soul, comrade! Guard the ring with your life; we may need to show it at the Venetian Embassy to reach Donato again. Say you bought the ring or won it dicing—say anything but the truth! We're at war now—it's a great game, but no time to talk. My own life hangs in the balance. I'm taking Achmet and going on to Rome—"

"You're what?" exclaimed O'Neill sharply. "Are you joking?"

"Aye, with death, every minute I'm here!" said Carbajal with energy. "I've turned you over to a party of noble Venetians—they'll bring you on to Rome by coach. You'll be well protected; I've arranged everything. But trust no one, lie like the devil's son! I've said you were a Spanish grandee, but gave no name. By taking the Leghorn road we've flung Raymond off the track—he'll stick to the

post-road via Florence. Your wound's been caught
in time—you'll be a sound enough man in a week
more."

O'Neill lay silent a moment, adjusting himself to
this astonishing complication. Donato gone, Carbajal going! He read the anxiety in the one blue eye
above him, and pressed Carbajal's hand.

"Good comrade! I'll be obedient—for the present. What program have you and Donato agreed
upon?"

"Program?" Carbajal laughed. "We're in the
grip of the whirlwind—time for nothing! Jump at
anything as it comes up! Just now, life's the great
thing for us all. At Rome, we're safe, but we'll have
the devil's own time reaching there. Donato will
get men and help there, and said he'd try to come
back and meet us on the road. Can't depend on anything, though, with Raymond after us."

"In the large side pocket of my coat," and O'Neill
pointed to his garments, "is a flat black casket. Take
it and keep it safe for me. I took it from Raymond
—letters he had rifled from the Queen of Sweden.
I count on her help in Rome to find the girl."

"Good! I'll take care of it, comrade. If anything
happens to you, Donato and I will look up the girl."

76

"You'll do that? Good man. If you haven't any plans—"

"None. We are dead men, therefore unhurried, with all eternity before us," and Carbajal chuckled grimly. "We're more anxious to enjoy our new freedom than to jeopardize it. You're a live man, with work to do, so we'll help you find the girl in Rome, and take such other action there as seems best. You'll help us in turn, should occasion arise. Our bond of union, and the one aim we all share, is to return to Corthia, eh?"

"Agreed," said O'Neill. "You think Raymond will follow us to Rome?"

"To hell, in one guise or another! He has allies, and he has himself. Does anyone know just who Raymond of Corthia is? I doubt it. He may be the Pope, for all we know! He wants you, he wants me, he wants Donato—and he wants us with all his heart! We're supposed to be dead—he kept us alive for his own purposes. Thanks to you, we're free. Will he follow? Needless to ask, my comrade!"

"I hope I killed that accursed Friar Dominic," growled O'Neill.

"You didn't. Now, I must get out of this town

77

in another ten minutes, or I'm lost, so no more talk. I've made friends with Achmet, and you need have no fears for him. Keep your tongue close—Raymond has spies everywhere. Farewell!"

"Farewell," said O'Neill, and smiled as he pressed the strong fingers of the one-eyed man.

Carbajal belted O'Neill's pistols under his cloak, after loading and priming them, gathered his few belongings, and was gone without another word.

In the courtyard, he paid the inn-keeper full reckoning, crammed his saddle-bags with food and wine, and ordered Achmet brought forth and saddled. He made careful inquiries about the road to Pisa and Florence, which he had no intention of taking; then, the Arab ready, Carbajal mounted and left the inn.

He rode circuitously about town, skirting the port and the canal to Pisa, cutting across the great piazza before the sea, stopping before the black-columed portico of the church to cross himself; then he turned suddenly and made his way to the south gate. He was bound for the hill road to Siena, thence the post roads to Rome.

Leghorn being free to all comers, and Carbajal having obtained a *bulletino* or bill of health, he had no difficulty in passing the guard. Round about the gates and outside them were vast throngs of country folk, gathered to watch a puppet show. Carbajal threaded his way slowly through the crowd, and here he came upon two horsemen, their beasts jaded and foam-flecked, who were pushing toward the gates. They came one on either hand of him, both men cloaked and muffled, dust-white, weary with hard riding across the level plain where lay the city.

Some indefinite instinct warned Carbajal barely in time—just as the man on his blind side drove in with naked stiletto. By a miracle of agility Corbajal evaded the thrust, although the blade caught in his cloak, and his wrench sideways caused the assassin to lose balance. At the same instant, the second cavalier was lunging.

Carbajal, reaching for his pistols, shot swiftly, desperately. By good luck the priming held, and the weapon roared, so that Achmet went plunging in air and the crowd scattered with shrill yells of fright. The second man was struck down by the bullet. Looking back at the other, struggling to regain his saddle, Carbajal caught sight of the bared lean face of Friar Dominic.

79

"Ah! If only my bullet had taken that devil instead!" he groaned. Then he put spurs to the Arab, and went flying down the road toward the hills, at a pace to baffle all pursuit.

CHAPTER IV

FINDING IS NOT KEEPING

BEFORE the move was made, O'Neill was given a sleeping-draught, and knew nothing of what happened until he wakened next morning and found himself in a room whose arched window overlooked the flowered courtyard of the Palazzo Borghi, now occupied by the Venetian party. Several incidents had transpired meanwhile, however—slight enough in themselves, yet cumulative in general result.

Angelo Donato came home without his balas ruby accompanied by a slender girl veiled in black lace, whom he led into the patio where Beatrice awaited him. The amber eyes dwelt upon him with amused curiosity as he came forward—these two were each a little afraid of the other, and between them was less of love than of mutual understanding and furtherance. Angelo caught the look, smiled, and presented Mary O'Neill to his lady.

"A foreigner, traveling to Rome, she fell into evil hands and was rescued by my correspondent, Signor Clarkson," he explained. "I offered to take her on to Rome in our company, and she accepted. She speaks no Italian, but you, dear one, speak fluent Spanish—"

Beatrice spoke it forthwith, and with a gesture sent Angelo away. The Irish girl threw back her veil, showed herself dark, slim, ruddy-lipped, blue eyes flaming like steel in the sun, and in the embrace of Beatrice abandoned herself to quick tears of gratitude.

Angelo went away smilingly, and after a time came back again, finding Beatrice alone. He sent away her women and sat beside her, and broke into soft laughter.

"This is amusing," he said. "Here I bring a woman to join our company, and I understand that you have brought a man to the same end! Decidedly, it is lucky that we are not lovers but partners —and therefore proof against jealousy. May I inquire as to the barbarian?"

"He is no barbarian but a Spanish don," she returned. "Tell me first about the girl."

Angelo shrugged. "My sympathy was stirred.

82

If she pleases Don Camillo, I have no doubt that he will take her under his protection—"

"So? And lend his influence to our business with Raymond, eh? You are clever, Angelo—but be careful! She says she is known in Rome."

"That is for His Eminence to worry over—afterward!"

Beatrice met his eyes, and a smile passed between them.

"I admire you more every day, my Angelo!" she said. "You always have an end in view, don't you? With me, it's different. I heard of this Spaniard, found he was alone, wounded, about to be butchered by local surgeons, and interfered. Of course, it is well to gain the goodwill of Cardinal Ludovici—"

Before the look in his face, her words died.

"Enough of lies!" he snapped, and caught her wrist suddenly. An unexpected gust of passion stormed in his eyes, and fear ripped athwart his sleek mask. "I saw him, saw the ring on his finger! What of it?"

"As yet, I don't know," she returned, and loosened her wrist from his clasp. "Quiet, my Angelo! There's been no chance to tell you—he won't waken until tomorrow. I heard of him, heard of the ring, went and fetched him here; that's all. He'll ride with us, and will be well as ever in a few days; his servant said he was a friend of Ludovici."

"Where is the servant?" snapped Angelo.

"Departed ahead to Rome." Beatrice smiled, and touched the slim dark fingers of her husband. "Come, come, be yourself! We'll have the story from him tomorrow."

"I know." Angelo's eyes were haunted. "And yet—that ring!"

"Precisely—the thing Carlo prized most in life, even above me!" she returned, an angry glow in her amber eyes. "That this Spaniard has it, shows Carlo is indeed gone—even had we not been sure of it already."

"Yes—and yet Raymond of Corthia might have played us false there," muttered Angelo. "He might have kept Carlo alive—he is a devil incarnate, that Raymond—"

"Not after Carlo drank the draught I gave him," and Beatrice sank back on her pillows with a slow smile. Angelo, before that smile, was heartened. He caught her hand swiftly, kissed it, and rose.

FINDING IS NOT KEEPING

"Right, my Beatrice! We pull together, as always. You can handle this foreign girl?"

"Like a child, so long as she is not suspicious. Let her suspect, and she'll prove most dangerous—did you see those eyes of hers? I warrant she'll knife Don Camillo."

Angelo only shrugged, as though that were the cardinal's lookout.

"We can spare a few prince-cardinals—they're thicker than fleas," he said. "I hear the new Pope has gone back on all his good resolutions, and is bringing his nephews into the game of politics. It's queer we've heard nothing from Raymond, after he wrote he'd meet us somewhere on the road to Rome! You don't think he'd betray us?"

"Of course, if it was to his interest," she returned coolly. "We must make it more to his interest to throw in with us, my Angelo. As yet, he knows nothing."

"I'm not so sure," said Angelo reflectively, and she frowned a little as she watched him. Angelo had his faults and his lacks, certainly, and was anything but a brave man; yet for this very reason his imagination often came in valuable. Bravery and imagination seldom go together, and the latter

85

quality was of supreme use to both Angelo and Beatrice.

"No, I'm not so sure," he went on. "The man Alfonso is at our Embassy in Rome, and Raymond certainly has spies everywhere. I rather imagine that Raymond will surprise us with his knowledge —so look out! He's almost certain to carry our game one step farther than we expect."

"Hm!" she returned. "Well, if you have genius, then I have knowledge of men. After we've met him and talked with him, I'll see if your estimate's correct—but what's this? A visitor?"

A servant was coming to them hastily. He saluted Angelo, and gave breathless message that at the gate was Cardinal Sainterre, traveling from Avignon to Rome with a single companion, who asked speech with Signor Donato. At this, Angelo threw up his hands.

"Another to join our company—these clerics are thick as fleas!" he exclaimed. "Well, bring him in. Do you wish to see him, Beatrice?"

"I am always curious," said the lady, smiling a little.

So presently the cardinal approached. He was a tall man with a fringe of black beard about his face

86

and a pronounced rotundity under his belt; his glance was very quick and active, and the black velvet under his cloak gave no hint of the prelate. His companion was a lean dark friar, who halted and let the cardinal come on alone.

"Greeting, my lord and lady!" The cardinal bowed somewhat awkwardly. "I heard that you were here, and shortly proceeding to Rome. As I am alone, save for Friar Dominic, and the hill roads are most unsafe, I beseech permission to join your party—"

Beatrice broke into sudden laughter, and Angelo gave her a sharp look. The cardinal cut short his address, in confusion, and also eyed the lady. She was quite composed.

"Undoubtedly, M. le Prince Cardinal," she said in French, "you have horses?"

"Two excellent mounts, madame," he replied in the same tongue.

"Suppose you tell us something," she demanded, a gay laughter in her eyes. "We were just speaking of you when you arrived, most opportunely, to solve our dispute. Our correspondence has all been carried on through agents, as you know, so we have not met you personally—"

Angelo looked as though she had gone out of her mind. The cardinal gaped, if a cardinal could do so vulgar a thing.

"But, madame, I do not understand!" he said blankly.

"You will," she said, with a little ring of laughter in her voice. "Come! Let me draw a knife across your belly, and if you haven't feathers for entrails I'll give you my sapphire pendant! So tell us whether Carlo is really dead or not, my dear Raymond."

Angelo, who had started suddenly, made a slight sign with his hand, and his two bravos loafed into sight across the patio. But Friar Dominic and his master stood staring at the amused Beatrice, until the lean friar uttered a grim laugh.

"I told you so, Raymond! And I win the wager."

The false cardinal tendered Beatrice a bow. "My congratulations, most beautiful! Your reputation is more than deserved, fair Beatrice. Well, you caught me; I'm Raymond, and I'm for Rome in your company, if you'll have me."

"By all means," said Beatrice. "Angelo! Stop making a fool of yourself with those two bravos.

88

FINDING IS NOT KEEPING

Send for chairs and table, wine and pastries, and remember this is Cardinal Sainterre—and speak French."

When it came to sharp action, it was easy to see who was head of the house of Donato.

Raymond was soon engaged in comfortable discussion with his hosts, Friar Dominic being relegated to outer darkness. Raymond had been in Leghorn since early this day, and knew what he was about in going to Rome in the guise of a cardinal. There, with the carnival, Lent and Easter ahead, a cardinal would provoke far less comment than would Raymond of Corthia.

"So the matter of your late beloved Carlo troubles you, eh?" he observed. "Banish all worry, my friends! He was taken in charge by my men, sewed in a sack with a fifty-pound shot, and was slipped into the ocean an hour after leaving Candia. As I think I wrote you at the time."

"His ring turned up here this morning," said Angelo, then became silent at a glance from Beatrice. The weather was stormy, and he was no Ajax to defy heaven.

"That's nothing," said the cardinal. "The ring turned up in Corthia the other day, too. An accursed Spanish don came along and played the mischief with all of us."

"I thought matters were better ordered in Corthia?" inquired Beatrice.

"Accidents happen. But I'll settle with that don myself, ere long."

Beatrice sipped her wine, eyed him, and played with the chain of topaz about her neck. She knew now why Raymond had showed up here; he had discovered all about her patient.

"Not before we reach Rome, my good cardinal! Neither of us are fools. Shall we play against each other, or in harness? We have large affairs coming to a head, as you may know, in which you'll be keenly interested. It rests with you to clear the air—or not."

"Hm!" The cardinal looked at her admiringly, and adjusted his false whiskers. "With a woman like you to help, I'd rule Italy inside six months!"

"With a man like you," said Beatrice flatly, "I'd be at dagger-points inside six days."

Raymond chuckled. "Well, we work together if that suits you! The Spaniard is here with you; I want him alive or dead. I have other affairs in

hand, but he's the most important, because he has
wounded my vanity, fooled me very neatly."

"Then he's a more remarkable man than I had
thought," said Beatrice, while her husband fingered
his chin and listened. "Well, you don't get him
this side Rome! I've promised to deliver him there
safely. What's more, I mean to do it."

"Why?" demanded the cardinal—exactly the thing
Angelo wanted to know, also. "Out of charity?"

"No, out of business," said Beatrice. She had no
intention of letting anyone know the truth about
that man with the one blue eye, and his threats, and
her own fears—least of all, Raymond. "Vitally important business. If anyone hinders, let him beware!"

"Threats, when so far from Venice?" asked the
cardinal with amused mockery.

"Try and see!"

"Not I, charming Beatrice!" The cardinal leaned
back and laughed. "I give you the don safe to
Rome. After that, you have no interest in his
future?"

"None whatever."

"Then it's a bargain. He's alone?"

Beatrice met his sharp gaze, and smiled slowly.

"So that's it, eh? You want the one-eyed man too, eh?"

"Yes. Is he here?"

"He's gone, as I think you very well know, Raymond. Who is he? Tell the truth, now."

"A servant who betrayed me," said the cardinal negligently. "No more. When do we set out from here?"

"Saturday morning—should reach Rome Monday night or Tuesday. Do you intend to wear that belly-pillow all the way?"

The cardinal clapped his paunch and laughed. "I was only testing you, charming Venetian. I admit myself conquered, in chains at your feet. You have no house in Rome?"

"The Venetian ambassador will have one ready for us," said Angelo. "We'll have some little business to transact there—shall stay until Easter."

"Business, eh? With me?"

"And others as well. With the ambassadors of Spain and Venice, and with Don Camillo."

The cardinal broke into laughter—laughter so amused and real that Beatrice eyed him sharply, divining a hidden jest.

"The 'painted face,' as he's called, eh?" said the

cardinal. "Painted worse than any courtesan of Naples, they say. Still, he has great influence in Tuscany, though he's been withdrawn from active affairs for a long while now. If you need his help, I can promise to swing it for you."

He met the gaze of Beatrice, and after a moment she nodded slightly.

"Thanks, my honest cardinal. We shall talk of it later."

The cardinal stretched out his legs and sipped at his wine.

"By all means. However, if you're tempted to have any dealings with Christina of Sweden while in Rome, I might advise you to leave her alone."

"Eh?" The amber eyes of Beatrice narrowed. "Why so?"

The cardinal shrugged and laughed. "Once bitten, twice shy! She has a name for wild intrigue, she plays at being a man, she has set half a dozen countries by the ears—I myself thought she'd be worth while. But I've changed my mind. After all, she's nothing but a woman at bottom, and a silly woman to boot; the kind to let alone."

"A publicity-seeker, eh?" Beatrice accepted the

advice gladly, knowing it came from a master at the game she was essaying. "Thanks, your eminence! However, she doesn't enter into my calculations in the least. Sweden's far away."

"Rome isn't," said the cardinal, and yawned. "She's got a fool love affair on with a cardinal and hasn't enough sense to destroy all letters. Bah! Leave her alone. But who's this astonishing creature? An angel, I'd say, except we have scriptural authority for believing that angels are all of the male sex—"

The others glanced around, following his eyes, and saw Mary O'Neill coming across the patio. Her blue-black hair melted into her black costume; and her eyes glowed out like blue stars, and in the great-hooped Spanish dress Clarkson had obtained for her, she seemed very small and demure and self-contained—and wondrous pretty. Yet more than one was to find something more than mere prettiness in Mary O'Neill, ere the race was run.

Beatrice rose, embraced her guest, and presented the cardinal. But when the latter would have bowed over her hand, she drew back suddenly, and her face became pale as death.

"No—no—ah, your pardon—I am not myself,"

94

she exclaimed disjointedly. "I did not know others
were here—"

"His Eminence accompanies us to Rome," said
Angelo, handing her to a seat. "Here, a glass of
wine—quick, Beatrice!"

The girl dropped into the chair, seemed near to
fainting, then rallied and with a laugh excused her
weakness. The cardinal's quick gaze probed the
courtyard, but Friar Dominic had vanished. A
servant brought word that two Moorish traders
were outside with rare carpets and shawls, and Beatrice ordered them admitted; thus, in another ten
minutes, the patio became a glory of color and rich-
ness, and the afternoon ran its course fluently, the
cardinal and Friar Dominic being assigned rooms
in the palace, which was large enough and to
spare.

The astute friar kept himself well out of Mary
O'Neill's sight, and if the cardinal needed any ex-
planation as to the girl's presence, he received it in
private from Angelo. He appeared, indeed, ironic-
ally amused over the whole situation, and made himself extremely agreeable to the Irish girl, who in
turn made frank amends for having greeted him in
such ill fashion. Small wonder, since in whatever

guise he passed Raymond of Corthia could exert a singular fascination for men or women alike.

When they were alone that night, in the great gilded wooden bed they had brought with them from Venice, Beatrice Donato said a word to her husband.

"Now, my Angelo, all caution! Guard your tongue with Raymond."

"He is our friend—"

"Bah! Raymond of Corthia is no man's friend. No one knows his secrets. He assumed that silly disguise in order that I might pierce it; he's a deep one, and you'd better let me play him. Each one to his own game, my Angelo—and this is mine, not yours."

To which Angelo assented, not without relief.

So were matters adjusted when, late the following morning, Yellow Brian opened his eyes to the warm winter sunlight and looked out from his bed upon the patio. He was alone; sitting up, he found his hurt newly bandaged and in good shape. Beside him on his bed, on a table, were food and drink, and he reached ravenously for them. Then he paused, stupified at sight of the black-clad figure walking in the patio beside the fountain, not twenty feet from him.

"Mary!" he exclaimed. Then, in Gaelic; "Mhuire! Mhuire! Is it you?"

The girl whirled, stared at him there in the arched opening, half dressed, a quilt wrapped about him. Her face went deathly white, and she signed herself with shaking fingers.

"Brian—a ghost—"

"Careful!" he exclaimed rapidly, at sight of a servant to one side. "Come here to my room when you have a chance—I don't think they know my name—"

She made a gesture of assurance and then turned away, dropping the veil over her face; for Beatrice Donato had just appeared and was coming toward her.

Brian withdrew from the arched window-opening. Alive and here, in good health—this girl whom he had thought lost in the hell of license and debauchery that was Rome! It was beyond credence, yet true enough. He could see her walking there, talking with Beatrice, until they both left his range of vision. Then, with an effort, he forced himself to readjustment.

"What matter how?" he muttered, overcoming his stunned bewilderment. "It's real—she's here—

97

that's enough! Did Carbajal know? No—he'd have told me. It's all sheer blind luck—another name for providence. Who are these Venetians? Well, I'll learn soon enough; meantime, step warily, talk little, keep on the alert! Something strange about all this."

He ate and drank. In the patio, after a little, he saw the figure of Cardinal Sainterre, now without the pillow-paunch but with whiskers hiding face, and Angelo with him; they too, passed, and almost at once O'Neill found visitors at his door. Ceccio came in, and after him Beatrice and Mary. He needed no warning to keep a guard on eyes and tongue, for at sight of the beautiful Venetian's face, in her liquid amber gaze, swift premonition came upon him. She bent above him as he lay, and her hand pressed him back when he would have risen.

"No, no, señor don—no rising until tomorrow—I am your surgeon here," she said in Spanish. "You do not know me? I am Beatrice Donato; my husband will come presently, being engaged in business. This is my dear friend who goes to Rome in our protection, Señorita O'Neill. Now let me look at your wound, and then we may talk. The salve, Ceccio!"

FINDING IS NOT KEEPING

Over her back, as she leaned to work on the bandages, O'Neill flashed one glance at Mary, and met warning in her eyes. He smiled a little, and looked no more for the present. She was real!

"Now we can talk," and her work done, Beatrice motioned Ceccio to clear away the dressings and salve, and took seat beside the chair of Mary O'Neill. "As yet, señor, we do not know your name."

"I am the Count Albujaras in Spain, though I have other titles no less barren than that one," and O'Neill smiled at the two women. "Brian is my name."

He gave it the Spanish pronunciation, so it might have been any word of like sound, and took the wine-cup Ceccio handed him, and drank. Beatrice eyed him thoughtfully, Mary with a lurking laugh in her blue eyes.

"I owe you great thanks and gratitude," he said to Beatrice, when Ceccio departed. "My debt cannot be paid with money, yet—"

"It may be paid with that ring on your finger," said Beatrice, and leaned forward to catch his hand and look at the ring. Then she looked him in the face, her fingers closing warmly on his, a sudden glow in her amber eyes. "I have a fancy for odd rings and jewels, and since this has no great value, give it to me and we shall be quits!"

"It is not mine; rather, I have promised to wear it always in memory of a dead man who was a good comrade," said O'Neill. "Even for gratitude, I would not break a promise, fair lady. Ask what you will of me, other than this—"

"Nay, this is all I would have." Beatrice rose abruptly, dropped his hand, and turned. "If a promise to a dead man is worth more than gratitude, I say no more."

She went rapidly from the room, as though angered. O'Neill looked at Mary, and saw her put finger to her lips, then rise and depart after Beatrice. He lay back on his pillows, and knew the fair Venetian had nearly trapped him—for he had been on the point of eager speech with this cousin of his.

Later that day he saw Angelo Donato, who visited him very courteously, made him hearty welcome to their company, and saw to it that his arms and belongings were cleaned and furbished. He had no other visitors, and indeed slept a great part of the afternoon. Toward evening Beatrice came again, alone this time, and caught at his hand as she sat beside him.

"You must pardon me," she said impulsively. "I was wrong—a spoiled child! And to beg your forgiveness—"

She kissed him quickly on the lips, then drew back and called Ceccio, and they changed the dressing. Astounded by all this, O'Neill said nothing whatever, but watched Beatrice. She set a flagon on the table beside his bed, and a great silver cup, bidding him drink of it during the night and forbidding any other nourishment until the morrow. Then, with a smile, she was gone and the door closed.

"Devil take her—what game is she up to?" Pondered O'Neill, disturbed. "Donato—that was the name of our friend who escaped from Corthia— where's the connection? This ring of common gray stone? It's past my understanding."

He gave up the puzzle, and presently fell off in a doze. When he wakened again, it was after dark. A blue-flickering night lamp lighted in the far corner of his chamber; he sipped at a bitter drink from the flagon, grimmaced, and put the cup back on the table.

After this, for a space, he was betwixt sleeping and

waking, until he was startled by a silent play of figures in the dim light. Like a ghost, a lean dark shape seemed to appear from nowhere, gliding across the floor toward the bed and window-opening. It paused for a little by the table, hung over the silver flagon, then retraced its way—only to stop abruptly, with a sharp catch of the breath. No ghost, but a man!

The man whirled, no longer silent, and darted for the open window-arch beside the bed, on its heels a second dark figure with bared blade. O'Neill, now awake, rose to one elbow, staring. The first intruder paused not, but went out of the window into the patio at one wild leap—and fell straight-way into the hands of two men who stood there. They fell upon him, and in the opening above paused the second intruder, watching. A word passed. The figure beside the bed turned, went to the table, took the silver flagon, and handed it down to the captors of the first intruder. A few words more, then the shape beside O'Neill laughed.

He knew Beatrice Donato was standing there.

She, too, jumped from the arch and joined the three below. The moon was high. In its light, O'Neill saw the scene clearly, saw the prisoner held, saw Beatrice holding the flagon to his lips, saw his face bared. It was the face of Friar Dominic. The false friar groaned, was forced to his knees, head wrenched back, teeth opened. Beatrice emptied the flagon into his mouth. A long moment passed— then slowly the captive figure of the friar went limp. They loosed him, and he fell face downward on the stones. Beatrice laughed once more, then was gone with her two men, leaving Friar Dominic there where he had fallen.

O'Neill sank back on the bed, sweating.

CHAPTER V

ONE VOICE IN A TREE, ANOTHER IN A FOG

"THE rascal put poison in my cup," thought O'Neill. "And, by the Red Hand of Ulster, he had to drink his own brew! Score one for Beatrice—but why? It means that she's against Raymond—or does it? With these Italians one can never tell. And Mary mistrusts her—"

His bewildered thoughts whirled and fell like a shuttlecock, as he was aware of another figure in his room, crossing swiftly to his bedside. He started up, and found Mary O'Neill at his side, gripping his hand; she knelt, and tears came hot on his fingers, and her voice broke out in sharp sobs.

"Brian—Brian—I had given up all hope of you! The one-eyed scullion promised to write you— Teague was murdered and they killed Hugh before my eyes—"

O'Neill drew her close, stroked her hair, calmed her with steady words, until presently ner sobs passed and she straightened up, trying to see his face in the dim light of the lamp.

"And now you'll take me away from all this, Brian?"

"You're safe enough now, little rose," he said. "We're all bound Romeward—"

She caught her breath sharply. "Don't you understand? Don't you know there's peril all around us—these people are not friends?"

"I understand precious little," confessed O'Neill. "But I think we're safe here. Signor Donato told me today that a French cardinal was going to Rome with us—"

"Ah, that man—that man!" she exclaimed swiftly. "He's no cardinal, Brian—he's the very man who killed poor Hugh! I knew him again the moment I saw his eyes. He was the leader of them all, there at the Black Bull—"

"Raymond of Corthia?" The words jerked from O'Neill. "You're sure?"

"Sure."

"Duar na Criosd!" swore O'Neill, startled. "Here, let me think—I'll tell you what's passed—"

The bearded, black-clad man whom he had seen—could it be Raymond of Corthia? All things were possible in this maze; bewildered, struggling for comprehension, O'Neill told of getting Carbajal's letter, of how he had come straightway, and of all that had taken place in Corthia and here.

"But what danger could there be here?" he concluded. "Look—there outside the window lies Friar Dominic—he tried to poison me tonight, and Lady Beatrice caught him in his own trap. That shows I am safe enough, and you are likewise safe with them—"

"I am not!" said the girl sharply. "Nor you, Brian! The woman is very beautiful, and very evil; I can feel it all the while. I am afraid to death of these Italians; we must get out of their hands without delay!"

"Well, nothing will happen you while I'm here," said O'Neill, patting her hand. "Let's put fears aside, little rose, and consider facts! It's not like you to give way to fear—you, who can handle a sword with any man!"

"I'm not afraid of the open—it's this secret intrigue, these lies, this feeling of being caught in a trap and held! But, Brian, you've grown in the

106

three years since we saw you—and I hear you've won fame in the wars under Don Juan—"

So they fell to talking of times past, and the Irish exiles in Spain—now scattered to the four winds. Orphaned long since, Mary had been left in the fostering of Brian's father, who was now dead. Behind both of them, indeed, the past was dead, and the future promised only what might be carved out of the present.

"Empty titles, empty honors, and wolves waiting to strip us of what little remains!" said O'Neill somberly. "We may talk of the Spanish ambassador and our friends at Rome, but there's no reliance to be placed on any of them, little rose; they'd betray us for a ducat of gold. Yet I think it's otherwise with Carbajal, and the man Donato whom I scarce know—we'll see. I've sworn to uproot Raymond, and Corthia with him—the three of us are agreed on it. I didn't know you were to be saved; but as for you—"

"As for me, Brian," she said swiftly, "I owe that debt likewise, and I join you in the oath. You should know that I'm no simpering maid—I'm an O'Neill, and if we're distant in blood we're close in spirit! But beware of these Venetians, Brian, and of this woman above all."

"Right." O'Neill leaned over and touched his lips to her hair. "We'll win through, Roisin Dubh, and we'll avenge Hugh and carve out some destiny for ourselves—so now back with you lest this place be still under watch! If you have any need of me, send me a gift of some sort, which will seem innocent enough to the Venetians. Christ keep you!"

"And you, Brian," she said, and so was gone softly.

When O'Neill slept at last, the still form of Friar Dominic remained on the stones of the patio.

It chanced that O'Neill saw and heard the morning's meeting between Beatrice and Cardinal Sainterre—it took place just outside his window, after the local authorities had carried off the body of Friar Dominic and the superficial investigation was done. Perhaps O'Neill's presence was forgotten—at all events, the two came face to face in the patio, and the false cardinal made the lady a deep bow.

"I trust," he said in French, and very suavely, "you were not incommoded last night by the suicide of that unfortunate man?"

Beatrice met his gaze with narrowed, challenging eyes—she was dangerous now.

"Bah! No evasions," she said curtly. "He left a poisoned drink for my patient, and I made him down it. You had full warning. Abandon subterfuge and meet the matter squarely! Is it to be peace or war!"

"Peace. I think we've too many larger matters in common, to quarrel over small things," said the cardinal. "The man hated your patient on his own account, and didn't consult me as to his intentions. Naturally, I shouldn't have allowed him to play with poison under this roof—one doesn't smell flowers in a perfume-shop! So far as I'm concerned, the matter's closed. Will you accept my arm! There's nothing more—"

They moved away, but certain words lingered with O'Neill. "One doesn't smell flowers in a perfume-shop!" A dark and grim hint, if accepted at face value, as to what Raymond knew of Beatrice. Doubtless, there was ground for Mary's intuitive fears of this beautiful Venetian.

Raymond knew, too, who O'Neill really was—would have learned this from Friar Dominic. This meant more peril, and Yellow Brian laughed to think how Carbajal had managed to land him in the very hands of the enemy. However, he appeared to be safe enough momentarily; yet what was to come of all—whither was he tending?

"Now that Mary's safe," he reflected uneasily, "I've no business in Rome—but must go there to meet Donato and Carbajal. Hm! I begin to think destiny must be at work in this apparently aimless jockeying. What connection can lie between these Venetians and Carlo Donato—it was of them he was afraid, because of them that he fled! Beatrice knows his ring. Good thing Carbajal warned me! And who's Carbajal himself, I wonder? Yes, it looks as though all these tangled threads would end up in some strong hempen rope—and it'll hang some of us yet if we don't look out. By the Red Hand of Ulster, I don't like this underground intrigue! Have to stick it out, though, until I can ride again. Fortunately, this wound is coming around in good shape."

Later in the morning Ceccio came and bathed him, aided him to dress, and took him out to the patio where Beatrice and Mary were sucking grapes while Cardinal Sainterre told tales of Avignon and Rome. O'Neill joined them, bowed to the prelate, and was commanded to the couch beside Beatrice. Presently Angelo Donato appeared, and the noon meal was served here in the fresh sunlit courtyard.

The tragic event of the night was not mentioned. Pulled into the talk, O'Neill spoke of Condé and Don Juan, and the campaigns in France and Poland and Flanders, and soon lost his reserve; here in the warm sunlight imagination lost power and fears died and intrigue faded away—remained only the great joy he had found in knowing Mary alive and at hand, so that the eager vibrance of the man leaped out past disguise. Beatrice, watching him, spoke with her odd hinted smile.

"You're very glad to be alive, Don Brian?"

"Today, very—thanks to you!" he answered, letting her see in his glance that he knew how she had saved him during the dark hours. "Aye, and if I can get free of my vow at Rome, as I think may be, I'll grant the request you made of me, with all my heart!"

"Ah! I have the power to release from vows," spoke up the cardinal, "if they be not of too serious a nature, Count Brian! So that, if I may serve you—"

O'Neill laughed. "All thanks, your eminence,

III

but this is a matter of my own conscience, and I fear only the Pope will be able to serve me. Perhaps you know Cardinal Ludovici?"

"Intimately—when in Rome, I dine with him each Thursday," responded the cardinal. "I am even now bound Romeward to confer with him in certain matters of state; as you may know, he is rather influential politically—"

There was a low, mocking laugh. The cardinal's words died, and he glanced about sharply, but all were as surprised as he. Then, in the silence, came a voice from behind the cardinal.

"You've heard that the scullion has escaped from the Black Bull, eh?"

The cardinal twisted about; no one was behind him—the patio stretched unbroken to the flowers and wall. Angelo leaped to his feet, so that his chair crashed backward, and cried out.

"Who was that? Who spoke, I say?"

The voice answered him, from empty air for all to see.

"Who spoke? Why, perhaps it was Carlo, perhaps a ghost!"

The sleek brown oval of Angelo's face became livid. The cardinal rose, crossed himself, stared from very wide and alert eyes at the garden. Beatrice, who had also changed color at those last words, suddenly flung up her hand, and her voice came with unusual harshness.

"The bird, tethered there—look! The one I bought the other day, Angelo—"

Indeed, in one of the flowered bushes was tethered a gay parrot on a thin silver chain. There was a pause, in which O'Neill spoke, frowning as though perplexed.

"Voices don't come from nowhere, my friends. Can the bird speak?"

"Fools!" came the same odd voice, but now from another corner of the patio. "Fools! It is your own hearts that speak. Seek me not!"

Now one looked at another, until Beatrice sent sharp words at her women, and Angelo shouted at the servants, and the cardinal went among the bushes himself, catlike, a dagger gleaming in his hand. But the blue eyes of Mary O'Neill went suddenly to the man on the couch, and caught the smile under his yellow mustache, and she leaned back in her chair and reached for more grapes as though she knew whence that voice had come, after all. None else guessed, however, and it was some little time before the search was abandoned. Uneasiness and even fear had been strewn across this pleasant patio, so that after a time O'Neill found himself alone with Mary. She, too, rose to depart, and stood regarding him with a twinkle in her eye.

"So the old tricks of boyhood still have their uses, Brian? All the same, we must be careful now —they're on the alert, and if they think there's any connection between us, no telling what will happen! Our friend the cardinal looked horribly startled— did the one-eyed scullion mean so much to him?"

"Obviously, though I don't know the secret myself." O'Neill chuckled as he thought of Sainterre's face. "That little trick of throwing the voice has served me well many a time. Yes, we'd better watch ourselves, little rose—we're on unsafe ground."

So she went away, and O'Neill dozed in the sun or smoked his pipe, and smiled to himself over it all. A childish trick indeed—yet it could throw these intriguing scoundrels into sheer panic! He felt a touch of contempt for the incident, and fell into musing thought.

"What can they mean toward Mary, how do they intend to use her? There's little philanthropy in this precious gang. I must play for time, get to Rome, join hands with Carbajal; then, with this cursed little wound in shape, nothing will so much matter. We can head for Corthia all together—"

Simple enough in the saying; but, as he well knew, Corthia was far away and getting farther each hour, as intrigue mounted and complications grew. Because of his brother Hugh, killed there by Raymond, he meant to push through his oath to the bittermost; yet he had come to guess that Raymond and Corthia and the Black Bull held darker things and more secrets than he yet dreamed.

During the rest of his stay in Leghorn, O'Neill found himself watched and circumscribed, Ceccio being ever close beside him, while Beatrice spent great time in his company. All this, he sensed, came not so much from suspicion, as from regard for his safety; he could guess that his safe delivery in Rome was for some reason of tremendous import to Beatrice—and no doubt Carbajal could have explained it. In memory, the one-eyed Carbajal took on stature, so that O'Neill began to look forward to finding the man again and probing his mystery. Of the pseudo-cardinal he saw little; Sainterre and Angelo had much business in the town.

So came Saturday and the start for Rome. As befitted his station, Angelo traveled in princely style. Beatrice and Mary and O'Neill rode in a great lumbering coach of green and gold, deeply cushioned and pillowed; sly old Ceccio and the slave girls followed in a second coach, while a wagon bore the huge gilded bed and the baggages. For reasons more practical than nice, the Italian hospices had only beds of iron, and he who would lie in safety and comfort must transport his own bed.

Angelo, his two bravos, and Cardinal Sainterre rode alongside or behind the coach, and postilions and equerries made up the procession to an imposing array. They left Leghorn by the hill road for Siena, thus cutting off a large segment of unnecessary road at the cost of a little rough going.

Reclining by the side of Beatrice, O'Neill regarded his distant cousin opposite and found himself no little amused by her manner. He knew very well that Mary O'Neill was no prim maid of Spain, bound up and hidden in vast hoops and furbelows, keeping a demure watch upon every word and act. Yet thus she seemed, and it rendered O'Neill thoughtful. The reason was here beside him, sleek and scented and lovely, and more than a little dan-

116

gerous. Turning to her, he found Beatrice watching him with sidelong gaze; a lurch of the coach threw them close, and he caught her warm, slender fingers in his.

"Well, fair lady of Venice?" he exclaimed gaily. "A bright golden crown for your thoughts—gold for the precious thoughts, the crown for beauty!"

He set in her hand one of the gold pieces looted from the Black Bull; his pockets were still heavy with them, and the large bag was in Angelo's care. Her brows arched, and the amber eyes studied him for a moment.

"Too much pay for such poor thoughts," she replied. "It was in my mind that Venice has need of captains, Don Brian. With the proper influence before the Council, one who has served under Don Juan of Austria might go far."

Eyes and voice showed more than the words. For an instant O'Neill was stricken dumb by the swift vision opened to him—to lead the forces of Venice against the Turk! Then the vision darkened; power, after all, might be bought too dear.

"Nay, Venice needs captains by sea, and a seasick admiral wouldn't be much good to her," said O'Neill. Then, as his jesting tone brought sudden

117

storm into her eyes, he added quickly: "Why does my safe coming to Rome mean so much to you, lady? Why should you bother to preserve my life, at great trouble and cost to yourself?"

"Because others want to take it, perhaps." Suddenly, savagely, she flung the gold piece out the window and turned upon him with a sharp flash of anger. "A fine recompense you make me—refusing my one request, then giving me gold and jests and a pack of lies, playing with me as though I were a child! Are you blind? It was a likely story about assassins following you from Genoa, when in reality you came from Corthia and it was Raymond himself who wanted your life! Now, if you refuse my friendship and aid, if you withhold your trust, if you treat me with disdain and contumely—look to it, Spaniard!"

Astounded by this outburst and by her knowledge, O'Neill made shift to parry her anger as best he could, while Mary watched them both, wide-eyed and uneasy. He explained how he had not dared to speak openly, being suspicious of everyone around; and with reason, as she well knew.

"Yet I have nothing to hide from you, dear lady," he continued. "As for Raymond, I have sworn to kill him and destroy his accursed robbers' nest. Friends of mine were caught and slain there. In passing through, I think I burned most of his town, and I hope to return and finish the work. Could I boast of all these things, in my condition?"

"You are either a fool or a great man," she retorted, "to remain in Italy while Raymond lives."

"But I'm bound for Rome," he said, feigning ignorance. "Raymond has no power there, and I have friends awaiting me."

She only shrugged at this. He waited to see if she would give him any warning that Raymond of Corthia was even then beside the coach and bound Romeward; but she shifted the subject, showed no more anger toward him, and fell to talking eagerly of the Carnival ahead.

He was glad enough to be off personal matters and to keep off them, for now he began to be aware of the peril in her; beneath her beauty he sensed hard and cold surfaces, as though emotion and sex and outward seeming would all be turned ruthlessly toward gaining some desired goal. Real womanliness was not in her, and he mentally compared her, soft and langorous and outwardly all that was feminine, with the demure girl opposite—who could

handle a sword better than most men if need
were.

Brian O'Neill had no genius for intrigue and was
not at ease in dealing with such ladies as Beatrice.
He was relieved when Angelo joined them in the
coach, after the noon halt, and gossiped busily of
Rome and the Carnival, the scandal of Queen
Christina of Sweden and Cardinal Azzolino, with
such matters. Angelo had turned some good deals
in Leghorn and was languidly pleased with life in
general.

It was hard upon sunset when the coaches and
horsemen clattered into Siena and sought an inn
close to the Porto Romano, the better to insure an
early morning's start; having concluded all his Tuscan business, Angelo was eager to get on to Rome
without pause. That night, for lack of space,
O'Neill shared a room with Ceccio, had his wound
redressed, and found himself rapidly recovering
from its effects.

Morning found them on the road again—but
without Cardinal Sainterre. That eminent prelate
had vanished, bag and baggage, during the night.
From the inquietude of Angelo Donato and his
hurried conference with Beatrice, O'Neill inferred

that the disappearance of Sainterre was as much a surprise to the others as to himself, and no very pleasant one. None the less they made an early start, and most of the morning rode through a miserable drizzle of mingled snow and rain.

Angelo had small liking for such weather, and after the noon halt at Torrinieri was heartily glad to enter the coach and give over his mount to O'Neill. The latter, warmly cloaked, was eager to try himself in the saddle of Angelo's excellent barb, and thought nothing of the weather; it was otherwise with the Venetians, who shivered and accounted him a little mad. O'Neill was well satisfied with his bargain, and found himself in very fair shape to ride once more.

As luck would have it, he arranged with Angelo to keep the horse next day as well, though he might have found room in the coach. Wily Angelo knew the road ahead and had scant heart for it. All the morning it climbed the rugged flanks of Mount Pientio, so that they struggled along the slow miles enwrapped in a thick fleecy fog, at last reaching the fort and hospice of Radicofani on the summit, there built by Duke Ferdinand. Clouds veiled the fort above and hid all the vast landscape around, being so thick that one could scarce see across the road.

When they had dined, O'Neill rose from the table early, to make certain his horse was being fed and watered. Just opposite the inn was a fountain, gushing into a great stone trough on which the Medici arms were carven. The horses, coaches and wagon grouped about this, and the north-bound diligence had just arrived from Rome, making somewhat of a crowd. O'Neill shoved his way through, saw to his horse, and was about to return to the tavern when a beggar muffled in dirty cloths pulled at his sleeve.

"Alms, signor!" whined the man. "Alms for a poor pilgrim laden with holy relics—alas, signor, I gave my whole wealth to the poor and have none left. Alms, as you love Achmet!"

O'Neill started at the name.

"I give no alms," he said curtly. "Show me your relics; perhaps I may buy one or two of them."

"They are in my bundle, signor—come out of the crowd, across the road."

O'Neill followed the beggar, who mouthed the virtues and rarity of his relics, across the way and to the corner of the inn. There, alone, the beggar stopped and turned, and a laugh broke from him.

"How goes the wound, comrade? Well enough, to judge from your looks—"

In the unshaven, dirt-smeared face revealed to him, O'Neill saw the dark and flaming eyes of Carlo Donato. He seized the man's hand joyfully.

"You! What does this mean, comrade? You need help—"

"Per Bacco, I need nothing!" The other laughed joyously, gaily. "I've been to Rome and back again —saw Carbajal in prison—"

"Eh? Carbajal in prison?" snapped O'Neill.

"Assuredly. He was entering town by the Vatican gate when Don Agostino, that rake-helly nephew of His Holiness, glimpsed the Arab and wanted to buy him for the Carnival racing. Our Carbajal was not polite, I gather, and swords were out. So Don Agostino took the Arab and clapped Carbajal into San Angelo; the Pope's nephew can do things in Rome, I assure you! I heard of it, saw Carbajal and learned about you, got word to his friends and mine, and posted hither on my own affairs. No fear, Carbajal's free by this time! But no more talk now— I've horses waiting below town, so come along with me, swiftly—"

"Hold on!" exclaimed O'Neill. "Whither bound?"

Donato jerked his thumb toward the thick fog below.

"Twelve miles to the Roman boundary—a precipitous descent that'll take your coaches all afternoon. I've men waiting me—you understand? If by chance one of those coaches goes over the cliff, I don't want you to be in it."

O'Neill shivered slightly. In the deep voice, in the eyes glowing from the dirt-daubed, stubbled face, he read terrible things.

"Wait!" he said. "Perhaps you know I sought a certain girl, presumably sold into Roman bagnios? Well, she's here, safe enough, and under the protection of Beatrice—"

"Better the protection of the devil!" snarled Donato.

"Perhaps. Yet Beatrice saved my life. Friar Dominic showed up in Leghorn, tried to poison me —she made him drink it. Raymond himself was there and started to Rome with us, but disappeared at Siena."

"Whew! That's news!" Donato whistled. "Saved you, eh? That was because Carbajal terrified her—threatened to bring me from the dead. It wasn't for love of you—"

"No matter. You shan't murder a woman."

The other drew back. "Shame, comrade! I'm a soldier like you; do I seem in your eyes so low and despicable—"

"Pardon, my friend!" broke in O'Neill quickly. "How do I know what you propose? It is none of my affair, yet because Lady Beatrice saved me from poison, I owe her a debt."

"Then heaven help you!" said the other gloomily, and his hand went to O'Neill's arm. "So she has impressed you, eh? She has visited you in the night, and put her lips to yours, and then fled? Ah, I know the wench's tricks! They mean nothing. She has no soul, that woman—"

"Bah!" said O'Neill, yet feeling the red come into his face. "I care naught what happens to her, and she has not fooled me a particle. But she is a woman."

"You're in Italy now, caballero," said the other with savage irony. Then his voice changed. "But I swear I'll not harm her, nor gentle Angelo neither! Go and get hold of that girl of yours, and fetch her; she can take my horse. Both of you disappear into the fog with me, understand? We've got to chance things. With Raymond on the road, anything's possible. Can you get her away?"

"Yes."

"Then I'll wait here. Ten paces, and we're gone in the fog. Hurry!"

O'Neill turned into the tavern court.

CHAPTER VI

FOG CANNOT HINDER A RESURRECTION

WHEN it was discovered that the Condé de Albujaras had disappeared, and the Irish girl as well, there was swift turmoil in the *osteria* of Radicofani. Once his first furious dismay and excitement were past, however, Angelo took charge and speedily narrowed things down.

Don Brian had procured no horses at the inn, and could have procured none elsewhere; a messenger to the fort above discovered no sign of the missing pair there. The north-bound diligence had changed horses and departed; although its passengers were numbered and known, the two bravos galloped after, overtook it, and made certain that neither Spaniard nor girl were in it. Meanwhile, the big gilt coach and convoy stood harnessed and ready to depart. The fog had thickened and one could scarce discern the stone water-trough opposite.

"It's obvious that they didn't set out afoot for

either Rome or Siena," declared Angelo, joining Beatrice before the tavern fire and downing the goblet of mulled wine she had made ready for him. He made a wry face, and continued.

"Their effects were not touched, however. She might abandon her clothes, true, but he would certainly not abandon twenty-five thousand crowns in gold, not to mention his sword and other things! She didn't appear to suspect anything?"

Beatrice shook her head lazily. "No. I think you'll find they went out for a walk and were lost in the fog. Will it lighten?"

"They tell me it thickens toward evening," returned Angelo gloomily. "Five thousand ducats and my balas ruby tied up in that skirt—and we must wait in this accursed fog until it pleases her to show herself!"

"Not necessarily." Beatrice was fully as anxious as Angelo to get out of the chilling dark mist and down into the lower country, and was tempted to take an optimistic view. "Leave Ceccio here to bring them on by the diligence—it will catch us at Acquapendente tonight. In this place, the girl couldn't lose herself long, and the gold in our luggage is hostage enough for the Spanish don."

Angelo brightened. "An excellent idea, my angel
—Ha, Ceccio! Inside here!" The little servitor
came in hurriedly, and Angelo gave him instructions
to wait. "If they turn up soon, hire horses or a
coach; otherwise, bring them by the diligence.
Spare no expense. Five thousand ducats lost in this
fog, not to mention my balas ruby—guard it well,
Ceccio!"

So it was arranged. After a delay of over an
hour, Angelo and Beatrice entered their coach, and
the cavalcade got off in the fog.

The twelve-mile stretch ahead of them, to Acquapendente and the plains of ancient Volsinium below,
was wretched and dangerous road, descending
sharply most of the way, so that the great coach had
to go slowly and with care.

While Angelo cursed the fog and mourned his
ducats and balas ruby, Beatrice was inclined to make
light of the matter. She held O'Neill in rather
spiteful contempt, and disregarded Mary entirely—
to her, the girl was a mere pawn, and she knew wily
Ceccio had the ability to take care of the matter,
having proven his worth long since. If Ceccio were
versed in the cure of bodies, he was still more versed
in their destruction.

A curious couple, this in the coach descending the sharp hill-road so carefully. Between them was less love than partnership; both ran to cold calculation and intrigue rather than to emotion. The untimely death of Carlo Donato at the height of his military career had left Beatrice a wealthy widow; courted by Don Camillo, nephew of the old Pope, the painted prince-cardinal whose sanctity was no deeper than the enamel on his face, she had learned barely in time of the Pope's death, and had turned to the alliance with Angelo Donato. Don Camillo married another and wealthier widow—an older one, content to leave him with his ladies—and the house of Donato waxed great in Venice and the Levant.

"I depended on this girl to win over Don Camillo," growled Angelo, as the coach rumbled on down the road. "What sort of man is he—you knew him, I think?"

"A marionette," and Beatrice shrugged disdainfully. "Behind his painted mask are wealth and power; yet few know him well. I saw him only a few times. Of late years he has lived in strict retirement. He is in Rome only at Carnival and Easter, as we learned."

"Yes, the nephew of the new Pope might not appreciate any political activity on the part of the nephew of the old Pope," grunted Angelo. "Still, if he will join us it means much—his influence will make us secure at Florence, and we need Tuscany on our side. I've hinted at things to Raymond of Corthia; he said he'd see us in Rome. With those two, and the Spanish influence thrown into the scales, we can defy the Pope safely enough. Particularly as we're assured that the Council will stand behind us. Rome will lose Ferrara rather than fight Venice."

"Bah! Rome won't fight anyone," declared Beatrice. "We have the man, the proofs of his identity, the backing—once the coup is sprung, the matter's ended. And what a scandal for Rome! Raymond must produce the proofs that he was set to ensnare and slay Alfonso, that Rome might continue to hold Ferrara; then what a scandal! Will Raymond do it? How far did you go with him?"

Angelo smiled and fondled his little mustache.

"I recalled history to him," he said suavely, enjoying the mere flavor of it all. "How Duke Alfonso died without heirs fifty years ago, Ferrara going to the Roman State. Then how word arose some years ago that a grandson of Duke Alfonso was alive; how he had learned his own identity and had gone to the

Spanish Ambassador with the evidence, asking the help of Spain to regain his estate; how the Spaniard betrayed the matter to the old Pope, and how this claimant Alfonso vanished mysteriously. I said he was undoubtedly dead. Raymond said he certainly was dead. 'But supposing he came alive—or another in his place?' I asked. 'Supposing this other had evidence of his identity, no matter how he came by it, and the backing of Venice and Rome? Supposing he had Raymond of Corthia behind him, swearing that instead of killing Alfonso he had kept him alive?' Well, this tickled our good Raymond, I can tell you!"

"What did he say to it?" demanded Beatrice, with swift interest.

"He said that all roads led to Rome, and that once in the city he would confer with us upon the whole matter."

"Suppose he betrays us?"

"He'd not dare—and he has nothing to betray. He evidently wants time to inquire just how far Spain and Venice might be behind us. He's a deep one, that rascal!"

"What did his eyes say?" queried Beatrice shrewdly.

"That he was mightily interested. There was no talk of rewards, but he'll want a sum—"

"Bah! Money does not interest that man," exclaimed Beatrice, and Angelo listened to her with attention. "If he saw a bauble, and wanted it, he'd murder a thousand—but he'd get it. He has no weak spot; he's invulnerable. That means one thing: he wants power! So prepare yourself for the demand. He'll give up Corthia and demand part of the Ferrara territories, or else a fief and dukedom from Venice. We could give him Istria."

Angelo whistled thoughtfully. It did not occur to him to question the judgment of Beatrice, which he knew to be above price—so far as men were concerned. From her early years Beatrice had toyed with men as with pawns. In a day when morality was a matter of personal preference, she trod the path of virtue; not for its own sake, but from a sexless realization that thus might her ends be better gained. If men were mad about her, she was mad about none of them, and with a diabolic penetration made use of their characters and desires to serve her own purposes. While she was sometimes wrong in her estimates, she was seldom wrong in her deductions.

Angelo, not having the gift of foresight, knew that Beatrice had probably prophesied the demands of Raymond to a hair's breadth. He smiled at the thought of their coming meeting in Rome. Angelo had gained great repute by being fortified in advance with his wife's opinions, and by being ever ready to act upon them. Thus, before meeting Raymond, he would confer with the Venetian ambassador and others, and could barter out of hand with Raymond —to the surprise of that astute nobleman, who would have counted on much delay. To those who did not know his wife, Angelo was ever an astonishing man.

"But who will rule Ferrara, behind our puppet Alfonso?" he asked reflectively. "Raymond may well ask for that."

"Not he," said Beatrice. "It's too close to Venice. Raymond is a sensible man—he prefers to be out of the way, inaccessible, and comparatively safe. This Alfonso is a meek little man, and will do what I tell him. He wills Ferrara to Venice, of course."

"Ah! He makes a will!" Angelo looked attentively at his wife. He perceived that she had gone well into the future of affairs with the Councillors at Venice—more so than she had confessed to him.

"Exactly," and she smiled languidly at him. "Do

you think Venice gives something for nothing, my
Angelo?"

"Hm!" said Angelo. "This puppet of ours will
have a short life, I fear. Well, I'm not interfering
in your affairs. This Alfonso will meet us at Rome,
eh?"

"At Rome," she said. "He's at the embassy now,
beyond doubt."

While they, thus profiting by the privacy of the
great coach, discussed their mutual projects in se-
curity, the cavalcade pursued its way along the savage hill-road, gradually winding toward the plains
below. The way was shaggy with trees on either
hand, now all adrip and ghostly in the windless mist,
dim as phantoms against the gray desolation of earth
and sky, with twining wreaths of fog creeping along
their limbs.

"I don't like this mist," said Angelo uneasily. He
looked out and shivered, despite the fur-lined coat
that wrapped him. "Especially on the road. One
can't see fifty feet—"

"An incident of travel," said Beatrice with a
shrug.

"An incident which might be turned to our dis-
advantage—ah! Name of the devil—"

A cry leaped to his lips.

The coach was turning a sharp elbow of the road. On their right, trees and rocks gave place to tree-tops alone—the hill-flank fell away here in a sharp precipitous descent. And ahead, scarce fifty feet distant, the road was blocked; figures were moving there in the fog, and behind them the lofty mass of a fallen tree cut athwart the way.

Horses pulled back, brakes squealing, the coach slid along the wet road on locked wheels for a little space. Shouts and oaths from the postilions gave warning to the coach and wagon following. The two bravos drew out pistols, in readiness; though seeing themselves trapped, they were brave enough.

Abruptly, the shadowy figures scattered and vanished, as the coach halted; then one man on horseback came forward slowly, showing himself unarmed, but wearing armor. He was a bullet-headed little man, whose accent showed he was a Genoese.

"My men are placed with muskets. Surrender, and no one shall be harmed. Refuse, and we give no quarter. Choose! You are taken in the rear and front."

A yell of lively alarm and dismay from the wagon

and coach behind, showed that bandits were there also. Surrounded, blocked off, evidently out-numbered and helpless in the fog, Angelo had no choice in the matter. He stood with his head protruding from the coach window, fright and anger stamped in his face.

"Is this robbery?" he demanded.

"It is robbery, signor," answered the Genoese coolly.

"Then we submit. Take what we have and clear the road."

"I am giving orders, signor, not you," was the response. "Our chief wishes to speak with you and the lady. You are not to be injured unless you resist. Our chief is close by. Come with me!"

Angelo hesitated; but Beatrice, who had heard the order, laughed softly.

"Obey," she said in a low voice, "and leave me to deal with this bandit chief."

"We submit," said Angelo, and gestured to his men.

There was a flurry of activity in the fog. The two bravos and the postilions were at once ordered back to the other coach and the wagon. The Genoese dismounted, two of his men joining him, and

137

bowed to Beatrice as Angelo handed her out to the road.

"One moment," he said, "and then I conduct you to our chief."

He stepped into the coach, and Angelo watched him in utter stupefaction and helpless rage. This coach, a long time in the family service, held a secret compartment under the seat, designed for just such emergencies as this. Without search, without hesitation, the Genoese pressed the spring, opened the compartment, drew out Angelo's gold coin and the jewels of Beatrice, and stuffed them all into his saddle-bags.

"Devil take you!" exclaimed Angelo, half stifled with fury. "You knew where to look!"

The Genoese laughed. "My master told me. He knows all things. Come!"

Bridle over arm, he led them to the roadside, then turned and waved his arm. His two men acted swiftly. From the other coach and wagon went up a sudden yell, and Angelo turned to see the four horses deliberately lashed, turned, sent at the precipice. It was all done in a moment—the shrill high scream of a horse, a wild crash, a thunderous reverberation from the hillside below, and silence.

138

FOG CANNOT HINDER RESURRECTION

Angelo and Beatrice were staring, horrified, incredulous, when the Genoese turned.

"Come! You are not to be harmed. In a few moments you may rejoin your people and go on your way. Come!"

They followed him by a path leading in among the trees. If this measure of destruction had been cruelly intended to impress them it had succeeded; Angelo was livid, and Beatrice was furious, her amber eyes glowing luminous—but they knew better than to provoke any ruthless vengeance by act or utterance.

Perhaps fifty feet from the road, a man was sitting above a tiny fire, a cloak hiding his head and body as he bent over, paying no heed to them. Behind and around, were voices and the impatient tread of horses, but nothing could be seen, so thick was the mist here under the trees. A dozen feet from the seated man, the Genoese halted his captives.

"They are here, Nobilissimo. All is done as ordered."

The chief waved his hand, and the Genoese stepped away into the fog. Angelo and Beatrice stood staring, puzzled by this affair; then Beatrice came forward a step or two and laughed.

139

"Well, my good bandit?" she said gaily. "At least you'll invite us to a glass of wine—since we've paid for it so handsomely?"

The chief rose, his face covered, and saluted them in the profound Venetian manner; if there were irony in it, there was more irony in his voice.

"Most noble Venetians," he said, at this voice Beatrice changed countenance and stared anew, "undoubtedly you know the laws of the Republic?"

"Somewhat," said Angelo uneasily. "Regarding what? Robbery?"

"No, galantissimo, regarding sumptuary dress, for one thing," said the chief. "You have paid a heavy fine for your gay clothes, for your silks and brocades and cloth of gold! Is it just?"

"This is not Venice," said Angelo sulkily, though Beatrice turned pale as death.

"But let us pass to other laws," said the chief, and sat down again. "Is it not the law that a noble may poison his adulterous wife, and poniard her gallant?"

"Yes," said Angelo. "But—but—"

The words died in his throat. Slowly the chief moved, raising his head, little by little taking away the cloak that hid his face. As it became more clear in the fog, a stifled scream broke from Beatrice, who shrank back and clung to Angelo's arm. Abruptly, Carlo Donato threw off his cloak and came to his feet, looking at them silently.

The incredulity and horror gripping them both in this moment was a sheer physical force beyond control. Here before them was the man who had died in Candia, to whom Beatrice had herself given the drugged cup—her husband. And as he had been in life, red-lipped, fiery-eyed, vigorous, a very eagle poised in flight, the glitter of a damascened breastpiece contrasting with the dark velvet dress and on his hand the little ring they knew so well.

Beatrice came near to fainting, but pulled herself together. Angelo lifted his hand and signed in the air, terror stamped in his face.

"Away!" he cried thickly. "Fiend or ghost—"

"Neither fiend nor ghost." Carlo Donato laughed a little, and held out his hand to them. "Look, there's my ring, made of stone from the Holy Sepulchre; would it be used by a fiend? No, no, dear wife and cousin, here I'm alive and hearty before you! And have you no other greeting for me than a blank stare?"

They had none, indeed, these two stricken beings, fear unutterable planted in them by the vision of this man come back from the dead. Neither of them doubted that he would take a hot and bitter vengeance to the utmost of his due, as indeed the custom and law of Venice allowed him; and as the reality of his presence grew clearer, as they comprehended more fully that Carlo Donato was here in the flesh, and they in his power, each reacted to it in different fashion.

Angelo tensed, gathered himself together, broke out: "Carlo! You are really alive, in the flesh—but why have we never known? We heard you were dead in Candia—Beatrice came home a widow—"

The words failed on his lips, lost body, died out; he stood licking lips with tongue under the impassive gaze of Carlo Donato. Beatrice, after one glance at her husband, shrugged and waited. She, too, was more collected, yet the mortal pallor in her face showed how she was facing the reality and dreading it.

"My dear cousin, and my dear wife," said Carlo Donato, with a smile that was no less terrible than his calm voice, "you need have no fear. I would not stain my hands with the blood of a woman, murderess and poisoner though she be; as for you, gentle Angelo, I'd rather spit a cat upon my blade and boast of it, than sully honest steel with your traitorous blood. No, no, you may go back, take up your journey to Rome, and fear me not."

A flicker of terror lightened the amber eyes of Beatrice.

"Carlo!" she cried. "What do you mean—you don't intend—"

"Exactly what I say, fair Beatrice," said Carlo Donato. "I arranged this pleasant little meeting merely to let you have the joy of knowing I am alive and in good health. You are married—gentle little doves! There'll be a pretty scandal in Venice when the news comes out, eh? I've taken your jewels and cash because I have need of them, and in any case they are my property. As for my other property, I don't doubt you've handled it well. When I demand an accounting, it'll be all safe, waiting for me."

He fell silent, letting the import of the words sink in. It staggered the guilty pair before him.

"But, Carlo!" ventured Angelo, wetting his lips anew. "When—when will—"

The red lips parted in a cruel smile. "When? Why, that's for me to suit to my own good will, dear Angelo! You and my dear Beatrice can live from day to day, from week to week, in anticipation of my showing myself to the Council and demanding restitution. Not of conjugal rights, perhaps—no, that would be going a bit too far, eh? Next time the poison might work better, and I prefer not to risk it. But you'll be glad to keep my dear wife in trust, Angelo, and my fortune as well. Guard it craftily, good cousin; I well know your honest heart and wise counsel! When we put little Ceccio to the rack and he tells all he knows—well, no more of that for the present. When? After I've finished some more important business that engages me at present. Thanks, dear Beatrice, for taking good care of the Spaniard. You need not hold rancor against him, for he was quite innocent of any share in the business; indeed, I carried him off and the girl as well, lest they come to harm. You, Tomàs! Come and take these two back, and in twenty minutes roll the tree from the road and let them go free."

So then, abruptly, Carlo Donato turned and strode off into the fog, and was lost to sight. The Genoese replaced him, and signed the two prisoners to follow. They obeyed, dumb, horrified, tasting already of the bitter cup that was to be ever before their lips night and day. Walking unsteadily, they were gone among the trees.

FOG CANNOT HINDER RESURRECTION

Carlo Donato came to where O'Neill and Mary were sitting, on a log near the group of horses. He waved his hand gaily.

"Finished!"

"Eh?" O'Neill looked at him narrowly. "And no blood let?"

Donato laughed. He was ever cheerful, this man, and yet at times there could come a terrible note into his mirth.

"Worse than blood! They now know I am alive, and that some day I shall proclaim myself to the world, tell the story of her treachery, take back my wealth and place. Figure it for yourselves! Shame and disgrace for her; for him, shame and disgrace. What punishment could be worse for those two, who live ever in the world's eye? Meantime, they wait —and the suspense drags on their very souls! Vengeance enough there, and then I shall have vengeance of another sort when we take Raymond of Corthia."

Mary O'Neill, who now knew the story of the man and his sufferings, stood up and took his hand and smiled into his fiery eyes.

"I respect you, Carlo Donato, for the man you are," she said simply. The Venetian flushed, and stooped above her hand. Then he straightened quickly.

"No time now to talk!" he exclaimed. "Your money and goods are already being packed, comrade. I have jewels and gold also, part of my own wealth regained. We must to horse, and spur for Rome full speed. Do you know, I am afraid that devil Raymond is ahead of us! If he left your party at Siena, it was for one purpose only—to get to Rome. I have the feel of events in the air, of big things brewing! Angelo and Beatrice are not here on any petty business affairs, I can assure you. Something's in the wind—"

"And Carbajal's in prison," said O'Neill brusquely. "These men of yours; can they be trusted?"

"Absolutely. They're lent me by Ser Mocenigo, the Venetian Ambassador, on my promise that I'd shed no blood—he doesn't want to be involved in any scandal of the Donato family. I return them the day we reach Rome, or the night of that day. I think this Tomàs is an accomplished assassin—"

"Mount, then! Let's be off. We'll need man's attire for my cousin, here, before we reach Rome. She joins us against Raymond."

"Eh?" Donato flashed the girl a look. "It's no woman's business—"

The girl spoke out sharply. "What happened to me at the Black Bull was no woman's business either!"

Donato laughed and put out his hand to hers.

"Agreed! Comrades, then—four of us instead of three. Mount!"

In ten minutes they were pushing their horses for the road, with Tomàs the Genoese and a led horse bearing their effects and plunder, and the others waiting behind to cover their departure. Indeed, they saw no more of these others, then or later, though the Genoese remained with them.

CHAPTER VII

CERTAIN CONVERSATIONS

O N Tuesday, second day of the carnival, O'Neill rode into Rome by the Vatican gate, Mary beside him muffled in a furred cloak. Carlo Donato and Tomàs presented passes and bill of health to the Swiss guards, and the four with their led horse were admitted without examination. The street beyond already spoke of carnival, being gay with masquers, decorations and mountebanks. Barely were the four inside, when up capered a man in red mask and domino, gaily waving a bladder at them.

"Into the Angel Inn on the right—swiftly!" he cried. "Pay toll in the name of carnival, worthy pilgrims—"

Donato would have ridden him out of the way, but O'Neill knew the voice, and interposed.

"It's Carbajal. Follow him!"

They turned aside, keeping after the fluttering

148

scarlet figure, and came into a tavern courtyard. The red domino pointed to stone steps mounting the wall, and mounted them, to disappear in an entry above. Donato followed, ordering Tomàs to remain and watch the horses, and the other two dismounted and climbed after him.

"Tired?" asked O'Neill, his arm under that of Mary.

"Enough. What a ride! I'm not used to the saddle yet—"

O'Neill laughed a little, and came to the upper floor. The red domino was there in the corridor, waving them into a room. Another man was with him, to whom Carbajal turned with a sharp order.

"Warn us if any come. Watch below!"

Wine and food were on the table, garments strewed the window-settle. Carbajal slammed the heavy door, and flung aside his scarlet vizard.

"Welcome, comrades!" he exclaimed, clasping hands with O'Neill. "We've no time for talk—but who's this you've brought?"

"A recruit," said O'Neill, smiling. "Mary, do you know the Black Bull scullion again?"

The girl drew away her cloak. Carbajal uttered a choked word of amazement, incredulity; he leaned

149

forward, peering into the amused features of the girl, then caught her hand and touched his lips to her fingers.

"A miracle, a miracle!" he exclaimed. "The starry-eyed Madonna of the Black Bull—"

"No miracle; plain cause and effect," and Carlo Donato laughed. "Here, let's at the wine and pastry —you did well to meet us here, Carbajal! We're famished—"

"I did better than you know," said Carbajal with grim intonation. He handed the girl to the seat O'Neill had drawn out for her. "It had to be done. I owe you thanks for my liberty, Venetian! Cardinal Ludovici had me out of prison in short order."

"And Achmet?" queried O'Neill. Carbajal threw out his hands.

"Don Agostino said to come and take him. Ludovici dared not do it—he's old, afraid to precipitate any crisis—"

"Hm!" O'Neill sat down and attacked the pastry. "We'll attend to it."

"Gossip later," and Carbajal's voice was urgent. "Snatch a bite and run! The devil himself is here, arrived yesterday!"

"Raymond?" O'Neill glanced up. "Aye, I thought he'd be ahead of us."

"I saw him enter, beard and all," said Carbajal. "He's watching for us; his men are stationed at the gate below. In another fifteen minutes he'll know you've arrived—then look out! I know this tavern well, so I've been waiting here. There's a way out, into another street. Eat, drink, change into the costumes I've provided, then we'll go forth and separate instantly. Thus, we may throw them off the track. Every moment here is peril."

"Right." O'Neill tossed down his cup of wine, and rose. "Where to?"

"Meet again at the Villa Ludovici—he's given me a house in the grounds. Use my name for entry."

"What name?" snapped O'Neill. Carbajal's one flaming eye glittered at him.

"Carbajal—still! We must separate at once—meet tonight after dark at the villa. Any errands can be done in the meantime."

"I must go to the Spanish Embassy," said O'Neill. "I thought we could all shelter there—"

"Heaven forbid!" and Carbajal laughed harshly. "Recognized there, I'm lost!"

"Then the Villa Ludovici tonight. You, Donato?"

"Agreed—I must go to the Venetian Embassy first. Our fair comrade here?"

"Brian and I stay together," said Mary, and smiled at the stare of Carbajal. "I'm one of you now—and I owe you a debt, Don Carbajal, for writing the letter and getting Brian here—"

"Faith, we're all in debt to each other!" and Carbajal laughed, almost gaily. "Come, enough time wasted! Costume, mask, and off. Tonight we can confer and settle our affairs. I've three men below, one here; O'Neill, take one as a guide to the Piazza di Spagna. Pick your own costumes. Who's the man with your horses, below?"

"My man," said Donato, "borrowed from Signor Mocenigo. I'll go to the Embassy and keep Tomàs with me until tonight. Carbajal, you take our baggage-horse, and watch him—he's got money and jewels aboard. I'll take the harlequin garb, and this blue taffeta for Tomàs."

"And I this black domino." O'Neill picked up a costume. "White domino for you, Mary—"

In three minutes they were garbed and masked

beyond recognition. Carbajal flung open the door and beckoned to his man outside.

"Stay with the black and white dominos—guide them to the Spanish Embassy. Forward!"

They descended to the courtyard, where three other men were lounging. Opposite the inn entrance was a large arched way leading through a corridor to another street. Bridle in hand, the party set off down this corridor, Carbajal the last. A number of loungers appeared and were about to follow when the tavern keeper appeared and closed a grilled gate in their faces, deaf to their oaths and threats. Carbajal slipped gold in his hand, and he vanished.

"Quick, now!" cried Carbajal to those ahead. "Into the street, mount, ride for it!"

No sooner said than done. O'Neill emerged into a narrow street, swung up into saddle, and with a clattering of hooves they all were reaching the next corner and separating; at once, O'Neill found himself and Mary and their guide alone. They spurred on hastily, fast as the guide could lead them, turning corners, taking street after street, until there was no doubt that any shadowers were flung off the trail.

An hour afterward, while outside the palace buzzed and howled the carnival, O'Neill and Mary were sitting with the Spanish Ambassador—a very suave and stately grandee whom O'Neill had met in Madrid, and who welcomed the Irish exiles warmly enough. Don Luis demanded all their story, and heard it out in silence; but O'Neill, watching him, saw the subtle flicker in his eye at the name of Raymond, and took warning. More, he changed his entire plan of campaign on the instant, abandoned everything he had meant to say, for he sensed unknown perils here around him. Nor did this feeling pass away before the very real sympathy of Don Luis, when Mary told of how young Hugh had been slain by Raymond before her eyes; behind the sympathy, O'Neill detected troublous thoughts and evasions.

"This is sad, very sad!" exclaimed Don Luis, when Mary had finished. "And all for the sake of a jeweled sword? Hm! You're sure it was Raymond of Corthia, I suppose, and not some bandit impersonating him? Yes, yes. Well, we'll have to take it up with the Tuscan court, Corthia being a fief of the Medici. We'd better demand the punishment of Raymond? An investigation—"

"Not at all," broke in O'Neill, somewhat to the astonishment of Mary. "I'll take up that matter myself, Don Luis; perhaps, officially, it would be better that you knew nothing of the affair. I doubt if an investigation would gain much, and you can help us in other ways."

Don Luis brightened a trifle.

"But such a thing cannot be let drop, my dear Don Brian! You are too considerate. Of course, I and my whole house and influence are entirely at your service. Whether you need money, justice, what not! I know this Raymond—he must be punished."

O'Neill smiled. It had flashed across him that Don Luis probably knew Raymond of Corthia very well indeed.

"I need none of these things, Don Luis," he said. "Only a discreet silence on your part. Where I do need and ask your help is in another and very different affair, here in Rome."

He went on to tell how Achmet had been seized by Don Agostino, how Cardinal Ludovici was helpless to get the restoration of the horse, and how the Pope's nephew laughed at any intervention.

"Now, as to the horse," pursued O'Neill, "I intend to get him myself, in my own way—which isn't a gentle one. Trouble may come of it. In such case, I ask only that I may place myself under your protection, and that you'll lend me your good offices with the Pope."

Hearing this, Don Luis waxed fluent and florid with assurances—this time entirely sincere. He had most excellent and weighty reasons for not stirring up any complaint against Raymond of Corthia; yet if O'Neill had insisted, it must be done, for the family of Tyrowen might be exiled, but were of too high rank to be ignored.

Hence the ambassador seized thankfully and earnestly upon the alternative, which would fully satisfy O'Neill. True, Don Agostino was the Pope's nephew and a presumptive cardinal, yet he was also a wild and reckless blade whose extravagances vied with those of the ancient Romans. His position had gone to his head, and he was not beloved. Don Luis could proceed against him with dignity and every success.

While these things were passing in one embassy, another not so far away was witnessing a different conversation, yet one containing a significant analogy. Grave old Signor Mocenigo, who represented the Republic of Venice in Rome, sat stroking his gray goatee and watching Carlo Donato, whom he had known from boyhood. Donato told of his companions, and of his meeting with Angelo and Beatrice.

"I'll keep your man Tomàs until tonight, if I may," he said. "The others will return today or tomorrow here. Well, now to talk of the future!"

Mocenigo nodded frowningly. "Naturally, Carlo, your first step will be to go before the Senate, set forth your identity, and make such demands as you —er—see fit—"

"Not at all," said Donato. The shaggy gray brows went up in surprise.

"No?"

"My first step will be to revenge myself. As you're aware—need I mention the case of your late uncle Andrea?—the law is quite clear in such cases."

"But, my dear boy," said Mocenigo uneasily, "there'll be the devil of a scandal about it if you have a stiletto put into Angelo and—"

"Nonsense!" Donato broke into a laugh. "My revenge doesn't lie in that quarter."

"Ah! Then, by all means, push it hard! Whither?"

"It's Raymond of Corthia I'm after—the man who kept me prisoned."

Mocenigo wriggled suddenly, as though a flea had bitten him.

"Venice stands squarely behind you," he said, with a rather unhappy air. "You, her bulwark against the Turk, her first captain, her proudest son! The Republic must champion your cause with all her power —she'll do it to the utmost, I promise you! Full reparation shall be exacted for your sufferings, be sure of that! Now, let's see—as I understand it, your wife poisoned or drugged you, eh? You were then handed over to assassins, who were in the pay of Raymond and took you to Corthia, Raymond hoping to make use of you later on. Naturally, you'd be a valuable prisoner—he may have intended to blackmail Angelo, who desired to marry Beatrice and was doubtless fully aware of the plot to get rid of you. Yes, that's Raymond's way! Hm! Perhaps it'd be best for you to face scandal, declare yourself before the Senate, and demand the punishment of Angelo and your wife. As to Raymond, that can come later."

Donato's eyes were opened by this abrupt volteface. He knew old Mocenigo well enough to suspect what was in the wind, and it rather amused him.

"Nonsense, why not be frank about it? I'm a

soldier, not a diplomat, and I can only comprehend what's said openly. Perhaps," he added drily, "you have an affection for this Raymond?"

"I detest the man!" said Mocenigo with asperity, and then sighed. "An unspeakable rascal—but, my boy, I serve the Republic, and at the present moment some rather delicate negotiations are revolving around this same Raymond of Corthia. You're safe enough, and I don't mind giving you a hint in confidence. It's a question of adding Ferrara and its territories to the Republic. Certain of the negotiations are being handled by your cousin Angelo, but his part is unimportant; I'd prefer to dispense with him rather than Raymond, just now."

"Ferrara?" Donato frowned. "But Ferrara belongs to Rome!"

"Since the last duke died without heirs. But, if an heir turned up and had the proper backing—you can conceive what might happen! I say no more. It's only to let you know that the moment is rather awkward for us to antagonize Raymond on your behalf—"

Donato leaned back, laughing. "But I ask no such thing! You misunderstood. See here—I don't want it known that I'm alive, for the present! I'll proceed against Raymond on my own account, with my friends, and I'm in no hurry to proclaim myself at Venice. What awaits me there? Scandal, a disgraced name, a traitorous wife, an empty future! Time enough to face it all when I've nothing else to do. Until then I'll attend to my vengeance in my own way for I've a heavier debt against Raymond than you know."

Mocenigo stroked his gray goatee and tried to hide the very complacent satisfaction that filled him. So long as his intrigues were not jeopardized, he quite despised Raymond of Corthia, and Carlo Donato could do as he liked.

"Not a bad scheme, my boy," he said paternally. "I'll write the Council that I've seen and talked with you—if I don't, others may. Between ourselves, I don't love that precious cousin of yours by half! Now, what can I do for you? I'm entirely at your command—letters, funds, hospitality, aid!"

"Ludovici isn't a diplomat," said Donato drily, "and is providing for us. And I've plenty of money, thanks."

"The old cardinal?" Mocenigo gave him a sharp look. "So you're not alone, eh? You don't want to say more about your friends?"

Donato shrugged. "To tell the truth, I don't know enough to retail! We've all been in a devil of a hurry—Raymond's in the city, is looking for us, nearly caught us this morning. I told you about the man who freed me, a Spanish don. Well, we're to meet tonight at the Villa Ludovici. I think the old cardinal's safe enough."

Mocenigo nodded thoughtfully.

"A wonderful old man, that! He has vast influence because he seldom uses it, stays out of political imbroglios, lives for his ancient marbles and bronzes. Still, don't lean on him too hard—he's old, out of date these days, and may fear to go against the tide. But you want something of me? It'll be my privilege, Carlo. Name it!"

"I want the finest shirt of Milan links that can be bought or stolen, for the man who freed me. For myself, nothing."

"There speaks the old Carlo!" Mocenigo was vastly pleased and showed it. He touched a bell-pull. "I have the very thing, luckily; a shirt of fine links made, they say, by Cellini in his younger days. Light as a feather, yet bullet-proof. A present to me from His Holiness last month. You shall have it, with my blessing—"

THE BLACK BULL

A servant appeared, and received his instructions with a bow.

While O'Neill was conversing with Don Luis, and Carlo Donato with the Venetian Ambassador, a tapestried chamber in the Villa Ludovici witnessed yet another conversation. The vast grounds of this palace, near two miles about, shut out all city noise and carnival merriment. The room itself held only couch and table and chair, and at the far end a pedestal on which stood the Dying Gladiator, esteemed as the rarest piece of ancient marble in all Rome. On the couch rested old Cardinal Ludovici—shrewd, kindly, wrinkled, with bright and penetrating eyes belying his white hairs, while Carbajal sat at the table talking with him over some very excellent wine of Sicily.

"You are the one person to whom I can come for advice and help," said Carbajal frankly. "As to help, I need little at the moment; I shall settle my own affairs with Raymond of Corthia. Advice, however, I need greatly."

The cardinal nodded gently, and his delicate, almost transparent old fingers played with a fine silk handkerchief, as he eyed Carbajal. The latter, garbed in black, had flung aside his red domino and

162

mask, and beside the black patch his one eye flamed out like a glowing sapphire.

"Help I could not give openly," he said. "You know what reply Don Agostino sent to my demand for the Arab horse. It shows that my day is past, my son. To stand behind you openly, I must bring upon my head the wrath of Spain, of the Pope, of all Rome; and I am too old for such a game. Yet here you and your friends have sanctuary while in Rome, and what I can give, is yours most gladly. What advice do you need?"

"You know what debt I owe Raymond of Corthia," said Carbajal. "I have told you who these friends of mine are. Should I seek out Raymond here in Rome, or should we do as we have sworn— in Corthia?"

The cardinal smiled to himself and sipped his wine. He was a wise old man, wise in many things, and if out of the active game it was not from any ignorance of what went on about him.

"Get out of Rome," he said gently. "It's no place for honest men. The Pope meant well and swore great oaths at first, but now—well, you can judge for yourself. The revenue from courtesans is of more worth than that from pilgrims! In Rome, this

163

Raymond is not the man you know. I dare not tell you who he is here—I only suspect. But a thing or two have come to my ears, most amusing hints, regarding what's going on. If I were you, I'd go slow; let me meet your friends, size them up, put my ear to the ground and listen!"

"I've heard a few things myself—in Corthia," said Carbajal slowly. "I'm not quite certain of details, but I know a huge game's at stake. For one thing, I was not the only prisoner in Corthia; again, Raymond was a trifle indiscreet in reading some of his letters. He's in correspondence with certain Venetians; with the Spaniards too."

"Raymond is no fool," and Ludovici smiled. "Half the great houses of northern Italy are indebted to him or afraid of him—in other words, he has power."

"And he knows we're here. He's after us."

"He's after bigger game than any of you, I fear," said Ludovici. "But you can trust me; leave it in my hands. The cruciform villa is yours, and my servants tell no tales. Make your friends welcome, enjoy the carnival, and leave your cause—"

"Bah!" burst out Carbajal, leaping to his feet and holding out his awkward arm. "I have no cause—

look at me! Deformed, bent by the galleys, an eye gone—death in life! I've nothing to hope for! Were I to claim my rights, the world would laugh."

"True." The old cardinal sighed a little. "True, my son. What, then, seek you?"

"Vengeance!" snapped Carbajal. "First on Raymond, second upon the Spaniards who sent me to the galleys, lastly on that vile Corthian tavern whose secrets would shake half Italy if made known! I tell you Raymond is plotting—"

Ludovici lifted his handkerchief, and his eyes glowed.

"Enough! My son, leave it to me. Meantime, I'm having papers and credentials made out in the name of José Carbajal, which will gain you respect wherever shown. My correspondents in Lucca will have ample funds to your credit. If you need men—"

"Men betray," said Carbajal bitterly. "Four of us are united—it's enough."

"Three men and a woman—against Raymond of Corthia? It's madness."

"All men die. I have nothing for which to live, except vengeance; if I die in the attempt, what matter?"

"If the others are like you, then it is not madness," said the old cardinal. "But here in Rome, I suspect your Raymond of Corthia to be another person, my son."

"A hint—give me a hint!"

"I cannot, though possibly I may put you on the road to discovery. You must leave Rome soon, though. Let me work a little, in secrecy. I can eke out your knowledge of that Black Bull Tavern of his, I think—but I must search my portfolios. Hm! There must be a key to the riddle somewhere. What can he be scheming?"

"Nothing small, whatever it is," said Carbajal, his one blue eye glowering in the waning afternoon light. "Spain and Venice behind him—Don Camillo, who represents Tuscany, somehow plotting with him —"

"We are a worn-out people, here in Rome," said the old man wearily. "Vice has battened on us, we have no more great men; the Church is rotten to the core. If a Pope does not arise to reform all things, what will come to us? We are in worse case than when the Goths descended upon Rome of old. The common folk are a diseased rabble. Our soldiers are mercenaries. If one strong, sure man swept into

166

CERTAIN CONVERSATIONS

Rome with slaughter and fire, the city would be his overnight—"

Carbajal stiffened. "Rome!" he whispered, his eye flaming. "Rome! There's the key to our riddle— Rome! I'll wager you Raymond is playing a greater game than even I dared to suspect—though I guessed the fate of Rome was somewhere involved in his plans—"

"I am tired," said the old cardinal, his head drooping. "Let me work, let me work, my son—"

Carbajal embraced the old man, donned his mask and domino, and went forth to watch the carnival; a hopeless despondency had come upon him with the last words of Ludovici. Tired! And this was the man on whom he had pinned all his hopes!

The afternoon was fast wearing away by this time.

CHAPTER VIII

ARAB, QUEEN AND CARNIVAL

ALL Rome was given up to carnival license, and here in the Corso was the heart of the play. This mile-long street running from the Porta del Popolo to the Piazza Venezia, under the Capitoline, was the maddest and merriest place in all mad and merry Rome, holiest and most licentious city of the age.

Brothel and palace alike were emptied into the Corso. Hidden behind costume and vizard, prince and outcast mingled in the wild throngs and rubbed elbows or flung confetti; perfume-filled eggs hurtled and smashed on every hand, musicians piped and fiddled, and the air was shrill with laughter. Fountains played wine, and who cared if the wine were of spoiled or soured vintage?

The courtesans in the palace windows vied with those in the street in laughter and gaiety, hurling

168

sugar-plums into the crowd and being bombarded in turn by passing nobles. Of these were many enough —princes and cardinals, ambassadors, dukes, even crowned heads, some well disguised, others easy to recognize by their trains of footmen and bravos. The Barberini brethren, Palestrini, Borghese—all the famous Roman names were here, by coach and ass and horse, most of the young bloods passing the entire day in mad racing from one end of the Corso to the other, all restraint discarded.

Late in the afternoon a chorus of shrill yells, drum-beats and trumpetings passed down from the upper end of the street—two Jews, stripped to loin-cloths and near to bursting with wine, were racing the length of the street. Not from choice, however; the carnival drew heavily upon the Ghetto for its entertainment and expenses, with a hand of iron.

The Jew-race ended with sunset, and brought a lull, the greatest treat of the day still to come. This would be the racing of riderless horses, barbs from Spain and Morocco, the prize being six pieces of samite subscribed by the Ghetto. The chief interest in this event centered in the start rather than the finish, and great preparations were being made at the upper end of the Corso, near the triumphal arch donated by the red-capped merchants of the Ghetto.

Here too stood the palace of Don Camillo, that great but little-known prince who was so seldom in the Eternal City. Adjoining his house had been erected a stand for his ladies and friends, and it was the object of much attention; this prince, once a cardinal, had reputation in the matter of ladies, and if the new Pope's nephew had outranked him as to wild debauchery, that only whetted popular curiosity. It was rumored, probably falsely, that His Holiness and cardinals would attend the show; the rumor was strengthened by the scarlet and gilt coach of Christina of Sweden, daughter to Gustavus Adolphus, passing up and down the street amid the cheers of the populace. Christina might be unpopular at home, but in Rome she had captured the imagination of the common folk, with her man's dress, her tempestuous character, and her way of yielding to any mad impulse of the moment.

With darkness, torches began to flicker, vendors of food and wine reaped rich harvest, and men took place beside high cressets, ready to light them for the race. Now the houses were lighted, and along the Corso and hills gleamed out thousands upon thousands of tiny colored lights—candles placed in colored paper lanterns, hung along each building by the hundred, from street to roof. The cressets were fired and into the guarded stand, amid a shrill cheering, came Don Camillo and his party.

Amid this riotous scene, two figures moved slowly —O'Neill in his black domino, Mary cloaked in her white costume. Luckily for his peace of mind, O'Neill was ignorant of the barbarous nature of the sport ahead, and waited patiently for the horses to be brought out. He and Mary fell into an eddy of the crowd, beneath the stand of Don Camillo, and stared up curiously with the rest of those around.

Lighted by the high cressets that flung a ruddy glare over the street, the gay party in the stand showed up clearly enough. Ladies and gallants, all were costumed magnificently, and masked to boot— all, that is, save one. Amid the laughter and talk, amid the hurtling sugar-plums and perfume-balls, the central figure stood out disdainful of all concealment; Don Camillo, clad in severe black, against which numbers of diamonds glinted fire. O'Neill regarded him with open interest, and nudged the girl at his side.

"Look at that face—a mask in itself! And calls itself a man?"

THE BLACK BULL

The girl laughed, and small wonder. Above an enormous Spanish collar, the head of Don Camillo seemed large and round; his hair was plastered down flat to his head, and his face was solid color, enameled rather than painted, since in talk or laughter it was ever the same and was innocent of wrinkles, movement, emotion. A large black mustache and goatee hid the mouth.

"He daren't wear a mask or he'd spoil the paint!" said the girl gaily, as Don Camillo bowed to the cheering folk, and then seated himself. "But, Brian —when are you going to the meeting? It's after dark now."

"Wait and see if Achmet shows up," said O'Neill. The man furnished them as guide had long since been lost in the crowd, but O'Neill knew it would be a simple matter to find the Villa Ludovici when necessary.

Even as he spoke, came a swirl, a wild yelling, with horns and trumpets adding to the din, and the throngs pressed back to leave the street clear. A number of horses appeared under the arch, and were led forward. Instantly a clamor of betting arose.

"The black, the black! Even odds on the black against the field!"

"Done! A crown with you—"

"Two to one on the white!"

"The white! The Arab! Don Agostino—three to one on Agostino!"

O'Neill shoved into the front of the massed ranks. There in the open street were the barbs—five of them in all, half wild, each held by two men. Their owners strutted and talked, and it was not hard to pick out Don Agostino; a drink-flushed young rake fluttering in a silken mantle, laughing and flinging sugar-plums as he walked.

Not at Don Agostino did O'Neill look, but at the magnificent white horse behind him—Achmet, excited by the noise and tumult, ears pricked forward. O'Neill's heart leaped to the sight of him, yet he restrained himself, waiting, at sound of a deeper roar going up. This was not for Queen Christina, whose coach was waiting fifty feet down the street, but for the men bringing in the saddles.

Suddenly a cry broke from O'Neill—a cry of incredulous horror and fury. One of the horses was being saddled, and this saddle was a heavy affair of plank, studded with nails. The horse screamed and began to plunge as the straps were drawn, so that

173

his keepers held him tightly, and another was brought to the work.

"The devils!" cried O'Neill, realizing now the sort of race going forward. Mary gripped his arm, but too late. He saw Achmet being led, saw two men waiting to throw that cruel saddle on the white back —and with an oath hurled himself out of the crowd and at the figure of Don Agostino.

"Achmet!" he shouted, and his whistle shrilled high.

Hitherto quiescent, the Arab suddenly whirled, plunged high in air, broke from his keepers, and darted toward O'Neill. The latter halted, put out a hand to the white muzzle, and faced Don Agostino, while sudden startled silence fell.

"Prince you may be," said O'Neill, "but you are thief and robber as well. This horse is mine—and I take him! Call away these torturers!"

One of the men caught at the bridle of Achmet, but O'Neill's fist smote him and he fell headlong and lay there.

"Liar!" screamed Don Agostino. "Hands off my horse—"

He flung forward, and a dagger gleamed in his hand. O'Neill, evading the passionate drunken rush,

174

knocked aside the dagger and gave Don Agostino one buffet that sent the prince reeling half across the street.

"This horse is mine!" rang out his voice sternly. "If—"

A sudden vengeful roar welled up from the crowd, and men were running with swords out. Then O'Neill heard a harsh voice beside him.

"Mad folly, comrade—'ware! Let Tomás take the horse—quick, Tomás!"

A red domino fluttered beside O'Neill, and as Carbajal cried out, the masked Genoese was on Achmet with one leap. The Arab plunged, whirled, scattered the crowd, and then with a tremendous bound clear over the heads of two men, was gone with a clattering of hooves. Gone, and not pursued either, for upon O'Neill were pressing in soldiery, weapons out while Don Agostino yelled them on and confusion ran high.

"Fight, now—fight!" gasped Carbajal, and O'Neill's sword rasped out as a blade drove in at him.

"Leave me," he exclaimed. "Look out for Mary —she's there—"

The attackers swirled back. A harlequin drove

into them from the side, scattering them, and Carbajal laughed again to his coming.

"I'll see to her," he cried, and so was gone, and
in his place stood Carlo Donato, sword flickering.

"Down the street, comrade!" he cried to
O'Neill.

For an instant the ring of attackers had been inde-
cisive. The mad flight of the white Arab; the blaze
of red domino aiding black, then replaced by harlequin—all this had momentarily confused them,
but the flash of steel steadied their heads. Don
Agostino was yelling orders, and the crowd scenting
blood backed up the orders. There was confusion on
all sides, but no way of escape for O'Neill. Beside
him stood Donato, masked, sword in hand and laugh
on lips.

"Now they're in at us," cried the Venetian gaily.
"Keep 'em from surrounding us—at them!"

"Break them," snapped O'Neill, and the two men
hurled forward.

Swords crossed, flickered, drove in and out. At
once a terrible yell of surprise and alarm went up
from the soldiers, for these, massed against two
skilled rapiers, could effect little—and the two men
were charging them. Down went a man, and an-

176

other, and through the gap broke O'Neill, with Donato at his elbow.

For an instant it seemed they were clear. Then, coming up the street, hemming off their escape, a wild rush of figures—some of the watch or *sbirri,* others of the Swiss guard, a number of officers in the lead. O'Neill glanced around, saw a great gilt and scarlet coach to one side, and leaped for it.

"Back against this, comrade!" he shouted, and the Venetian was beside him and whirling with a joyous laugh.

"Come, Swiss dolls—here are real soldiers for you! Ah—then take it—"

The stamp of feet, the click of blades, the wild roaring of the crowd—and behind them the coach rocking on its high springs, yet saving them from rear attack. Side by side, Venetian and Irishman engaged the circle that hemmed them in, the men-at-arms holding back and letting their officers plunge in first.

One plunged indeed, with Donato's blade through him, and as the Venetian stooped to free rapier, another drove in a deadly lunge. The rapier bent and shattered on the gay harlequin-costume, and Donato drove up his hilt into the man's face.

"Steel coats!" rang out the cry. "Conspiracy! Conspiracy!"

Someone loosed a pistolet, but it went wild. O'Neill had two of them on his hands now, officers both, and he answered Donato's laugh with a ringing shout. Steel touched throat—one of them gone, coughing on the stones—the other pressing in, rapier clinking, giving O'Neill thrust for thrust. Skilled swordwork here, while Donato held the left side and the plunging coach-horses fended off attack on the right; scrape of blades, hot oaths, a bedlam of voices all around. The officer drove in, staggered sideways, went to his knee, and was shoved away as another replaced him and leaped in at O'Neill.

Something else came, too, infinitely more dangerous—a long hooked halbard-head, reaching for Donato's legs, barely missing him. The *sbirri,* the street police, were now on hand; but the mob turned on them savagely, scattering them. The halbard reached in again for Donato's legs.

Then, abruptly, the coach door opened and out between the two defenders leaped a figure, darting bare-handed on the halbard and swinging it aside.

"Cowards!" a shrill trumpet-voice leaped at the ring of soldiery. "Bullets and spikes on them you cannot touch—back! Ho! To me, Sweden, Sweden! Help for brave men! Here's help for you, my Spanish don—"

Man's garb, woman's cloak, steel poniard in hand, Christina flung herself at the steel line in front. Well they knew her, these Swiss, and drew away from her mad attack, while a wilder, fiercer yell mounted from the mob around. For a moment there was sudden peace about the coach, and Christina turned with a laugh to O'Neill.

"I recognized you, mask or no! Did you get that box for me?"

A laugh broke from him, at this speech, coming at such a moment.

"Yes, I have it, Your Majesty—"

A wild howl of delight from the mob, a swaying thrust of bodies, and then came a glare of light and the whole crowd split apart, leaving the dead men on the stones. Don Camillo, with his torchmen and guards, broke through to the coach. He was very stately.

"Come," he said calmly to O'Neill and Donato. "Safety in my house yonder—quick! Back to your coach, lady. Musketeers are coming from the gate. Swift!"

179

"Who the devil are you, painted face?" snapped Christina, staring.

"Don Camillo, lady," and he bowed to her.

Just then Don Agostino staggered up with a howl of drunken fury. Don Camillo turned, tripped him up, hurled him as he fell—all done in the flash of thought, in one lithe, unexpected movement. Agostino fell headlong and lay senseless, while the crowd yelled in shrilly eager approval.

"Camillo! Camillo! Well done, Camillo!"

"Come, fools!" Don Camillo swung at O'Neill and Donato. "To the house with my men—I'll fend off danger—"

Next instant, O'Neill and the Venetian were being hurried across the street, while Christina flung herself on Don Camillo with one eager embrace ere he could shove her away. From the archway came bursting the musketeers, rending the crowd apart mercilessly with staves and gun-butts. Too late, however, to catch their prey, for the massive iron gates of the prince's palace clanged shut; O'Neill found himself in the courtyard of the palace.

"Did you see him?" Carlo Donato swore a wondering oath as he sheathed his naked blade. "Did you see that painted doll act? By the Cross, com-

rade, he was a thunderbolt! Who'd have thought it
of such a man? And that woman seemed to know
you—"

O'Neill laughed happily, and clapped the Venetian
on the back.

"The Swede-queen? Aye, she knew me well
enough! We're moving in high company tonight,
my friend! Good swordplay of yours; it's a joy to
stand beside a man like you!"

"I'm nothing to you," declared Donato. "How
you handled that blade of yours! Hola! We'll
effect something in Corthia, I can tell you!"

A door opened before them, and led in by an
officer, they passed through a number of extremely
handsome chambers and so to a large room draped
all in cloth of gold, and lighted by a great lamp of
alabaster.

"If your lordships will wait here," said the officer
to his masked guests, "Don Camillo will come presently. This is his library. I'll send in refreshments.
Are either of you hurt!"

"Not touched," said Donato. "Thanks to good
Milan links!"

The officer smiled, bowed and withdrew. O'Neill
stood looking about the room.

"This is a strange library, comrade! By the Red Hand—look at those scimitars!"

Upon one wall, against the gold hangings, were crossed two Moorish blades. Damascened and with gold hilts, they were studded with blazing diamonds, while the scabbards were crusted with rubies and pearls in a most intricate pattern. Donato examined them and whistled thoughtfully, then swung about and drew out the hangings from another wall. Behind, was revealed a row of bookshelves going to the ceiling.

About the room stood a divan and a few chairs. Against the far wall, its windows covered by cloth of gold curtains, stood a huge table of oak, and on either side of it against the windows was a large oaken arm-chair, intricately carved. Upon the table were papers, and over the papers, strewn carelessly, were large gold coins by the score.

"Our prince is careless with his gold," observed the Venetian, and dropped on the divan, with a sigh of relaxation. A servant entered and set down a tray, bearing wine and cakes, and departed again. O'Neill poured wine into silver goblets, handed one to Donato, and was lifting the other when Donato sprang to his feet and checked him.

"What's the matter?"

"Caution! We're in Rome, my friend," said the Venetian earnestly. He pointed to the fireplace opposite, where a small fire was burning, above thick ashes. "There's the place for our wine! I tell you, there's something queer about all this!"

"Suspicious? Of what?" queried O'Neill. "This Roman saved us."

"After the Swede-queen intervened, yes. Bah! We were safe enough, once she leaped out with us!" Donato crossed to the fire, and carefully emptied his goblet into the ashes. Then he darted to the lamp, held up the goblet, examined it carefully. He turned and beckoned, and held out the silver cup. "Look at it!" he said in a strange voice. "The stud!"

O'Neill obeyed. Inside the cup, at the bottom, was a stud or round knob of silver, as though forming the bottom of the goblet. O'Neill touched it with his finger, and it moved. He looked up.

"A receptacle—for a drug?"

"Exactly. The wine's good, but the cup holds poison. That was precisely how my charming wife removed me, comrade, from her path of ambition! Now what do you think of our host, eh?"

O'Neill said nothing, but poured his own wine into

the ashes, found a similar knob at the bottom of his own cup, and replaced it on the tray. After all, suspicions were not proof; there might have been no drug in that moveable knob of silver. Donato continued, pulling aside his torn domino to reveal the chain-shirt underneath.

"I got a present for you today, comrade—and it saved my life. Your old mail-shirt is good; this is super-excellent. Cellini is said to have made it. Fortunately, I slipped it on. You'll honor me by accepting the present—"

"With all my heart," said O'Neill, then turned. "Ah! Here's Don Camillo."

The prince entered, alone, bowed slightly, and stood regarding them.

O'Neill was close to him now; light struck upon him from behind, where light came through the open doorway, and from the alabaster lamp in front. Perhaps because of these contrasting shafts of light, O'Neill perceived a curious and startling thing. A portion of Don Camillo's left cheek showed a distinct woven texture.

He looked again, steely eyes narrowed and alert. He could make it out now, though it was clever in the extreme—the painted face was a mask of silk, painted and powdered to a skin-like appearance. Only across that one cheek where something had rubbed, did the silk texture reveal itself. At edges of nostrils, about the eyes, at ears and mouth, it was cunningly molded so that it melted into the skin, and ran down to the high Spanish collar. Then the hair, too, must be false—goatee and mustache, shimmering raven locks above, heavy black brows!

Through O'Neill's realization, broke Don Camillo's even, emotionless voice.

"My dear Harlequin," he said, addressing Carlo Donato, "I should like a few moments of private speech with this Black Domino—"

"Nothing you may say," broke in O'Neill quickly, "cannot be heard by my friend."

"So far as you are concerned, true, but not so far as I'm concerned," said Don Camillo. His lips moved slightly, but no face-muscles showed on the surface of the mask. "So, if Signor Harlequin will retire into the adjoining room—"

Donato bowed. "We owe you a debt, Don Camillo. I cannot be churlish."

The prince waved his jeweled fingers. "Messer Carlo Donato could never be churlish."

Stupefaction held the two masquers. Donato's

hand slipped under his robe, but Don Camillo pointed at the other hand and spoke suavely, although rather stiffly.

"Perhaps I mistake. Yet that ring with the gray stone was once famous; Carlo Donato is dead, and I spoke of him as one famed in life for his very courteous chivalry. Since you wear his ring, I honor you by believing that you partake his nature."

A hint of irony in the plausible words caught O'Neill's ear, but Donato, without risking further exchange of speech, glanced down at his ring, bowed again, and went to the door. He closed it behind him and a latch clicked.

Don Camillo walked to the table, seated himself, poured wine into one of the silver cups, and drained it.

"Bah! What a vile crowd out there!" he exclaimed. "Four men dead, five wounded; there's the devil to pay about it all."

"I can promise you," said O'Neill, "that Don Luis of Spain will undertake to satisfy the Pope as to my part in the affair."

"Perhaps," said the prince. "Meantime you're safe enough, having been unrecognized. Will you remove your mask?"

"When you remove yours," said O'Neill, laughing. The prince regarded him with that oddly unchanging expression, and raising a hand, felt his face very carefully.

"You have sharp eyes, or—ah! On the cheek, where that damned Swedish vixen embraced me! Well, I assent to your request. Come, pull up that chair, make yourself comfortable. If I'm not mistaken, your name is O'Neill and you're the Count of Albujeras in Spain, and own a greater if less substantial title in Ireland. Well, draw up the chair and let's talk."

Don Camillo began to push away the golden coins strewn on the table, and to sort through the papers, as though what he had just said were of small moment.

O'Neill was swift to see that both he and Donato were somehow known to this man, and the perilous mystery of it appalled him. He reached in silence for the nearest chair, to which the prince had pointed; it was one of the massive oaken armchairs with widespread arms and ancient black carved wood. To his effort it did not move. He put out his strength and turned it to face the desk, irritated by its great weight.

187

"Abominable old furniture, eh?" said Don Camillo. "Well, it's comfortable enough at least, and has its virtues—yes, I'm glad to say that it has its virtues. Most things have, if one only knew how to turn them to account—"

O'Neill found something terrible in the man—in this unemotional and impassive creature whose face and head were a living lie, in the quiet voice so eloquent of restraint. He recalled how Don Agostino had been sent down senseless, as by a thunderbolt. A sense of danger, of deadly and imminent peril, seized upon him.

"You did well to pour that wine in the fire," said the prince. "Well, sit down, sit down—it makes me nervous to have anyone standing about. Let's be comfortable at least—"

O'Neill sank back into the big chair, resolved to pierce into the man, solve this mystery. Then as he laid his hands upon the arms of the chair, something happened. A click, a sharp movement as though the ancient black oak were alive—the carvings had moved, indeed. His wrists were enclosed, his thighs and knees, a carven band was about his neck. He strained forward, and found himself straining against immobility.

"Yes, all things have their uses," said Don Camillo, with a quiet chuckle. "So you wish to see who
I am, my dear Don Brian? Very well. Suppose
you tell me first, where I can find a certain one-eyed
and somewhat warped rascal who was until lately
scullion in the Black Bull of Corthia? Eh?"

CHAPTER IX

ONE CITY—TWO DUKES

A BELL tinkled in soft interruption. Don Camillo struck another upon his desk. The door opened, and a servant appeared.

"The report, Excellenza—all is quiet. The *sbirri* were beaten away by the crowd, but the soldiers cleared the street. Don Agostino was taken home. There is no investigation."

Don Camillo nodded carelessly. Street fighting was no great matter in Rome, where even street murders were common affairs.

"The man out there—he made no trouble?"

"None, excellency. He went into the room."

"And you opened the pipes?"

"At once. He beat the door for a little, but is quiet now."

"Have him brought in here."

The servant withdrew. Don Camillo smiled as he looked at his captive in the chair.

190

"Poor Donato! We really must not let him perish under the charcoal fumes—he is far too useful as a prisoner, and it's a dog's death for a brave man."

Helpless to move hand or head or foot, O'Neill yet saw how Don Camillo was hugely enjoying his own cleverness. There was the one weak point, his sole chance—play sluggard of wit, pretend to understand nothing, watch for some opening!

For his own case, the reality of the trap was cruelly simple, and Donato's also. The Venetian had been ushered into a room where hidden vents spouted charcoal gas; such contrivances were all the rage, and any sophisticated Roman would scarcely have been caught by these elementary gins. Not the traps, however, but the man—here was the staggering factor! What reason was behind it—and who was this masked man who apparently knew everything? The answer burst swiftly enough upon O'Neill, yet was difficult to comprehend.

Now two men carried the limp shape of Donato, still masked, into the room, and at a gesture from Don Camillo dropped him beside the table and retired. Don Camillo looked at O'Neill and spoke calmly.

"There—you see? Two reunited; and presently the third. Where is he?"

"Would I tell you?" said O'Neill.

"Hm! That's what I'm wondering," said Don Camillo reflectively. He poured more wine and sipped it slowly, watching his prisoner. "Would you? I'm afraid not. And would you be of more value living or dead?"

"None in either event," said O'Neill.

"No? Hm! I think that old fox Ludovici is mixed up in this somewhere."

O'Neill, gradually readjusting himself to realities, wasted no time or effort on questions. It was all horribly plain now, as he met the bright, sharp eyes peering at him from that emotionless mask of a face. He had looked into them ere this, and such eyes were rare in Italy.

Where was the real Don Camillo, then? Was this man merely playing the part for the moment—which seemed improbable—or was he in reality Don Camillo? Everything was improbable, unreal; the only real thing about it all was the probing stroke of those dark eyes—the eyes of Raymond of Corthia.

"You're wondering too, eh?" Don Camillo

laughed softly, amusedly. At the tone, at the words, O'Neill started slightly; was his very thought being read? "I like you, barbarian; I like the way you burned Corthia under my nose! And you're wondering how I could play the part, eh? Tut, tut! It's always the most fantastic and improbable thing which is the easiest to carry off. Surrounded by my own men, my own friends, risking nothing except the stares of the common herd—easy enough. You know me now, eh? Don't play the fool—I could read recognition in your eyes."

"Aye," said O'Neill.

"Well, it's easier to bargain than to use torture, with one like you," said Don Camillo cheerfully. "Come, I'll bargain! Your life and Donato's here, for that one-eyed scullion. Where's your rendezvous here in Rome?"

"Ask Donato," said O'Neill grimly.

The other looked at the Venetian, who lay face down, huddled and limp.

"Not I. The price isn't high enough, eh? I'll raise it." The dark eyes struck at O'Neill sharply. "I'm not the fool you take me for, Don Brian— you could trick Beatrice and Angelo, all very nicely, but I know all about you and that girl. Now, then, shall I set out and find her, and then make you talk? Speak up."

The steely note in the voice—here was Raymond of Corthia speaking, suddenly flinging away all assumed character. Here was a man above other men, conscious of mastery more than they knew, abruptly revealing the dominance and power within himself. Yet O'Neill laughed.

"Why try to make me think you a fool, Raymond?" he said. "Set me free, give me a sword, best me if you can; and if you can, I'll betray my friends."

"Nonsense!" Don Camillo threw back his head and laughed heartily. "I've no intention of killing you—before you speak!" He leaned forward and pointed to the carven oak of the chair above O'Neill's head. "You see the griffin there? One little pressure on his horns, and you're free. It's worth a word, eh? Then shall I look for that scullion at Ludovici's villa? Or elsewhere? You know who he is?"

"I wish I did," said O'Neill. "Who is he?"

Don Camillo laughed at this. "What, questions? Answer, first. At the villa?"

"If you like. I don't know where it is, nor do

I know your friend Ludovici, so please yourself. Why not ask Don Luis of Spain?"

Don Camillo stared at him, suddenly immobile, and drew a deep breath.

"Eh? Eh? If I thought Don Luis would betray—but no, he'd not dare! You've a ready tongue, my friend; perhaps a red-hot needle passed through it would serve my purpose after all."

"You murderous dog!" said O'Neill calmly. "You murdered my brother, a boy—you'll pay for it! You and yours. Not one of your men gets quarter at my hands. Look to it!"

"What's this?" The other chuckled. "So my little cockerel is crowing, eh? Fine talk for one in your position! However, I think you might prove dangerous, and I'd better take some caution against you—"

The little bell tinkled again. Don Camillo struck his responsive note, and the door opened to admit the same servant, announcing a Signor Umberto. Don Camillo started.

"Ask him to wait—"

"He cannot wait, excellency," said the servant. "He says it is most pressing and that he can only stop five minutes."

"Admit him, but search him first for weapons."

In a moment, a little furtive man scurried into the room, and stopped short to stare at the apparently dead figure of Donato, and at O'Neill in the chair.

"They're safe, or soon will be," said Don Camillo drily. "Your news? I suppose you saw this man in the chair at the Embassy, eh?"

The little man nodded. Under his black cloak he wore the livery of Don Luis—a spy, then, making report!

"Yes, excellency. But the one at the Embassy, of whom I wrote you—that man is Don Alfonso, and Don Luis means to make him Duke of Ferrara!"

By this awed, startled tone, the spy expected great things of this message, but Don Camillo only flung back his head and laughed.

"No news in that, Umberto," he said. "How did you get it? Who was talking?"

"A Venetian, a noble named Donato, who was with Don Luis." The spy spoke sharply, swiftly, in quick-breathed words. "They spoke of you, of Mocenigo the Venetian Ambassador, and of Tuscany. They want to make sure of Don Camillo at once. Donato had brought him a slave-girl and lost her; he will try to see Don Camillo tonight or tomorrow—"

The false Don Camillo waved his hand.

"Good—the warning shall be well repaid, Umberto," he said. "Soft lights—they'll do the trick."

"But the plot, excellency! This heir to Ferrara—"

"Tut! I know all about it," said Don Camillo, laughing again. "Run along, and when my men sack Rome you shall have the pick of the spoil! You're one man who can keep his tongue between his teeth—do it!"

The spy bowed himself out, and Don Camillo turned to O'Neill with an abrupt change of front— figuratively speaking.

"There! You heard—what of it? Will power tempt you, and intrigue, to forget this mad scheme of vengeance?"

"Yes," said O'Neill. "When you're dead and Corthia a heap of ruins."

"Bah! Why didn't you try it, there in Corthia, or later in Leghorn? You knew who I was—that girl guessed it or read it in my eyes! Why not?"

"I bide my time," said O'Neill.

"Then you've bided it too long, fool that you are!" snapped Don Camillo. "Kill me, indeed—

you! Give you a sword, indeed—saints bless us!
If it weren't for disarranging this mask with sweat,
I'd do it this minute, and kill you at the third pass
as I did that puling brother of yours. Well, that
sword is in Corthia now, and it's a fine blade; I'll
use it often enough when you're dead. You can
take the charcoal fumes and reflect—go in hale and
strong, and come out with shriveled lungs and
heart, like this carrion—" and with his foot he
stirred the inert Donato.

"Fools—petty creatures, you and Umberto and
the rest of them!" he went on scornfully, beginning
to stride up and down the room. "You, to talk of
killing me, of taking vengeance! What's vengeance,
after all? An appetite appeased, an excuse to let
blood; does it give any satisfaction, repay any debts,
put anything into pocket of body or soul? No. The
wise man knows better—turns matters to good use
rather than become a destructive agent. Little petty
things like you, who haven't vision—bah! A
soldier taking orders, and you'll be one still when
I'm ruling Rome."

O'Neill's face was wooden, expressionless, his
gray eyes half veiled; but he caught a slight movement on the part of Donato—as of one shifting a

strained position. And then, without warning, a leap from the very floor as Don Camillo came close. The inert figure came up like a steel spring, a stiletto flashed, drove home, and Don Camillo went staggering across the room with one hoarse cry.

Whirling like a flash, Donato leaped for the oaken chair, put his hand above the head of O'Neill, and pressed. In his face was no drawn suffocation—instead, a laugh of exultancy. With a click, the framework of the chair opened, and O'Neill flung himself from the accursed thing.

Then from Don Camillo broke a whistle, high and shrill.

Uninjured, he stood by the opposite wall, reaching for one of the Moorish blades hung there. O'Neill darted to the door and swung the huge key in the lock; he still had his sword, and caught it forth of the sheath. Donato swept to one side.

"At him, comrade—now's the time—"

Don Camillo had not taken down the scimitar, however. Instead, he had merely pulled at it, then caught the heaving hangings and slipped behind them. O'Neill guessed what was forward; a dismayed oath broke from him as he dashed at the wall, struck the hangings aside, held them out. In his very face came a click and slam of wood, as a massy door drove shut. Don Camillo was gone.

"The windows—swift about it!" snapped O'Neill, putting away his weapon.

He ran to the windows behind the desk, and Donato was with him, breathing curses. Here were great windows, the gardens just outside. They swung one open, and Donato leaped, O'Neill following him swiftly. Behind them came voices, shouts, a shrilling whistle.

"He wore steel too, eh—it's popular!" exclaimed Donato. "Good thing I held my breath and kept nose to floor in that cursed room—this way, comrade! Wall or nothing."

They were back in carnival now—a tiny garden walled about, houses rising high, carnival lanterns gleaming like stars on every side. Before them rose a wall, topped with iron spikes, heavy vines masking it. Donato leaped for it, gained foothold, went up like a monkey, and O'Neill came after him more heavily, the vines breaking down under his thrust, yet affording foothold enough.

Together they came to the spikes above, and carefully swung over. A street was below them, a narrow street where lanterns glimmered and carnival throngs passed with laughter and singing. O'Neill shouted in warning, held himself clear of the spikes, and jumped. He landed without hurt, and a thud beside him told of Donato's coming. With shouts and cries, the crowd scattered.

"This way!" cried Donato, and together they broke into a run.

Two minutes later, in the Corso itself, they halted, edged into a quiet nook, and drew breath. Donato was laughing, and O'Neill responded to that gay laugh, as he clapped the Venetian on the back.

"Well played, comrade! Tragedy turned to farce —eh? You knew he was Raymond?"

"I know the devil wore a steel shirt; that dagger-thrust numbed my arm! A house of tricks there, eh? Well, it's nothing to the Black Bull—if he'd had us there, we'd not have come away so easily! Takes a soldier to know when to run, I tell you! Let's get out of this cursed mob and find Carbajal. Rome's too hot to hold us now—I learned today my boasted protection was poor stuff against Raymond."

O'Neill thought of what he himself had learned this night, and agreed.

The little cruciform villa in the Ludovici gardens was itself a gem, and housed the rarest gems of painting and antique statuary collected by the old cardinal over many years. In a little room on the ground floor, where the most exquisite inlaid wood-work vied with the rare marbles in their niches to catch the eye, a table was set out with food and wines; the servants had been dismissed, though they were trusty enough, and here beneath the lighted candelabra sat the four who had escaped the horns of the Black Bull of Corthia.

"And what now?" demanded Mary O'Neill, from the table's head. "Achmet's safe, we're all here—and why? If there's so much danger here, why did we come?"

Donato broke out laughing. "Why indeed? I have a suspicion that we're all innocents. Rome's the center of the world, the abode of great men, the house of refuge! We all had friends here—eh, comrades?"

Carbajal barked out his curt laugh, more sardonic than usual, and his one blue eye rested on O'Neill. The latter chuckled.

"Council of war, comrades! Are we all agreed

against Raymond and Corthia, or have any of us changed?"

"Agreed," said Carbajal, and Donato nodded.

"Then be frank," said O'Neill. "I talked with the Spanish Ambassador today. He would grant anything and everything, but when Raymond's name was mentioned, he fell cold."

"As did Signor Mocenigo of Venice," put in Donato drily.

"Faith, that same chill affects everyone!" added Carbajal. "It's not fear of Raymond—it's some plot in the air. Statecraft offsets everything else."

O'Neill glanced at Donato, received a curt nod, and spoke.

"We learned tonight what's going on, unless it's rank madness," he said. "A spy came to Raymond, and made report. Your cousin, Donato, seems behind the affair; apparently he has the backing of Venice, and that of Spain also. It seems there's a man now at the Spanish Embassy, named Don Alfonso, who's heir to the dukedom of Ferrara—"

"Eh?" said Carbajal, leaning forward. "What's that again?"

O'Neill repeated the statement. "This man is

to be made Duke of Ferrara—which means a coalition against Rome. Further, Raymond spoke once or twice of ruling Rome; perhaps his ambitions run to this height, madness though it seems—"

"Madness? Not a bit of it!" snapped Carbajal, with sudden energy. "Rome is rotten to the heart, a tottering shadow upheld by Swiss and German mercenaries. With five hundred real men at his back, a man like Raymond could begin blood-letting at midnight, and by dawn hold the city in his grip! Add to this a usurper seizing Ferrara, with Venetian backing—and the Roman state would go to pieces in three days. Tuscans, Spaniards and Venetians would slice off the outlying territories to add to their own holdings; the Spaniards would take the Pope under their own protection, making Rome into another Avignon, and Raymond would take the city and what remained of the state. Simple? Bah! Given the proper backing, it would be child's play for Raymond!"

"And he has the backing, evidently," said Donato.

"But he also has four enemies," and Carbajal's blue eye swept about the table like a dancing flame. "A woman, a Venetian, an Irish-Spaniard—and Carbajal. We have money, and if we need men

we can always get them. I propose that we ride out
of Rome at dawn, head for Corthia, and destroy
that accursed place while Raymond's here."

"Destroy it—how?" put in Mary O'Neill.

"With any means to hand. We've time enough
to discuss means. Our first aim is vengeance; our
most bitter blow at Raymond will be to destroy his
eagle's crag, and smash this little plot which he and
Angelo Donato are hatching."

"Say Beatrice, rather," spoke up Carlo Donato.
"You're right, Carbajal! Break this fine scheme,
and we break the man. Then we ride north at
dawn?"

"If so agreed," said Carbajal. "I'll have further
information tonight from the cardinal perhaps, more
than I already know about the Black Bull—well,
Brian? Why the laugh?"

O'Neill smiled at him. "Who are you, Carbajal?"
he asked.

"I? A dead man," said Carbajal. "A dead man,
in whose place another is now being raised. A man
without a name, whose name another bears falsely.
It that enough?"

"For me, yes," struck in Donato uneasily, and
made O'Neill a slight sign. He put out upon the

table a glittering heap of fine steel links. "Here, Brian, is my present for you; it saved my life tonight—may it save yours!"

O'Neill spread out the shirt and caught his breath as he realized its exquisite work, the glitter of gold running through the fine mesh of steel links, the pliant softness of it, and the feathery yet absolute protection it afforded.

"More worthy a prince than me, comrade," he exclaimed. "With all my heart, thanks! Yet I've an old one of my own, good enough—with your permission I'll give this to our new comrade, here. Wear it, Mary! Tomorrow you'll be no longer a woman but a cavalier—so wear this, and we'll have less fear for your safety."

"Excellent!" Donato lifted his wine-cup. "A health to our fair comrade—a health to Monsieur! Monsieur Chemise-de-fer!"

Amid the laughter, Mary O'Neill's eyes sparkled gaily—then O'Neill put out his hand and met the blazing blue eye of Carbajal with stern gaze.

"Carbajal, have I failed you? Am I a comrade or not? Keep your promise, for I claim it now. We know what's afoot with the enemy, we know our work, we know why fate drew all the threads of events together here in Rome. We're united; so either trust us or leave us."

Carbajal's sardonic laugh rang upon the room.

"Aye! You want to know why I've suffered, why Raymond kept me prisoner like his other captives, why he'd give his right hand to get me back again, especially now? Because I'm the real Alfonso—heir to Ferrara's dukedom. Donato there knew me of old."

Silence settled on the room; after what they had just heard, this seemed a miracle, too incredible to be swallowed. Yet the eager nod, the curt assent of Donato, showed it was truth. O'Neill drew a quick breath.

"So this is the key to the riddle!" he exclaimed. "No wonder that devil's afraid of your escape, afraid to have you at liberty—the real Duke of Ferrara!"

"Bah! As though I could publicly interfere with him—poor crippled fragment of a man!" said Carbajal bitterly. "As though I'd come out and declare myself, to be jeered down, laughed at! No, no—let him fear me, and he's right enough there. But for me there's no future, no Ferrara, no dukedom. Carbajal alone exists."

207

"But Carbajal has friends," said Mary O'Neill softly, and touched the shoulder of the one-eyed man, and looked into his sapphire eye. Under her regard, the blue depths of that single orb glistened, and a tear shone on Carbajal's cheek; abruptly, he caught her hand, touched his lips to her fingers, and then rose.

"I must see Ludovici," he said. O'Neill checked him.

"I've an errand to go, since we're off in the morning. It's not yet midnight. Where's the black wooden case you brought on to Rome for me?"

"Upstairs with our things. I had it back safely when Ludovici got me out of jail."

Carbajal turned to the staircase, and presently was back with the ebony casket. O'Neill pocketed it.

"Come along, then, and get me a guide. Mary, better get to bed; I'll be back after a time. No danger in this trip."

"I need fresh air," suggested Donato, with a laugh.

"You need sleep," said O'Neill, and shook his head. "No company, thanks."

"Eh? Why such secrecy?" demanded Mary O'Neill bluntly enough, her eyes anxious. "You were the first to say we should have no secrets—"

O'Neill laughed at her manner. "Because I hope to have a pleasant surprise when I see you all again —good news for one of us, at least. We'll see later. Ready, Carbajal?"

They left the little building, and headed for the villa entrance to get a guide from among the guards. Carbajal touched O'Neill's arm.

"You told me at Leghorn about that casket, remember. You're going to Christina?"

"Aye," said O'Neill.

"Well, look out for yourself!" came the gloomy warning. "She's an unstable vixen and carries no good luck to anyone. She's surrounded by thieves, flatterers, intriguers, lovers—all the scum of Roman society. She disappoints everyone."

"She did Raymond, at all events," and O'Neill told about the love-letters and how he had gained them. "But cheer up—I'm looking forward to the day when you and Don Alfonso of Ferrara meet each other!"

"So am I," said Carbajal, and growled in his throat.

CHAPTER X

A S he followed his guide through the carnival-mad streets toward the Palazzo Rospigliosi, where Christina of Sweden was installed in some state, O'Neill's hopes were high. Great things should come of this interview, he reflected, though it was not for himself he went seeking. Unstable the lady might be, but she was at all events a queen—and he could ask of her what he would.

"I'll put a heavy spoke in Raymond's wheel," he thought, "and at the same time gain a high friend for poor Carbajal. Christina is close to the Pope, can get Alexander's personal interest for Carbajal, hates Raymond, and can effect an arrangement by which, when all this business in Corthia is ended, our Carbajal may at least have some future to look forward on! The man has some excuse for bitterness; we'll see if we can't lighten his burden a bit!"

At the palace, a line of coaches were entering—
obviously some entertainment was going on. Leaving the guide to await his return, O'Neill followed
a fat cardinal up the steps, and at the door took
one of the letters from the ebony casket, which was
unlocked.

"Give this to Her Majesty," he said to one of the
fantastically uniformed Swiss guards, "and say the
bearer desires to see her immediately."

"Your name, excellency?"

"None is needed."

The man departed, and O'Neill was ushered into
a salon amid a throng of nobles and prelates, where
his mask and domino made him conspicuous. In
five minutes the Swiss came back and bowed low to
him.

"Will your excellency follow me?"

O'Neill strode through halls and rooms filled
with all the spoils of Sweden and Germany—for
Christina had not left home without stripping Stock-
holm of everything brought thither by her all-con-
quering father, Gustavus Adolphus. He came at
last to a room where Christina was being but-
toned into a gown of red and black velvet by the
same little valet O'Neill had seen upon the highway;

and as she came to him, with an eager exclamation, he bowed over her hand and then extended the ebony casket. She took it, and turned.

"Go!" she said to the valet, "and close the doors."

When they were alone, O'Neill removed his mask, and she looked at him curiously, counting the letters in the casket between glances. A sigh of relief broke from her, then she laid the box aside and came quickly to him, and seized his arm.

"How was it done? I did not look for you so soon—after that affair in the Corso! You weren't hurt? What a fight it was!"

"And what a rescuer who came to our aid!" exclaimed O'Neill. "As to the letters, the matter is best forgotten, Your Majesty. I owe you thanks for your intervention tonight."

"Bah! If I'd had a sword instead of a dagger, I'd have done something worth while!" she flashed out. "It was Don Camillo who broke up the party. He got you off safe?"

"I'm here," said O'Neill, with a shrug. "Since I'm forced to leave Rome in the morning, I brought your letters tonight."

"How did you get them?"

"Told Raymond you had sent me for them," and he smiled. She frowned absurdly.

"And he?"

"Gave them up with a laugh."

"The mocking devil!" She strode up and down the room, and then came to a sudden halt before O'Neill. "How can I reward you? Wait—I know! You shall have a colonel's commission in my army, in the crusade I'm raising against the Turk!"

"Unfortunately," and O'Neill bowed, "I am in the service of the Emperor, Your Majesty, and must beg to decline your offer. If I may ask your help—"

To his utter amazement, she drew back as if he had struck her, an oath on her lips.

O'Neill was ignorant that he had touched a spot which the Pope himself dared not press too closely. At the moment, Christina was spending every possible effort and coin, in her madly impulsive way, to engineer a great crusade against the Turk; she was writing rulers, making treaties with Mazarin and Modena and Venice, raising men—and being gently but firmly rebuffed on every side. The queen in her was stung to the quick by O'Neill's lack of diplomacy, for she had begun to realize her failure, and the same wild pride which could cause her, like Charles II of England, to have a treacherous servant executed in her very presence, now swept her into an overwhelming fury of rage.

"So because Raymond laughed, you dare to flout me!" she cried out, passionate storm in her eyes, shaking her fist in the face of the man to whose aid she had leaped an hour or two previously. "You jeer at me, a queen without a country—at my efforts to raise all Christendom against the infidel! Shut up, you spawn of hell—shut your cursed mouth! Stand here and mock me, will you? Get out! Leave my presence—go to the devil!"

She ended with a volley of camp-oaths flaming between her lips, her face convulsed by stark madness, and advanced on O'Neill as though to claw at him with her bare hands. He, bowing, turned his back on her and strode to the door, heart hot within him.

"Wait!" she cried suddenly, with a changed voice. "Wait! After all, I cannot forget that you have served me—"

O'Neill turned. "Your Majesty, I have not served you," he said coldly. "I have only aided a woman who seemed to be in distress. As to serving you,

SMALL MEN PROPOSE, GREAT DISPOSE

I beg that you will allow me to leave such matters
to your valet."

And he stalked out of the room forgetting to re-
place his mask, nor remembering it until he en-
countered the curious stares of the guests at his white
face and blazing eyes. Outside, he found his guide
and beckoned him, and started for the Villa Ludovici
again.

Carbajal had been right, then; better have left
Christina of Sweden alone! Yet it was a shrewd
blow, a stiff blow; the very fact that O'Neill had
sought nothing for himself, made his anger and
disappointment the greater. He raged at himself,
at Christina, at all Rome, and so came home again
in bitterness. He found Carbajal sitting up for
him, over a wine-flask.

"Ha, comrade!" The one-eyed heir to Ferrara
leaped up at sight of him. "You saw the lady?
Name of the devil, what a pair of eyes on you!
What's happened?"

O'Neill reached for the wine and gulped at it.

"Made a fool of myself," he said sourly. "I
meant to ask that woman to use her influence with
Pope Alexander on your behalf—and like an ass,
I offended her dignity somehow before I had spoken

215

ten words. First thing I knew, she was storming at me like a camp-follower. I gave her a cud to chew on, and came away."

Carbajal broke into laughter, then sobered and laid his hand on O'Neill's shoulder.

"Thanks, comrade," he said, his deep sapphire eye flaming softly. "Thanks! So it was for me you went? You're a good fellow! But leave the queens and lesser women alone when you search for gratitude, comrade mine. Let Rome alone. Let 'em all alone! It's few people in the world a man can look to for honesty and trust; there are four of us under this roof, and farther none of us dare seek. Failure? You've not failed—you've only proved the truth of what I've just said. Be content, comrade! You and Donato and I and Monsieur Chemise-de-fer—ha! There's a quartette for you to knock the props from under Raymond of Corthia or the devil himself! So forget it all, drink another glass with me, and look at the fine old parchments Ludovici has dug up for us—some plans of the Black Bull and its secrets!"

He shoved a roll of parchments on the table, and his enthusiasm drove thought of the late encounter from O'Neill's head.

With the following morning, a sorely battered

SMALL MEN PROPOSE, GREAT DISPOSE

Don Agostino came to the Villa Ludovici, a score of
Papal guards at his back, and demanded speech
with the old cardinal. He had it, and had no good
of it. Ludovici suavely disclaimed knowing anything about a white Arab or its owner, and had
heard nothing of any street fighting the previous
evening; he even urged Don Agostino to come and
see some new antiquities he had just unearthed in a
corner of his grounds and which were being installed
in his little cruciform villa. The end of this matter
was that Don Agostino went away sullen and perplexed, but empty-handed, to plunge anew into the
gaieties of the carnival.

Two days saw these gaieties become madder and
ever madder, and then came the night of the fireworks, maddest night of all the carnival.

San Angelo was surmounted by a huge pyramid of
lights, bonfires were everywhere in the streets, and
the palaces of princes and ambassadors gave enormous displays of ingenious fireworks. That before
the Spanish Embassy was particularly noteworthy,
as showing a huge dragon outstretched, and above
the dragon were the Papal arms in triumph. This
piece lasted a long while, with squibs and crackers
detonating by the thousand.

By the light of this firework, rather than by that of the single candle burning on the table, an upper room of the Spanish Embassy was quite well lighted. Here by the window sat stately Don Luis himself, looking out complacently upon his costly display. Behind him was a man of perhaps forty, handsomely dressed, whose face behind its trimmed auburn beard showed a certain bold effrontery and truculence masking real weakness, and whose blue eyes were mildly protruding. Seated at the table, dressed all in black, was Raymond of Corthia, and near him were Beatrice and Angelo Donato.

The cheers and tumult outside redoubled in volume. Raymond, sorting out some papers, glanced up abruptly and spoke to Beatrice in a low voice, using a northern dialect. By the single candle at his elbow, his lean dark face took on odd highlights.

"Yes, our friends left Rome early yesterday morning. You need not worry. I learned of it at once, and luckily had pigeons with me. Orders have been sent out. Your man will be looked after."

The amber eyes of Beatrice glittered at him angrily.

"Then you lied when you said he was dead long ago, drowned in the sea by your men!"

218

Raymond shrugged. "It was so reported to me. Bribery, perhaps—who knows?"

"Or Raymond, perhaps—who knows?" The low voice of Beatrice was dangerous. "You're said to hold more than one prisoner there in Corthia, hostages against the future, men who may be worth more to ambition as captives, than as corpses. Perhaps you thought Carlo of more value alive than dead, eh?"

Raymond regarded her intently for a moment, and laid his papers aside. It was a crisis, as he very well recognized; she might throw all intrigue overboard and turn against him at a moment's notice, or without notice. The others could not readily catch their words nor understand the northern dialect used— Angelo excepted. He stared at them, white-faced.

"Dear lady," said Raymond, "the answer to all this matter is very simple indeed. Suppose the real heir to Ferrara—the real heir, mark me—were also in my prison among those you mention. Eh? Suppose, I say. In such case, am I worth more to your ambition as a friend, or as an enemy? Take your choice."

Angelo caught his breath at this, and the eyes of Beatrice widened.

"Ah!" she said softly, and then laughed. "Agreed! You are a wonderful man, Raymond."

"You are a wonderful woman, dear Beatrice," he said, smiling. "And further, I shall take it upon myself to rid you of this incumbrance, your late husband."

He took up his papers again, but now the amber eyes of Beatrice were no longer calm. The hint that Raymond might hold the real Don Alfonso was not at all preposterous, since he had certainly held Carlo Donato; he might be bluffing, but she knew better than to take any chances.

"My dear Don Luis," said Raymond quietly, "since I hope to leave Rome early in the morning, shall we arrange our affairs?"

"Ah, yes, yes, with all my heart," exclaimed the ambassador, and turned his chair about to face the table. "More lights?"

"I need no more. My own man watches the door —good. Let's go about it in orderly shape without evasions; a matter of business, my dear señor don. Hm!"

His quiet voice dominated the room. The suave Spaniard drew back from the light and leaned over, as though watching the fireworks below; perhaps he did not want chagrin to appear in his face, for he was a proud man of the Sidonia line, and here it was very plain he was not in the seat of the mighty.

"This is not business," spoke out Don Alfonso, chidingly. "It is politics."

Raymond looked up at him a long moment. "My lord duke," he said smoothly, "politics is a most un- healthy profession; that of business pays better and involves longer life. I must strongly advise you to become a man of business."

"Am I to take orders from you or from Don Luis?" demanded the other.

"That," and Raymond smiled, "is what we are now about to settle."

Don Alfonso relaxed sulkily in his chair, for Don Luis had stepped heavily on his foot.

"I pray you," pursued Raymond, "let me be cor- rected if I am wrong. As I understand this affair, Don Alfonso is the heir to the dukedom of Ferrara, now incorporated in the Papal states. He has full proofs of his identity, which is recognized by letters from the ambassadors of Spain and Venice; in case he comes to power in Ferrara, he will be at once recognized by the Grand Council of Venice, and the court of Madrid. Correct?"

"Yes," assented Don Luis. "But we must not forget Tuscany. The Medici are not what they were —but they have power."

"I can answer for Tuscany," spoke up Angelo Donato, and upon him the eyes of Raymond rested with a certain humorous glint. "I've interviewed Don Camillo, and he authorizes me to say that his influence, which is great in Florence, will be thrown to Don Alfonso. He has even given me letters to his relations in Tuscany, or has promised to give them."

"That's another matter," said Beatrice sharply. "I think I'd better see Don Camillo myself—"

"No need," broke in Raymond smoothly. "He's with us; we need not fear Tuscany, for I have influence with him also. Let's proceed to the program. It is, I believe, that Don Alfonso show himself in Ferrara and seize the city. Unfortunately, he'll be unable to do it alone. What force will he have?"

"At any agreed date," said Don Luis heavily, "one hundred arquebusiers will be found in Ferrara— trained Spanish troops, ready to throw off disguise and obey Don Alfonso."

"On the same day," said Angelo Donato, "four hundred German and Swiss mercenaries will be provided in the same fashion by Venice. With five hundred men who know their business, one could conquer Rome itself—much less Ferrara!"

"Exactly my thought," and suddenly Raymond broke into laughter of unfeigned amusement. "Exactly my thought, Messer Angelo! Since you have everything so nicely arranged, may I ask why I'm dragged into the affair, or how needed?"

"Justification," said Don Luis. "None must know Spain is in this affair. You must provide proofs that you were engaged to kill the real Don Alfonso when he first appeared; that, instead, you kept him alive and well; that you now produce him! Throw the onus upon Rome and Spain."

"Also, you're needed as manager of the business venture," and Angelo smiled. "Business must be entrusted to good hands; yours are good. Such a coup would fail with the wrong man heading it, and must win with the right man. You're the one man in Italy to handle it."

"I thank you—and I agree with you," said Raymond. "Now, have you considered that when news of the coup reaches Rome, as it must within a few days, the whole force of this state will be loosed on Ferrara?"

"Not with Spain urging against it," said Don Luis. "Not with Venice and Tuscany behind Don Alfonso—"

"Perhaps not, and perhaps yes. You talk of probabilities, when we must have guarantees! The most important part of the whole affair is this aftermath," said Raymond briskly. "That brings us to my own share in the venture. I offer, not a perhaps, but a certainty! I'll undertake to leave Ferrara and most of its territory entirely in the hands of Don Alfonso and his five hundred men; and I'll guarantee further that Rome will not only leave him in peace, but will acknowledge him and make alliance with him inside of three weeks."

This astonishing offer broke upon his auditors like a bomb.

"Eh? Eh?" exclaimed Don Luis. "You can guarantee this? You?"

"Exactly," said Raymond of Corthia. "At a price. I am a business man, you comprehend."

"But how?" demanded Angelo Donato. "How can you guarantee such things?"

"After you agree to my price, I shall tell you."

"Name the terms, then!"

"Immediate recognition by Spain and Venice, and

the use of the Spanish troops now in garrison at Naples, in case I need them. That's all."

Angelo stared at him blankly, but the amber eyes of Beatrice widened in slow comprehension. Don Luis blinked at the lean, dark, powerful face under the candle-light, and frowned.

"I'm afraid I don't understand," he said slowly. "Recognition—of what? Of whom?"

The stabbing eyes of Raymond swept them, amusedly.

"Recognition of Raymond of Corthia as Duke of Rome, Protector of the Pope—and chief business man of Italy."

These ironic words brought stunned silence upon the room.

Poor Don Alfonso swallowed hard as he stared at this adventurer, to whom he was as the vulture to the eagle. Angelo Donato leaned back in his chair, jaw fallen; Don Luis frowned, his suavity completely rent asunder. Only Beatrice, meeting the keen dark eyes, smiled slightly to herself and gave him one curt nod, as of approval.

There was no doubting the cool assurance of the man. In word and look and calm restraint, Raymond of Corthia showed exactly what he was—

intrepid yet careful, able to do what he proposed in full confidence, yet a little disdainful of those who stared at him. His personality dominated them all.

"Do you mind telling us," said Don Luis, with an effort at sarcasm, "just how you propose to occupy such a position?"

"Not in the least, señor don," answered Raymond. "One hour after Ferrara is fully in the hands of Don Alfonso, yonder, I set out for Rome—whither my men will have preceded me. The news from Ferrara will set the city in turmoil. That same night, I strike. Perhaps I should say that I will not only have my own men from Corthia, but certain Tuscan troops as well, and perhaps others—perhaps others. Between midnight and dawn, most of the Swiss and the *sbirri* will be killed, and certain of the palaces will be thrown open to sack and rapine by the populace. I shall not molest San Angelo; those of the city troops who escape, will shut themselves up in that castle. Instead, I shall seize on the Vatican, whose armory will equip forty thousand foot and horse, and the Pope will become a prisoner in his palace on Monte Cavallo. At his direction, the castle of San Angelo will surrender to me, and the affair is finished. It depends on a thorough blood-letting to begin with—and, I assure you, I shall not neglect this point."

"This is madness!" exclaimed Don Luis energetically.

"Bah!" Raymond leaned back in his chair. "No platitudes, dear señor don."

"I cannot permit it, cannot countenance it!" went on the Spanish ambassador. "I do not doubt that you can carry out your program—"

"Then it is not madness?" and Raymond smiled at him.

"I say it cannot be permitted!" said Don Luis firmly. "This holy city, this focal point of the Christian world, put to sack—the head of the faith a prisoner—"

"Nonsense," said Raymond. "This holy city has been sacked a dozen times. I propose to sack only certain of the cardinals' palaces. This chief brothel of the Christian world needs a cleaning, Don Luis! It's an outrage on Christianity, to look at it from that angle; why, I shall be a reformer, a second Savonarola! Nor will the Pope be a prisoner long —he'll soon fall in with my plans, I can promise you."

"I cannot countenance it," said the Spaniard with stiff vigor.

"No? But the kingdoms of Naples and Sicily are held by Spain, feudatory to the Pope. Suppose they become Spanish fiefs, eh? Then Spain no longer has to pay annual tribute of forty thousand crowns. There's an offer—think it over. What about Venice, Signor Donato?"

Angelo looked rather frightened, since he had to speak before witnesses. He looked from Don Alfonso to Don Luis, then looked at his wife, which he might better have done in the first place. What he read in her eyes assured him.

"I think," he said hesitantly, "Venice will not oppose this, Duke Raymond. That is, in case Rome will relinquish all claims to Ferrara, now or later."

"Gladly," said Raymond, and smiled at Beatrice. Then he turned to Don Luis. "Well?"

The Spaniard hesitated. Well he knew that his decision would sway the fate of Rome—for there was no question of Raymond's ability to carry out his scheme. The horse guards, the Switzers and other troops, were all mercenaries; they were rotted to the core, could not be depended on, and like the whole city, would shriek at the first grip of any

228

strong fingers that clamped down on Rome. And there was no weakness in Raymond of Corthia.

"I cannot assent," said Don Luis sternly. "It would outrage Christendom!"

"Bah!" said Raymond, and laughed a little. "Very well, then; may I present an alternative?"

"Ah! By all means," said Don Luis in some relief. It was of short duration.

"It is, that I shall do without Spanish recognition. You know Christina of Sweden? An excellent woman, full of intrigue! We shall undertake to drive the Spaniard out of Naples—a patriotic endeavor! We shall first set Don Alfonso on the throne of Ferrara—not this Don Alfonso who sits here, but another and less handsome man, who was thought to have died some years ago—"

Don Luis started slightly.

"Wait!" he said. "Wait, Raymond—let us think this over again. Christina—really an excellent woman, but given to mad impulses. Do I understand that you threaten me?"

"Not in the least," returned Raymond. "I cherish you, Don Luis, as a great man, a diplomat of the first rank, a statesman who is far too clairvoyant to make any mistakes of policy. Do you know what my first acts will be, when I have mastered Rome? To expel all the courtisans, obtain a bull enjoining poverty on all cardinals, and organize compulsive military service for all citizens and nobles."

"Hm!" said Don Luis, startled anew by such a program. He remembered that this man was of the Medici family; with Tuscany and Venice backing him, Raymond might go far. Then there was the hint about a real Don Alfonso—

"I believe," said Don Luis, "that my master the Emperor might fall in with your views. I shall have to write him, of course—"

Raymond laughed. "Afterward, Don Luis, afterward! You have only to assent here and now, or else refuse. Shall I be so fortunate as to have your backing?"

The Spaniard sighed. "Yes. But, I warn you, Rome will not brook such reforms!"

"Yes? I omitted to say, among my projects, that the first shall be to re-establish the Roman usage of the Tarpeian Rock as a jumping-off place for those who do not agree with the existing status of business. My administration will be strictly a business one," and Raymond smiled thinly. "Now, since all such details are arranged, let us pass to the more

immediate program. Has any date been settled for
the installation of our good Don Alfonso in his
heritage?"

"None," said Don Luis, eyeing the speaker
askance. "When you like, Duke Raymond."

Raymond glanced at Angelo, who merely shook
his head.

"Ah!" he said reflectively. "It's left in my hands,
eh? Let me see—we're at the beginning of Lent,
and Rome is full of pilgrims who'll remain until
Easter, and will then hurry home. Let's put it for
the Friday following Easter. Does that suit?"

The others nodded, although frowningly. This
brisk settlement of dates was not in accord with the
sound traditions of Italian intrigue.

"I may say," went on Raymond, "that only we
five are aware of the exact program, and it would be
most regrettable if any news of it should leak out.
Regrettable, that is to say, for the one responsible
for the leak. Now, I propose that Don Alfonso return with me to Corthia, tomorrow morning. Also
I should be glad to have you as my guest, Signor
Donato."

"I?" said Angelo, startled. "But there are arrangements to make at Venice—"

"Which Lady Beatrice can make excellently. I, too, have arrangements to make; you and I should visit Mantua, Parma, Modena and perhaps Milan, to discuss matters of business with these states. You'll enjoy yourself, I promise you, and being in company with me, you'll find fair entertainment and a fascinating bit of statecraft. I rather imagine, too, that your visit in Corthia will not bore you greatly."

Raymond accompanied these last words with a wink, which Beatrice did not observe. Angelo looked about for help, found none, and gave assent. Raymond looked at Don Alfonso.

"So it's agreed, Alfonso?"

The prospective Duke of Ferrara nodded, none too happily. He quite understood by this time whose orders he was to take.

CHAPTER XI

THE little wayside inn, on the post-road from Florence to Modena, was not a post-house. It was merely a tiny stone building on the hillside, with a court and stable and three rooms above the wine-shop. All around were savage and desolate hills, peaks serrating the horizon on every hand, not even a farm-house in evidence. The gnarled peasant and his loutish son who conducted this inn, alone, were savage as their native hills. There was not a woman on the place.

Certainly none would have suspected the sex of Mary O'Neill, as she helped Brian saddle Achmet this clear, cold, sunny afternoon. Beneath the furred cloak, which blurred the lines of her figure, showed a sword and leathern jerkin; her cap, too, was leather, and her shortened hair did not betray her.

"Then we start in the morning?" she demanded. "I'm all right again."

O'Neill nodded. "We'll be fit enough then, little rose. I'll exercise Achmet and be back in an hour. Donato's asleep, and Carbajal is poring over those plans of the Black Bull he got from Ludovici. You'll be glad to get off?"

"Yes. I don't like this place, and like our host even less."

"He's harmless." O'Neill laughed, swung into the saddle, and headed Achmet out up the mountain road. Mary O'Neill stood looking after him a long while.

Three days they had been here, thanks to spoiled meat at their last halt, which had sickened them all. Another ten miles and they would leave the post-road and strike off through the hills, down to the plain, and to Corthia—a scant three days ride distant.

As the girl stood gazing after O'Neill, who had now vanished up the way, she saw two men afoot come out into the road and stand there. One of them waved his hand, as though to another on the hillside below. Then they sat down and began to munch food. Whence had they come, out of this savage wilderness?

At a step, she turned and saw Carbajal approaching from the steps that led to the rooms above. He was grinning.

"Ha, Monsieur!" he exclaimed, giving her the name they had come to use. "That was the Arab going out for exercise, eh? You should see Donato —the poor devil woke up vomiting and is going to be well enough by morning, once he's rid of the evil. I'm a new man already, and you're looking fit."

"Oh, I had the lightest touch of all," and Mary laughed. "I'm quite all right. Had I better look in on Donato—I might help him—"

"I gave him a hand. Better leave him alone; you're too new a soldier to absorb his fine cursing. He's an artist, that Venetian! Can you use that sword you wear so becomingly?" he added, with a curious look.

She laughed again. "A little. Do you want to warm up?"

"Ah!" Carbajal threw off his cloak and whipped out his sword. "To it, Monsieur! Knowing what sort of a chemise you wear, I shan't worry about touching you once or twice—"

Mary O'Neill bared her sword. They took position and crossed blades; Carbajal's one vivid blue eye widened abruptly and an exclamation broke

235

from him, then he drove in a hot attack as though
bent on testing the fine links beneath the girl's leather
coat. Laughing, she yielded no inch, and the blade
in her hand not only clung to that of Carbajal, but in
another moment had him parrying desperately.

Out into the sunlight, watching them, came the
inn-keeper—a burly ruffian, his red hair sticking out
at angles from head and jaw and jowl, his red
cheeks shining, his little red eyes glittering. He was
not handsome, but he laughed a bellowing laugh at
sight of the sword-play and stood arms akimbo,
watching, until Carbajal disengaged and leaped backward, and thrust away his sword into scabbard.

"Whew!" exclaimed Carbajal, panting. "Enough
of it—I'm no swordsman, and in another moment
I'd be at your throat for blood! You're a devil with
the blade, Monsieur!"

"No, I'm a pupil," she answered. "Hello—our
friend wants a word with you."

The inn-keeper advanced to Carbajal, who alone
of the four companions could understand his barbarous hill dialect. He grinned and gestured to the
building.

"You're a soldier, you of the one eye!" he declared
heartily. "Come with me and I'll show you a sword

236

—sell it cheap, too! A real sword. It belonged to the old Marquis of Mantua, and is said to be of Toledo steel. Come along and I'll show it to you— takes a soldier to appreciate a sword like this one! It's down in the cellar with the wine."

"Soldier? Not I," disclaimed Carbajal, readjusting his eye-patch. He looked up at the open window of Donato's room, which overlooked the courtyard, and lifted his voice. "Ho there, Venetian! I'll bring you a sword to look at presently—buck up, you rascal!" Then, turning to Mary O'Neill: "Will you come look at the blade?"

She gave the inn-keeper a glance and shook her head.

"Not I, thanks—I prefer the fresh sunlight just at present, for my stomach's sake."

"Come on, then," and Carbajal clapped the burly host on the shoulder. "Muscles—not a man, but an ox! Lead the way. I'll look over your wine-bin while we're there, too."

"I have sent that lazy son of mine to see if he can help your comrade," and the whiskered ruffian jerked a thumb at Donato's window.

The two men stamped into the building and disappeared.

THE BLACK BULL

Mary O'Neill put up her sword and rearranged her garments, then walked out to the gateway and sat down on a bench there. She glanced up the road and saw three figures there now, clumped at one side the road where there was a pile of stones. Road-menders, then—these post-roads were well kept up!

Thought of Carbajal's amazement brought a glint to her eye and dimples to her cheeks. Why should she not handle a blade well, whom old Teague had trained almost from childhood in all manner of arms, along with Hugh O'Neill! She rejoiced in the swinging freedom of her man's garb, enjoyed the part she was playing, and looked ahead with heart-hurried eagerness to what might await at Corthia. There was destruction and death of men awaiting, true, but death lay on every road these days, and Irish exiles were not accustomed to easy paths— besides, old Teague and young Hugh lay there outside the Black Bull, flung somewhere into the earth unshriven, murdered, forgotten! Her nostrils quivered at the thought, and a flame gathered in her eyes.

Presently she rose, looked again up the road, saw that the three men had vanished, and wondered about them. She walked back into the courtyard, and came

238

to a halt—from somewhere in the house sounded a crash. The stables, perhaps—she turned, to see if the horses were all right, and then caught a queer sound from above, and looked upward. What she saw there left her white-faced, petrified.

At Donato's window was the arm of a man, a naked hairy arm, clutching the window-ledge. Nothing else.

Another crash—the arm whipped about suddenly, vanished, appeared thrusting into air, then clutched anew at the ledge. She knew instinctively that a man was there, struggling—but what man? The arm leaped away once more, then a hand rose and fell, and steel flashed in the cold winter sunlight. Almost at once, there was a heavy thudding fall, and the arm hung limp over the window-ledge, and the dagger falling from its hand struck on the stones below and tinkled at her feet. She stared upward, fascinated by that terrible limp, sagging hand. It had all passed in the fraction of a moment.

A sudden frightful sound wakened her—Donato's voice. Then she saw his head at the window, above that limp arm and hand. Not his arm, then—the inn-keeper's son! Donato saw her, put a hand to his throat, his eyes bulging, and uttered his choked

239

words again. He had been nearly strangled, obviously.

"Danger—danger !" he gasped out, and she could see him stagger. "Tell—Carbajal—look to it—danger—"

He fell out of sight then, and his voice was stilled.

The girl's heart leaped—Brian gone! The enforced stay here, her presentiments of peril, the evil aspect of the place—everything confused her for an instant. Carbajal, then—she swung about, clutching at her sword, gripping it out of scabbard. A heavy foot scraped the stones, and across the threshold of the doorway came the inn-keeper, grinning.

"Where is he?" Mary O'Neill flashed at him, blade in hand. "Carbajal! Carbajal!"

The burly ruffian before her snarled an oath, then lifted his voice in a roaring yell, as though calling others. At the same instant he whipped out a knife, parried her sword aside, hurled himself upon her.

An evil moment for him—the pommel of the girl's sword struck him heavily across the eyes, staggered him. His left hand had caught at her cloak, however, and his knife drove home, struck her between the breasts as he pulled her toward him. A cry broke from her, echoed by his angry oath as the knife slid sideways from the steel mail—then she had jerked her cloak free, leaped backward, and was at him with the point.

Quick work, desperate work, no time to weigh chances or take half measures! Life hung in the balance, death lay in the turn of a wrist—in and out flashed the rapier, and the yell that burst from the burly host had another note now. He flung himself bodily upon her, madness in his red eyes, blood upon his breast—spitted himself on the rapier and tore it from her hand as he whirled sideways and crashed down upon the cobbles, still cursing as the breath fled out of him.

"Carbajal!" Leaping clear, Mary O'Neill lifted her voice, and there was no answer.

The dying man there on the stones half lifted himself, tore the steel out of his great body, hurled it savagely at her, and then fell back again. The rapier dropped almost at her feet, and as it did so, she heard the thud of footsteps from the road. She caught up the weapon, and saw two men running in at the gateway, cloak about arm, sword in hand—running for her, eyes upon her, exchanging a swift word with each other as they came.

"Carbajal!"

Desperation in her cry now and it brought a laugh from the two of them as they drove at her, one from either hand. She evaded them, slipped away, gathered herself to meet the assault, back to the wall beside the doorway. Their silence, their deadly rush, showed all too clearly that a trap had been sprung. The swords clicked, the pommels rang—she was engaging one of them, keeping away from the other with rapid footwork.

One drove in suddenly, swiftly, and his point tore at her side, sent her reeling, though unhurt.

"Mail!" cried one. "For the throat only—"

Deadly blades, these two, deadly merciless eyes over them. A little panic shook her, then was gone; she steadied, held one of them engaged, avoided the other. She danced about deftly, light-footed, avoiding the treacherous steel licking at her from one side, keeping both men in pursuit of her about the courtyard. It was hot and furious work; stamping of feet, click and ring of blades, sharp panted oaths filled the courtyard. She was back against the doorway now, slipping ever to one side and away, tiring fast.

"Dogs!" cried out a voice behind her. "Assassins —death to you!"

It was Donato, staggering out into the sunlight, half naked, the ghastly pallor of sickness in his face, sword in hand. He hurled himself on the two, caught them unprepared, ran one of them through the body. The second leaped back, then turned abruptly and took to his heels, and was gone at a run out of the inn yard.

Mary O'Neill put a hand to the wall behind her, stood sobbing for breath, unable for the moment to speak or move, so abrupt had been this deliverance. Donato dropped his blade and put hand to throat, in an acute spasm of sickness.

"Horses!" he cried. "Get the—horses—out of here—"

A groan burst from him. He turned, and went staggering away into the tavern and was lost to sight. Seeing the trap clearly enough now, realizing how the whole thing had been planned out, Mary O'Neill was stabbed with keen fear. She woke to action, darted to the gate, looked up the road. The fleeing assassin had disappeared. No one was in sight. What of Brian, then? And—Carbajal?

This wakened her. Carbajal, indeed! She flew back across the courtyard, avoiding the two dead men there, and dashed into the inn, seeking the cellar.

Desperation speeded her, but her first panic had worn away now; she was cool enough, and finding the cellar door standing wide, darted down the steps. At the bottom she tripped over a limp figure, could see nothing in the darkness, but knowing it was Carbajal under her hands, seized and dragged him up the steps.

As she came to the top, a mutter broke from him, and he stirred into life. Then he came to himself suddenly, sprawled across the floor, and leaped to his feet.

"What the devil!" he cried out, staring around with his one blue eye. "Where is he?"

"Oh!" The girl leaned back against the door-post. "You're not dead—"

"Eh? You here?" Carbajal peered at her and rubbed his face. "That scoundrel hit me—had a fist like a ham! Where is he?"

"Dead," she said. "His son—tried to kill Donato —there were men outside—"

Carbajal comprehended everything, saw her knife-slashed jerkin, and with a growl swung toward the doorway of the courtyard. He looked out, turned to listen to the groans of Donato, and then the Venetian spoke.

244

THE ROAD TO CORTHIA

"That you—Carbajal? To horse! Find Brian—
I'll be all right—in a minute—devil take all
stomachs!"

With his words came the smash of a musket-shot
from somewhere not far distant.

Carbajal darted into the court, caught up Donato's
sword, and ran for the gate; close at his heels was
Mary O'Neill. When the road opened out before
their eyes, another musket rang from the hillside,
and they could see the belch of white smoke. And
there before them was O'Neill coming down the
road, the splendid Arab extended at full gallop—
then, suddenly, three more puffs of smoke from the
hillside, the ragged report of three muskets thun-
dering.

Achmet leaped high in air. One frightful cry
burst from Carbajal, then he was gone, running up
the road; but the girl stood wide-eyed, unable to
move for the horror that seized upon her. The Arab
was down now, down in a crashing fall—a fall ending in a convulsive tremor and the death of a broken
neck—that hurled O'Neill out of the saddle and a
dozen feet distant.

Four of them there, and Carbajal running at them
alone, a howl of fury upon his lips. They broke

245

from cover and came for him, steel flashing, but not all together—this was their mistake. For Carbajal hurled himself upon the first man, struck up sword, caught throat and went to earth, worrying his quarry. He rose alone, as the second was upon him, and their blades crossed. The third and fourth came up, running at Carbajal from the side—

Then O'Neill was staggering to his feet. A pistol roared from his hand, and one of them went down to it. Carbajal drove steel through his antagonist at the same instant. The fourth and last man was cut off from the hillside; he whirled and broke into a run down the road, naked sword in hand, eyes flitting about in search of refuge. Mary O'Neill drew back from sight, tore off her cloak, wrapped it about her arm, and waited.

His feet came pounding down the road. Like a frightened rabbit he bolted into the inn courtyard, saw the figure awaiting him, and thrust blindly, a desperate cry on his lips. Fending the lunge with her wrapped arm, the girl grappled with him, threw her weight against him, and brought him down with a crash.

He fell underneath her, his sword knocked away. She had one swift glimpse of a gold chain about his

246

neck, the glitter of rings on his hand—then his fingers found a poniard and whipped it up at her. Pierce the mail it could not, but the thrust of the blade in her side shoved her away, and with a violent effort the man twisted loose. She clutched at him— and a reeling half-naked shape intervened, fell upon the man, bore him down again. Donato laughed wildly, then Carbajal was running in, and O'Neill after him.

"Don't kill him!" snarled Carbajal, and drove the man's head back on the stones so that he relaxed and lay limp. "I know the rascal—here, tie him up—"

It was done, and they stood staring on one another, until O'Neill groaned a little and sank down on the bench by the doorway.

"Achmet—poor Achmet!" he said dully.

"Bah! Better the horse than you," exclaimed Carbajal, panting vigorously. "Good work, I call it; five of them, and this rascally inn-keeper and his son! And all bagged. Donato, you and Monsieur here deserve our thanks, per Bacco!"

"Monsieur, not I," said Donato, "Ha! I feel better—"

"Then go and find their horses," said Carbajal, with one sharp glance at O'Neill, who sat dejected and limp. "On the hillside somewhere—we'll need 'em. Off with you!"

Donato growled a little, then laughed and started off. Mary went to the side of O'Neill and caught his hand.

"Hurt, Brian? That was a fearful fall—"

"It was nothing," he responded, and drew a quick breath, and patted her fingers. "All right, little rose! My heart's sore for Achmet—but better him than you. It's sore for poor Hugh, too—another item in the score against Raymond. What's happened here?"

Between Mary and Carbajal, he was soon informed. He looked at the senseless man who lay bound on the stones, and his gray eyes hardened, and his hand went to the poniard at his belt; but Carbajal intervened with his sardonic laugh.

"No, no—wait a bit! I know this rascal; one of Raymond's most trusted lieutenants! And he knows me. We might use him, comrade."

"Ah!" O'Neill's eyes quickened. "Right, Carbajal, right! Mary, sit down and take it easy, and don't let him suspect you're not a man. We'll put this fellow to the question—aye, use him indeed! There were five of them, you say? Excellent! It

248

may be here's the very thing we need. Come, Carbajal! He's stirring—"

The prisoner was stirring indeed, and opened
his eyes to glare at them in realization of his
plight. The glare soon died away, however, for
Carbajal stripped off his eye-patch and stood looking down, and acute terror leaped into the captive's
face.

"So you know me, gentle Santinelli, honest good
Captain Santinelli?" he said with soft and terrible
mockery. "You remember the scullion of the Black
Bull, do you?"

"Santa Maria!" gasped the captive. "Aye, I know
you. Kill me and ha' done with it, then—no torture,
for the love of the saints!"

"Oh, no torture! And who was it hurled mar-
row-bones at the scullion, eh?"

O'Neill rose and came forward. "Had this man
any hand in my brother's murder?"

"Not he," said Carbajal. "He was elsewhere at
the time."

"Then he's yours," and O'Neill shrugged. "Do
you want to slit his tongue? Better yet, roast his
feet in the oven, inside there."

"No, no, our good Santinelli is going to earn a

quicker death," said Carbajal, and his blue eye glimmered at the captive. "Eh? You'll talk?"

"Yes," said Santinelli.

"A coward, like all his breed—the bravo breed," said Carbajal in scorn. "Come, then, speak! There were five of you in all?"

The captive nodded, and licked his lips. He was thin, sharp in the face, but the arrogance was clean fled out of him.

"And Raymond sent you to head us off. Where's Raymond?"

"Should be in Corthia now. We had pigeons from him."

"Oh! Was he coming from Rome alone?"

"With friends, the letter said. A noble Venetian and others."

"That's Angelo Donato—and others, eh? It grows interesting." Carbajal leered. "Would he stop in Corthia or at the Black Bull?"

"In Corthia, I suppose," said Santinelli, sulkily. His sulk vanished abruptly when Carbajal stooped, picked up the knife fallen from Donato's chamber-window above and felt the point of it. "Don't torture me—"

"Then don't glower at me," snapped Carbajal.

"You dog! Who's in charge at the Black Bull now, and how many men?"

"Gaspard the Swiss, and two others," said Santinelli. "A second letter came when I was leaving, with orders about bringing in all the men and getting others from Mantua and Milan, but I know little of it."

O'Neill caught the arm of Carbajal suddenly and pulled him back to the bench where Mary was sitting.

"Here's the game ready to our hand!" said O'Neill crisply, his gray eyes agleam. "Wait—Donato! Come over here!"

Donato was just turning in at the gate, riding a saddled horse and leading four others. He dismounted, let the beasts go to the watering trough, and joined his companions after one glance at the prostrate Santinelli.

"Just five of them," exclaimed O'Neill, "and five of us—take their hats and cloaks, tie this rascal firmly in his saddle, and ride for the Black Bull! All we needed was the opening, and now we have it; queer if we can't turn it to our advantage somehow! Raymond's gathering men, getting a force together—the four of us must strike in swiftly, before he has done much."

"And he's bringing friends to Corthia," put in Carbajal with a grin. "Donato, there's your cousin, if you want him! And if my Alfonso of Ferrara comes along, we'll have a pleasant meeting. Once we hold the Black Bull—ha, we'll have Raymond in a forked stick, I can tell you!"

"Agreed!" Donato's eager eyes flamed in his white face. "Then we'll not go to Lucca and seek men—"

"Bah!" exclaimed O'Neill. "Santinelli's worth an army—if we play him right! You're able to ride? Then take their horses, cloaks and hats—let's be off!"

"And—Achmet?" put in the girl softly. "He's dead, Brian?"

His eyes were hard and cold as he looked at her, and if he winced, he did not show it.

"Let the dead bury their dead. They've paid for Achmet—and now there are other debts to be settled. Get your things—get ready!"

Twenty minutes later five horsemen, bearing four led horses, rode out of the mountain inn and headed for the Corthian road. The leader glanced once at a white blotch off to one side the road, and the strong hands that held his reins trembled a little.

CHAPTER XII

IF O'Neill's little party covered a three-day stretch of road in less than two days, it was done with cold reason—and with destiny spurring them hard.

O'Neill was neither a fool nor a madman. True, he meant to have two things out of Duke Raymond; life, and the old sword of the O'Neills, but he was not letting this lust for vengeance rob him of a cool head. Mary was safe, and he meant to keep her safe, and himself too if possible.

Carbajal, he saw clearly, was utterly careless of what happened so that his vengeance was glutted. Donato, while reckless enough, was too much the soldier to fling himself away, yet had nothing for which to live. Impetus would count for a great deal, wits would count more, and most of all would count time—hence, O'Neill rode hard for Corthia. Against

253

Raymond, four were better than any army, yet they must strike before Raymond's men began to gather for the blow that would make him master of Rome.

Just what that blow was, they could very clearly visualize. O'Neill and Donato had overheard the key to it all while in Don Camillo's palace; with this key, Carbajal could unlock some of the secret doors that had baffled him—for he had caught many a chance word in the Black Bull.

"They're all in on it," declared Donato thoughtfully. "Beatrice, with Venice and old Mocenigo behind her; Don Luis of Spain, and no doubt two or three princes and a cardinal or so to boot. If Raymond installed this false Don Alfonso in Ferrara, then swept down and made a bold stroke for Rome itself—who'd go against him? No one except Modena or Tuscany. Raymond could laugh at all Italy except the Medici, for by blackmail and other means he holds most of the royal houses in pawn. His weak point is Tuscany, or Modena."

"You forget Don Camillo," said O'Neill drily. Carbajal spoke up.

"But how? The man is *not* Don Camillo, merely because he wears a mask and painted face! And how often could he wear such an outfit and pass muster?

254

No, no—there's some dark deviltry in this business that we don't know!"

"Then ride on and unearth it," said Mary O'Neill, laughing, and they did so.

As to the Black Bull, wily Carbajal kept to himself the plans he had received from Ludovici, as well as what he already knew; the place had secrets, he would say with a grin, and if he didn't know them all, he knew enough to give his comrades a very handsome surprise once they mastered the inn. It would take mastery though.

"It'll get mastery," said O'Neill grimly. "Your Italy, my Carbajal, is like Rome itself—rotten, rich, shrieking at a pinch, its work and fighting done by mercenaries, ridden by memories and old dreams, its wars mere imitations and mockery of war. Step in and shed blood with a ruthless blade, and Italy will fall. Just so with Corthia and the Black Bull! Give 'em the point and thrust home—and the day's won."

"Probably," said Carbajal. "And I'd not be surprised if that were exactly what Raymond had in mind for Rome. A stern hand, a good blood-letting, and that holy city would be shrieking for mercy at his feet. Well, we'll carry it to him first—with luck!"

So, having spare mounts, they pressed the pace hard, while the hapless Santinelli, tied to the saddle, groaned and suffered heavily. And late on the second afternoon they came into the post-road for Pisa, at that very cross-roads or rather fork, where O'Neill had first set eyes upon Christina of Sweden. The sun was close to the western hills.

"Safe enough so far," said Carbajal, his sapphire eye roving about in keen satisfaction. "Any watchers among the hills will take us for Santinelli's party. Now what? We should be at the Black Bull soon after dark."

O'Neill nodded and drew his horse alongside that of their prisoner, and looked into Santinelli's face with cold and pitiless eyes.

"I'm going to offer you a chance for life," he said. "At the Black Bull, call Gaspard and his two men to see the catch you made—fetch 'em out to us. Understand? You're to be of service to me, and I pay for service. Also, I pay for treason. If you fail me," and he tapped Teague's sword, "you get this in the belly."

Santinelli's jaw fell, and his eyes widened. "You're going to the Black Bull?" he quavered. "But others may be there now—"

"Shut up!" snapped O'Neill. "You understand?"

"Yes."

O'Neill turned to Carbajal. "Ride beside him, and watch him closely."

They struck out along the side road leading to the Black Bull and Corthia, and after a little sighted an empty ox-wain approaching, led by two peasants. Santinelli was pushed up beside O'Neill, tied hands concealed by his cloak. That he was well known became evident when the peasants saluted and got their team out of the way. He asked them for news, at O'Neill's bidding, and whether they had halted at the tavern.

"Not we, nobilissimo," said one of them. "We took a load of timber to Corthia—the work is getting in hand now, and carpenters have come from Lucca and Mantua for the rebuilding, and timber is needed."

"Duke Raymond is there?" demanded Santinelli.

"Aye, with friends—they say great feasting is going on, and much preparation—for what, I don't know. Couriers and messengers are flying in all directions. I heard from one of the guards that an envoy from the Duke of Modena should arrive tomorrow."

O'Neill tossed the man a gold piece and they rode on.

"From Modena, eh?" O'Neill glanced at Carbajal, his eyes speculative. "You know the roads—wouldn't that envoy come this way?"

Carbajal grinned. "Right, comrade! He wouldn't come with any flourish of trumpets, be sure of that—Raymond isn't courting publicity yet. And this would be his shortest way to Corthia."

O'Neill nodded, and smiled to himself. Perhaps destiny had chosen to be generous toward him, he thought—well, it was high time! His scene with Christina still rankled.

Twilight drew down on the hills, and darkness was at hand when they came to the long descent above the Black Bull. O'Neill called Mary to him.

"Ride on down to the inn, little rose. If only two or three are there, go in and order wine—you're a courier for Corthia. If more are there, however, ride back and warn us—we'll have to change our plans."

She road on down the hill with a word of assent, and O'Neill waited to give her time. Donato pressed up to his stirrup.

"Eh, comrade—I've waited for a little word.

258

This fellow Gaspard, now—I know him to my cost!
He's one of Raymond's torturers. A lame brute
with stone for heart. I don't object to forgiving my
enemies, up to a certain extent, mark you, but it
goes against the grain that a rascal who has usurped
the functions of Satan should have the grace of a
quick thrust into eternity."

O'Neill laughed. "What do you want to do—torture the man?"

"Bah! I want to hang him. This Santinelli is a
born hangman."

"You shall."

O'Neill took the prisoner's reins, and rode down
the hill, Carbajal and Donato with him. They
sighted the dark bulk of the Black Bull below, and
saw a few lights glimmering, but no sign of Mary.

When they came down to the courtyard entry, the
spare horses clattering along behind, a man was just
setting a new-lighted torch in a socket, in order to
take away Mary's horse to the stable. The party
turned in upon the stones, and Santinelli lifted his
voice.

"Ho, Gaspard! Gaspard! Bring out everybody
and see what catch I've made. Where the devil
are you?"

"It's the captain!" shouted someone inside the inn, and in the doorway appeared a large figure, limping a little as he came forward.

O'Neill saw Donato approaching the man under the torch, saw Carbajal dismount and turn toward another man who was running out from the kitchen entrance, and himself rode on to the inn doorway where Gaspard stood. Santinelli perforce accompanied him.

"You, Santinelli?" growled the man in the doorway. "You've had luck?"

"The best of luck," said the prisoner cheerfully. "Come here and look at the loot!"

Gaspard limped out and approached the two horsemen. O'Neill, who held a pistol by the barrel, struck down savagely and knocked the man in a senseless heap.

A yell sounded. Carbajal was upon his man, Donato had the third cornered; steel clashed, and Mary O'Neill came into the doorway, watching. One of the men yelled again.

"The cresset, Ludovic—light the signal—"

"Light it yourself," laughed Donato, and thrust him through, so that he fell with a cough. O'Neill swung out of the saddle and saw Carbajal coming toward him, wiping sword on cloak. Mary O'Neill spoke out quickly.

"Just the three of them here—I saw no others—"

"I'll look," said Carbajal. "You heard what that fellow shouted about a signal? They've probably put a cresset on the roof—the light could be seen from Corthia—" and he darted into the building and was gone.

"Here's your friend Gaspard," said O'Neill to Donato. "Tie him up and take care of him, while I'm putting up the horses. Monsieur, we'll appoint you chief cook; see what you can find in the kitchen and cellar. We deserve a feast tonight!"

So saying, he began getting the horses into the stable, across the courtyard, pausing at the horse-trough on the way.

Eight animals to water, unharness and feed, made no quick task, but now time was of small account. Exultation filled O'Neill as he worked; the first blow was struck, the Black Bull was his, with all its unguessed secrets! He did not know, or care particularly, what those secrets might be—they could wait.

His exultation passed into a certain grimness, however. He could not forget that here under this roof old Teague had been knifed in the back, that on these courtyard stones his brother had been murdered by Raymond—the blood still staining them, perhaps. On this thought he perceived Carbajal coming, and swung toward him.

"Those two are dead? Good. We'll have to bury them later. There's to be no quarter given, you understand? Spare none of them—"

Carbajal, understanding, touched his arm. "Comrade, comrade!" he said softly. "You lost a brother here. What did I lose?"

"Well?" snapped O'Neill, already ashamed of his growled outburst.

Carbajal laughed and slapped his shoulder. "Out of the black mood, comrade!" he cried with energy. "You don't know yet what we've won here—but you will soon! Food and wine is what we need; come on, we'll clean up this job, and get in to where Monsieur has found an excellent dinner waiting. Dinner for half a dozen at least—there's mystery for you!"

"For half a dozen?" repeated O'Neill. "You think others are coming?"

"Others are here," and Carbajal broke into sardonic laughter. "Let 'em wait—time enough! Oh, I'll show you a pretty thing or two, comrade mine! I showed Donato a cell with chains in the wall, and he has Santinelli linked there with Gaspard. Otherwise, the place is empty and ours."

O'Neill wondered if the man were a little mad, not knowing what all this mysterious talk was about; but he was too tired to care now. Weariness was on him, not only of the body, but the weariness that comes with strain ended and over. The quick, sharp stroke had fallen, and the Black Bull was taken— and now was reaction. What all of them most needed was wine and hot food.

And these, as Carbajal said, proved to be ready in some quantity. Mary O'Neill had heaped a fire in the great hearth, lighted torches, and decked a table in the inn-room. When the two men had washed and came in, they found Donato helping her to bring bread and wine from the kitchen, and capons from the spits, with a great roast that was done to a turn. O'Neill wondered anew for whom all this provision had been made ready, but he only laughed at Carbajal's exultant mystery and took the place awaiting him at table.

"Ours!" he exclaimed, looking around the somber room. "The Red Hand of Ulster has crushed the Black Bull—here's luck to the rest of the game, little rose!"

Mary's eyes laughed at him as she lifted her cup, not wholly in mirth either, and drank.

"Lamh laider an uachtar!" she cried in Irish. "The strong hand on top, Yellow Brian—and destruction to all this dark place!"

She hurled the pewter mug, so that it thudded into the fireplace. The others did not understand her words, but her mood was plain enough; Donato broke into laughter, Carbajal chuckled almost gaily, and triumph lifted their spirits into wild exuberation. So they attacked their meal, and when at length he pushed back his chair, got out his pipe, and lighted the tobacco with a brand from the hearth, O'Neill felt like a new man.

"There's Santinelli to feed," he said.

"And perhaps others," said Carbajal.

"Others?" O'Neill looked at him, and the sapphire eye glimmered luridly. "Hm! Well, finish with what's to hand. Where's this torturer?"

"Leave him for the moment," put in Carbajal, rising. "Donato isn't the only one who has a word for Gaspard! Here are the keys I took from his belt," and he showed a huge ring of keys. "Torches, now! With what I know already, and with what

264

Ludovici helped me to, we'll see something. Torches, comrades!"

The suppressed eagerness of the man, his air of mystery, gripped at them all. He waited while the three of them got torches from a pile ready-made in one corner, then he swept his one slightly crooked arm toward the rear wall of the room.

"A secret door there somewhere, but I can't find it, never could," he said. "No matter! Come along outside, and light your torches in the court. We'll look for Charlemagne's stone—there's the hint for us. I know the entrance there well enough. Thank Ludovici!"

They followed him to the courtyard and lighted the torches at that flickering out near the great oak tree. O'Neill saw now that, as he had suspected, it was a question of a cavern in the hillside and secret chambers; and he waited amusedly while Carbajal found the cross-marked stone which, men said, had been laid in mortar by the hand of Charlemagne himself. In fact, O'Neill felt rather scornful as to any possible revelations of the place.

Carbajal examined the stone by the torch-light, then uttered an exultant cry and thrust a huge key in between two of the stones. The key turned under his thrust, and he shoved; a six-foot section of the wall swung in—a door built up of stones, cemented into a backing of iron. Directly ahead of them showed another door, this time of iron-bound oak.

"Now we have it!" exclaimed Carbajal, fitting key to lock, throwing back a bar, and shoving on the inner door. "Feel that draught of air—look at the torches! Other entrances to this little drawing-room, comrades—somewhere up the hillside, perhaps. No telling. None were shown on Ludovici's plans, anyway. Lights there, link-men! Lights!"

"You've not been here before?" queried Mary O'Neill.

"Not I," said Carbajal, and bore on the door.

It swung widely open, flew back with a great crash against the rock wall, and sagged on a smashed hinge. Carbajal laughed at the damage—O'Neill remembered afterward how he had laughed in this moment, and wondered. Ahead of them showed a passage that seemed to pierce the very heart of the hillside. To right and left were doors fitted to the stone-work, half solid rock, and Carbajal paused.

"I'm not sure," he said, jingling his keys, "but if I'm not mistaken, we're about to find the answer to more than one riddle here! That devil Gaspard was

266

not placed in charge of the Black Bull for nothing, you can be sure—now for it! All the locks well oiled, hinges free from rust—I thought so!"

The door on the right swung in to his hand. O'Neill, pressing after him with a torch, uttered a sharp exclamation as he saw what was in the room here. His cry was echoed by another and sharper cry from the darkness.

"No lights—devils that you are, back with the lights!" wailed the voice. O'Neill halted, thrust back Mary and Donato. Peering ahead, he could see two figures against a wall, heard a dull clink of iron links. Carbajal chuckled in his dry way, as he tried his keys.

"Not we, friends—the devils are dead, and here's freedom for you! Shut your eyes, now—give me a light here, Brian! That's better. There's one free; now for the other one. Any more of you about here?"

"No more of us," quavered a voice. "Is this some fiend's jest—who are you?"

"Friends, and it's no jest—there you are!" Carbajal stood back. "No more of you, eh? Must have brought you out here from Corthia. When?"

"Yesterday," came the response, "or last week. Raymond sent you to release us?"

"And hang his men? Not likely. Come along into the tavern; wine's waiting, and food, and horses if you want to leave."

The two of them came stumbling forth, tears on their cheeks, prayers and blessings on their lips. O'Neill glanced at Donato and Mary, jerked his head toward the tavern, and all returned as they had come—not without a last look up the cavern passage, though.

By the time Carbajal had brought up his two half-blind and staggering companions, there was meat cut and wine awaiting them, and the pair fell upon the food and drink like wolves. O'Neill considered them frowningly. One, he perceived, was a spare, oldish man with a white stubble of beard blurring the lines of his face, and a broken air; the other, younger, had a long and ragged brown beard and a certain burly defiance in his manner. O'Neill lighted his pipe and nodded to Donato.

"Bring out that fellow Gaspard, and get a rope to hang him with, after I speak a word or two with him."

He said this, perceiving that the two released prisoners were suspicious, terrified, incredulous of their liberty. But, instead of obeying, Donato came

268

around the table, staring at the younger man all agape in the light from the cresset beside the hearth and the lamp hanging from the rafters. And the brown-bearded man, looking up, started to his feet with a harsh cry, and crossed himself.

"Body o' death—no! It can't be—not Donato the Venetian, the captain of galleys—"

"But it is," and Donato laughed suddenly. "And sink me if you haven't the look of John Doria of Genoa about your eyes—"

The other stared blankly at him. "Carlo Donato!" he breathed. "Donato—alive!"

Donato whirled on the others. "Doria—the Genoese captain who fought me like a brave man!" he cried, eagerly, gaily. "Another of Raymond's victims, eh? Here, Doria—formerly we were enemies, but now we can drink together. Nay, I'm flesh and blood, man! Here's my hand on it—"

The two men gripped hands. Then the older captive shoved forward, peering at Donato.

"Eh? Carlo Donato, eh? I saw you once at Venice—don't know me? That was before this black devil Raymond carried me off and flung me into his dungeons—Camillo—"

"Don Camillo!" shouted Donato. "Here—"

He glanced around in surprise. Carbajal had quite vanished. Mary O'Neill was swinging out into the courtyard. O'Neill himself was frowning a little, and as Donato introduced him, he nudged the Venetian.

"Gaspard—quick with him!" Then, to the two rescued men: "Signori, will you be seated? I am about to ask you to sit in judgment upon a prisoner whom I have taken here."

"But we do not understand all this!" exclaimed Don Camillo. "Who are you, señor Spaniard? And why are you here?"

O'Neill waved aside the questions. He was quick to see that neither of these men was of the calibre to aid him; the more they understood, the more dangerous they would become. And soon enough they would be anxious only to get away. Therefore, he had no idea of letting them know his exact weakness.

"I am here to help you," he said, and lifted his voice to the doorway. "Ho, Carbajal! See that the outposts are in place, and order the men to light no fires! Where is that prisoner, Donato?"

"Coming," said Donato. In the corner, he had swung open a door, and presently came back into sight, leading the halt Gaspard, now adorned with manacles at wrist and ankle.

The other two swung around, and exclamations broke from them at sight of the torturer. Gaspard stood before them scowling, his brutal features showing no emotion, save a puzzled frown at sight of O'Neill. He said nothing.

"Do you know this man, Messer Doria?" demanded O'Neill.

The Genoese exploded with a volley of hot oaths. "Know him? I have seen the devil use boot and rack—"

"And you, Don Camillo?"

The old man nodded, fear in his eyes. "Aye, señor, aye! The torturer."

"And you, Donato?"

"I?" Donato stood before the hulking Gaspard and bared his teeth. "Ask him if he knows me, comrade! Look at him! There's answer enough."

"Take him out and hang him to the oak in the courtyard," said O'Neill. "Signori, will you see justice done while I have horses prepared for you?"

He rose, went to the cell, and ordered Santinelli forth. The bravo came, and O'Neill freed him, then pointed to Gaspard.

"You've kept your bargain; I give you your life. But you haven't earned liberty. Hang that man yonder, and you earn liberty—when it pleases me to give it."

"And supper?" queried Santinelli, rubbing his wrists and rolling an eye at the table.

"And supper."

"Then give me the rope—sapristi! The quicker the better, say I."

O'Neill went outside, found Carbajal, and spoke softly.

"Keep your eye on Santinelli—I'll get horses ready for those two. You want to get rid of them? So do I. That Genoese looks treacherous."

"He is," said Carbajal, grimly. "But he's of a great family in Genoa. Raymond picks his victims well! So this explains everything about Don Camillo, eh? With his own men around him, Raymond could pass the thing off well enough—and with Don Camillo in his hands, he was safe from Tuscany. A fine system, this of Corthia!"

O'Neill laughed, and went on to the stables.

Twenty minutes later, the Genoese and Don Camillo mounted and rode for Pisa—thankful to get away alive, asking no questions, caring only to get free of the Corthian grip. And Santinelli, eating and drinking in his prison cell, had earned his supper, as the long shadow swinging on the oak in the court-yard bore witness.

In this fashion was the Black Bull taken.

CHAPTER XIII

WEARY as all of them were with hard riding and excitement, the departing hoof-beats had hardly died into silence up the hill when they were looking one at another in tacit questioning. Then Mary O'Neill laughed suddenly.

"Come—who's as curious as a woman, eh? Brian, you're bursting with curiosity! Lead on, Carbajal—we all want to see what further secrets are in this place of yours! We have all night to sleep. You don't think anyone will come from Corthia?"

The three men exchanged a look and a shrug.

"We can risk it," said O'Neill. "Tomorrow—well, tomorrow's another story."

"You don't expect to do nothing here indefinite-ly?" asked Donato.

"We've been fairly busy so far," said O'Neill drily. "Over tonight and tomorrow, rest and sleep.

274

Tomorrow night—strike at Raymond! On with
you Carbajal, or I'll fall asleep on my feet."

Carbajal, nothing loath, led them across the courtyard, now darkly ominous, to where the door of the
caverns stood open. Again the torches flickered.

"I don't like that draught of air!" exclaimed Carbajal uneasily. "It shows there must be other entrances—well, here's for the doors. Ah, unlocked!"

He had no further use for his keys, indeed, since
only the prison-cell of the whole place proved to have
been locked. Raymond kept no treasure in these
caverns.

If no treasure, however, there were other things
more to the point. The underground passage led
into a perfect maze of ancient chambers, partly hewn
in the hillside, partly natural; one after another, these
caverns yielded up their secret—prosaic secrets
enough, for the most part. One room was racked
high with muskets and pistols, another with bolts
and arbalests, another with leather jerkins and steel
caps, and so through the whole range. Equipment
was here for an army, from horse-trappings to lead
bullets, nor was there any lack of such food as could
be salted down and stored. One of the last chambers into which they penetrated was piled to the roof

with kegs—and Carbajal slammed the door in all haste, lest torch-sparks somehow reach the powder waiting here.

Another room contained chair and table, and a huge oak secretary against the wall, with lamps and taper-holders about. The secretary was locked fast, and nothing short of broad-axes could have smashed it open.

"Raymond's room, doubtless," said O'Neill, glancing about. "Here, it may be, we'd find some of his levers by which he blackmails half Italy—if rumor speaks true! No time to search now, however. How far does this cavern run?"

"To hell, by the looks of it," and Carbajal held up his torch, so they could look on along the passages. These appeared endless. "Want to see more?"

"Bah! Let's out of here and get some sleep. We'll have need of it this time tomorrow night."

It was not difficult to trace their way back to the entrance, since the main passage was larger than the others and quite distinct. When they came to the courtyard and the cold night air, Donato shivered.

"Ugh! A deadly place, comrades. Shall we close this opening? If Raymond's men can get in by another entrance, we might be taken in rear here."

276

"Not tonight—they'd have no reason," said O'Neill. "And we'll chance things until tomorrow. As for burial, we can bring those dead men into this prison cell and leave them there; I'll guarantee they'll be buried soon enough!"

So it was done, and extinguishing the torches, they returned to the inn. Making sure that Santinelli was safe in his cell, they sought the chambers above —all save Carbajal, who made his bed near the hearth in the great room.

"Any plan, comrade?" asked Donato, as he and O'Neill were making ready the chamber they shared. "We're well rid of those two whom we released— yet news of it will come to Raymond—"

"Not before tomorrow night," said O'Neill. "And by then we'll finish. Yes, I've plan enough—but let it hinge on what turns up! Do you realize that Raymond has been getting ready for years past? These arms and munitions cost good hard money. Now he's preparing a great stroke, he's gathering men—and the four of us are here to quench all his ambition at one swoop!"

"We haven't done it yet."

"An army couldn't do it—but the four of us can. You'll see! Sleep tight."

The room was plunged into darkness.

Morning broke clear, cold, sunny, when creaking of cart-wheels and shouts of men brought O'Neill down to the courtyard. He found that Carbajal had closed the gates, and had removed the body of Gaspard from the oak tree. The passing carts were laden with timbers and building material for Corthia, where the work of rebuilding the fire-gutted place was going forward fast.

"And not bad for Raymond either," commented Carbajal, as he watched O'Neill splash in the horse-trough and then shave. "He gathers men on every hand—and abruptly, over-night, his army of workmen is transformed into an army of soldiers! Not that he'd want an army here. He'll throw his force into Rome quietly, around Easter when the city is crammed with strangers—oh, he's a crafty man, our Raymond! Where's Donato? and Monsieur?"

"Snoring," said O'Neill. "Let 'em sleep. That envoy from Modena wouldn't be along until afternoon, so we've time enough."

"For what?"

"Preparations. Get torches and come along."

Carbajal obeyed, and O'Neill led the way into the

278

hillside passage. There was no danger that any of the passing country-folk would want to enter the Black Bull, while anyone coming from Corthia would find entry barred and must waken Donato. So O'Neill felt safe enough in leaving the place unguarded momentarily.

In one of the rooms where muskets were racked, he halted his companion.

"Get a dozen of these out under the oak, and a load of pistols. No telling what'll happen tonight, so we may as well be prepared for emergencies."

"Hm!" said Carbajal, his blue eye probing at O'Neill. "I wish I knew what you had in mind to do!"

"That depends on catching the envoy from Modena. At the present instant, I'm after powder for these arms, and a flask of bullets."

"Then for the love of the saints have a care with your torch!"

O'Neill laughed, and strode off up the passage. So far as the torch was concerned, he was safe enough, for the passage was set at intervals with holders high in the wall, where torches or tallow-dips might be placed. When he came to the powder-room, he found one of these holders opposite the door, and put his torch in it. With the door open, he could see into the room well enough.

He had brought a cleaver from the inn, and attacked one of the kegs, smashing it open and dumping the powder about the other kegs, and running a heavy train of it to the door and so on down the passage—not in the center, but in the angle of the wall at the right, where it merged into the shadows. The keg empty, he replaced it, opened another, set his torch on down the passage in another holder and continued the train of powder along the angle of the wall. Somewhat to his relief, O'Neill found a portion of candle in one of the holders, for which he exchanged his sputtering torch—the combination of sparks and powder was bad on the nerves. The thought caused him a grim laugh.

"It's different now from my first coming to the Black Bull!" he reflected. "Then, nothing mattered —Hugh gone, Teague gone, Mary gone! Now I have Mary at least, and if I get my sword again and serve out Raymond his due—well, life's ahead!"

When he came out to the sunlit courtyard, Carbajal was sitting under the oak tree arranging pistols and muskets. He cocked his one blue eye at O'Neill and watched the latter bring the powder-train to the outside door, then chuckled.

"Going to blow the Black Bull to hell?"

"Aye," said O'Neill, and set down the half-empty keg. "Here's powder. Can we fasten this outside door shut?"

The outer door, a mask of stone against iron, could be barred and locked from the inside, but could not be held closed from the outside except the key was turned due to its construction. The hinges of the inner door were smashed and sagging.

"Then leave the passage open," said O'Neill, with a shrug. "There's no telling what will happen; if we shut the door now, we can't open it in a hurry—best leave it, and in case of emergency we'll have the passage and caverns as a refuge. Here's a flask of bullets I pocketed, so let's get to work loading your arms."

Mary, it proved, was already up and busy in the kitchen. Donato made his appearance, doused his head in the horse-trough, and watched the two of them at work loading until O'Neill sent him to feed and water the horses. The work was about finished when Mary came out with word that it was close to noon, she had a meal nearly ready, and Santinelli was shouting from his cell. O'Neill went in to him and opened the door.

"Well?" he demanded, looking at the bravo.

"Do I have to hang another man, signor, in order to eat?" demanded Santinelli, who had largely recovered his natural bluster. "And when comes the freedom you promised?"

"Tonight," said O'Neill. He had no intention of letting the man become aware that Monsieur Chemise-de-fer was a woman. "Come out for half and hour, if you like, and then back to your cell and noon meat."

Santinelli swaggered out, warmed himself in the sunlight, and seemed vastly amazed by the opening into the hillside. He had known nothing of it, and professed entire ignorance of the caverns. In this O'Neill took him to be a liar, and Donato confirmed the opinion when the bravo was returned to his prison-cell.

"Santinelli's one of Raymond's captains," declared the Venetian. "And you can be sure Raymond isn't the only man in Corthia who knows about these passages! However, no matter."

Matter enough, as things fell out; but of this they had no prescience as they fell to the meal Mary set forth. Over the excellent wine Carbajal produced from the cellar, O'Neill ordered the Venetian to saddle a horse and ascend the hill, and to wait at the cross-roads for the Modena envoy.

"But we don't know he'll come this way!" objected Mary.

"Luck's breaking for us," said O'Neill, laughing. "Have faith! If the man has any large company with him, Donato, pass the time of day and say nothing. Otherwise, say Raymond sent you to meet him, and bring him here."

"So!" said Donato with a shrewd glance. "You want to make use of this envoy, eh?"

"We'll see," and O'Neill smiled. "Give him until sunset. If he doesn't come then, we'll make other plans. If he comes, I'll set my scheme before you all."

"Fair enough," said the Venetian, and departed.

When they had closed the gates after him, the time dragged. O'Neill was tempted to penetrate the caverns, yet dared not risk so prolonged an absence, for now, while he hoped to avoid crisis until after dark, it might be forced upon him at any moment.

The afternoon was half over when Mary came out to where O'Neill was sitting on a bench near the gate, idly puffing at his pipe, and dropped beside him.

"You'll not tell me what you have a mind to do?" she demanded, smilingly.

O'Neill laughed. "With all my heart, little rose!"

"What, then?"

"Take you to Vienna—and tell you all that's been in my heart the three years since we parted—"

"Silly! I mean about Raymond," she exclaimed, color coming into her cheeks—though her eyes held steady on his.

"We're not talking about Raymond, but about what I have in mind," said O'Neill. "And the chief thing I have in mind is—"

"Your sword, that Hugh was bringing you!" she broke in swiftly. At mention of the dead boy's name, her manner changed swiftly. She put her hand on that of O'Neill and regarded him seriously, gravely. "Brian—not now! Let all that wait until we reach Vienna; not here, now, in this place! It terrifies me. Perhaps because Hugh was killed here under that oak tree, perhaps—"

"Right, little rose." O'Neill pressed her fingers. "Right. And if anything happens that I don't get to Vienna, then—"

"Then," she interposed, "you'll know that I had something to say to you, also—"

And leaning swiftly over, she kissed him on the lips—and then was gone with a quick laugh, dancing into the inn, waving her hand to him from the door, and caroming full tilt into Carbajal as the latter emerged.

"Hola!" cried Carbajal hastily. "A pleasant enough surprise, Monsieur, except for the mail-shirt —devil take me if I like you in man's garments as well as I did in your own! And I'm not yet quite blind, either, and if I see more than I should have seen of what passed out there—"

"Why, then, you get your own reward!" she exclaimed, and pressing her lips to his cheek, was gone merrily. Carbajal grinned and came out to O'Neill.

"A kiss of pity—no, no, of comradely friendship," he exclaimed. "A heart of gold, that woman! No news from Donato?"

O'Neill came to his feet, head on one side, listening.

"Aye—Donato or others this moment! Stand by your shot over there while I swing at the gates—"

He went to the wide gates, while Carbajal darted

to the loaded muskets under the oak tree. Donato's voice reached in a clear hail, as O'Neill tugged at the gates and swung them apart; he looked out, to see three horsemen drawing rein—the Venetian and two strangers. The Modena envoy had walked into the trap.

All three came into the courtyard, dismounted, and Donato grandiloquently presented the two strangers to O'Neill.

"Don Brian, I have the pleasure of presenting Ser Guido Marucchi of Modena, and his esquire. I've told them Duke Raymond sent us to meet them here, and promises to join us later—"

O'Neill bowed, and Marucchi, a vain and pompous little man, laughed heartily.

"A good story, that, about Raymond and the two ladies of Rome! Since Messer Donato says the wine here is excellent and we see for ourselves how good is the company, we'll be only too glad to await him, gentlemen, with you. I hear my old friend Captain Santinelli is here too."

"If not drunk," said O'Neill. Already Donato was swaggering into the inn, and Carbajal led away the horses, aping a servant's airs. "Donato! Bid Monsieur keep his room, and do you fetch out some of that Muscatello we found. Come, Ser Guido, and we'll do our best for you—we had to kill the rascally inn-keeper last night for under-cooking a capon, but I think we can make good cheer—"

The two gentlemen of Modena were obviously sleek courtiers and not soldiers, and found the rough ways of Corthia alarming. It was clear that Donato had taken occasion to warn Santinelli, for the latter came out of his cell, greeted the envoys cordially, and kept his tongue between his teeth. All five settled down at a table, and when the heady wine of Montalcino was opened, O'Neill made the bravo a significant gesture.

"Drink the cellar out!" he said heartily. "By ill luck, I can't join you at it, having a malady of the stomach which prevents much drinking—"

"That have not I," said Santinelli, catching his cue, and Donato broke out laughing.

"Nor I! Here's a health to Modena—bottoms up!"

So it started, and in twenty minutes the two messengers had forgotten their business and were applying themselves to the bottle with right good will. Mary kept out of sight and, O'Neill trusted, out of sound as well, since the rafters echoed to the mirth of jests better suited to the camp than to her ears.

Then O'Neill fell to work at pumping, wanting more than the mere letters Marucchi carried. He soon found that neither of the envoys were known personally to Raymond, though Santinelli, who had been in Modena some months before, had met Marucchi there. Satisfied of this, O'Neill threw out broad hints as to the plans of Raymond, and the sleek, half-drunk knight of Modena tapped his nose significantly.

"Ha, señor Spaniard! It's not hard for us to guess a thing or two!" he hiccuped. "Here you are, here's a noble Venetian, and our lord the duke has sent us with letters of the utmost importance—well, well, mustn't talk too much, eh? All the same, we'd not be surprised to meet a certain gentleman from Ferrara, I can tell you! And if he goes back to Ferrara—well, there'll be two hundred men from Modena to take his orders. The house of Este must stick together—"

A little deft questioning, and O'Neill had what he wanted. Raymond was getting backing for his catspaw—getting Modena behind him for the attempt to seat the false Don Alfonso in Ferrara. His own stroke at Rome was probably being held in the background, unguessed by any.

Another half hour saw Santinelli hanging low above the table, the esquire under it, and Marucchi singing a maudlin song. Donato had drunk enough, and more than enough, but he came to his feet when O'Neill rose in disgust, and with Carbajal led the protesting Santinelli back to the cell. O'Neill looked at Marucchi, and with a short, sharp blow knocked him sprawling. He lay quiet on the stones. O'Neill bent over him, then rose.

"Carbajal! Mary! Come along, now. Carbajal, tie up these two swine and chuck them into a corner. Donato! Souse your head in the trough, close the gates, and join us. Sharp about it! Bring candles with you, Mary; it'll be dark soon."

O'Neill was afire with eagerness now—impatience tugged hard at him, as he tore open the letters he had taken from Marucchi and spread them out on the table. He could not read the crabbed Italian hand, however, for the letters were not in Latin, and had to wait until Carbajal and Donato had joined him at the table, with Mary. Carbajal deciphered the missives readily enough, and chuckled drily.

"Good! Raymond gets aid from Modena—two

289

hundred men promised. He's to furnish equipment and take them under his orders until Don Alfonso holds Ferrara, when they take orders from Alfonso. Modena guarantees recognition and support. You see? Clever Raymond! He doesn't need to spare a man to Alfonso!"

"Clever, indeed!" said Donato. "He seizes Ferrara, probably with Venetian troops to help, and then steals away to Rome, where all the men he can rake and scrape together are awaiting him. A bold stroke —and he holds Rome! You see? And nobody dares interfere. The House of Este would throw him out of Rome—but Raymond has set Don Alfonso there in Ferrara, and Este is blocked. No telling where his intrigue runs with Venice and Spain, but I'll wager he has them behind him!"

Carbajal looked up at O'Neill suddenly, and in the gaze of that lurid sapphire eye was something that checked speech.

"Per Bacco! Do you remember," he said, pointing to the floor, "how that rascally red-faced ruffian died—and what he said as he was dying? About you, and Rome, and destiny—I told you then the man was fey! He had second sight, comrade! And it's come true. Now it's you who stand between Raymond and Rome, if he but knew it!"

"Not I," said O'Neill. "All four of us."

They looked at him, expectantly. He filled and lighted his pipe, unhurried, seeing now with growing clarity what must be done this night. The others waited—Mary frowning a little, Carbajal blinking at him eagerly, Donato sipping again at the wine, reckless of what might come.

"All I want, first," said O'Neill, "is to reach Raymond without interference—get hold of him, put point to throat and hold him in my power! You see? All of us, except Monsieur here, are too well known to him and his men; we couldn't hope to do it. But he's expecting these envoys from Modena. We'll be taken straight to him. If we can fool him just long enough to cheat his guards and get a dagger to his skin—then his guards are helpless to intervene."

"And kill him there?" exclaimed Carbajal.

"No—kill him here, where he slew my brother," and O'Neill nodded toward the courtyard. "Carry him off out of Corthia. Play the same game he must have played with Don Camillo and others. He'll go with us, and he'll order his men not to intervene, if he knows that I'll meet him here sword in hand.

He's bursting with confidence in himself, thinks no swordsman can stand against him."

"But that's the sober truth!" exclaimed Donato. "I know well enough I couldn't stand against him— the devil has an arm of steel! Is that all you mean to do—carry him off?"

"It's enough," said O'Neill, looking at him for a moment.

"Name of the devil, it's a tremendous big order— like all simple things!" swore Carbajal, and chuckled. "Yet it would work, aye! The crux of the whole matter lies in getting to him personally. He's well guarded, that man, and if he suspected a thing, the attempt would be suicide. I see now why you wanted those envoys from Modena—ho! You're a crafty one, comrade! It'll work. But as you say, we're all too well known there to reach Raymond, even calling ourselves envoys. One look from him, and he'd know us. It won't do to merely get past the guards—we have to reach the man himself."

"You don't," said O'Neill. "You remain here, have the horses saddled, keep the gates closed, keep your matches lighted and your shot ready—that's your end of it."

"And being a woman," struck in Mary suddenly, "I suppose I'm to bide here too?"

O'Neill met her hotly scornful eyes, and smiled.

"You go as Marucchi the envoy," he said, and she changed countenance at that. "I shorten my mustache, shear my hair, daub mustache and brows and hair with black from the fireplace yonder—and I can get across a room to Raymond's side before he knows me."

"And I?" demanded Donato, his eyes eager. O'Neill puffed at his pipe.

"You," he said, "go as Carlo Donato of Venice—yourself. With a rope about your wrists, a prisoner. Of course, you can fling off the rope when need be—the point is that sight of you will catch Raymond off guard, bewilder him, keep his thoughts from us—"

Donato smashed his mug down on the table, in wild and furious glee.

"There's a strategist for you!" he shouted. "Ha! To my arms, comrade!"

"To your own," said O'Neill, and rose. "We want to be off at once, and catch Raymond at dinner if possible—to work! Well, comrade?"

Carbajal had gestured uncertainly, his sapphire eye gloomy.

"After all, it's a desperate game to play, a mad risk—"

"Bah!" O'Neill laughed. "Are we merchants gabbling on the price o' cloth? Risk, yes! It's win or lose everything."

"But," objected Carbajal, "if you reach Raymond you should kill him—"

"And then be shot down by the guards? Thank you, comrade, I prefer to live if possible."

"He'll over-reach you. He's crafty, that devil! And if you get to him, he may tell his guards to shoot and be damned to you!"

"The right man would; that's the risk," said O'Neill, with a nod. "We risk it in any event— that's why he has guards! It's a mad scheme, out of reason, illogical, improbable—like all simple things, as you said just now. But it's that or nothing, for me."

"Hm!" said Carbajal. "And what of me? What about that unknown specimen of garbage who calls himself Don Alfonso of Ferrara?"

"Oh!" said O'Neill. "He comes back with us too —for an introduction to Carbajal."

The dry, sardonic chuckle of the one-eyed man made sufficient answer.

CHAPTER XIV

THE night was uncommonly warm for February, even though winters were never harsh in Corthia, and Raymond had set forth an open-air feast in his gardens that would be long remembered by his guests. To further banish any chill, great round drums were set here and there, fed with charcoal and giving off a fierce heat.

Along the trees and the walls glimmered paper lanterns, many-colored, and two huge bronze candelabra bearing candles large as torches were set to light Raymond's festal board. This table was set close to the marble pool, so the feasters might fling scraps and watch the carp and lampreys rise to the bait, with splash and flurry of water. The ground around was soft and gay with bright rugs and carpets, so that this seemed more some vast banqueting hall than the open air. Any guards were invisible among the trees, and no sounds came from the gutted shell of the town around the palace, for all work of rebuilding was stopped at night lest it disturb Raymond.

If the Duke of Corthia had no weakness for the ladies, at least his palace was well supplied with them, and the three who shared his board with Angelo and Alfonso of Ferrara were well calculated to enhance the enjoyment of all concerned. That Angelo was having a very good time in his sleek way was quite obvious. Alfonso, too, had a partner to his liking, found the wine much to his taste, and vaunted loudly what he would do when he occupied the seat of the mighty at Ferrara.

Raymond sat at the head of the table, said little, listened much, and paid attention to the excellent dinner that was provided. His chosen companion of the evening, a slim dark-eyed Greek girl he had brought from Candia, laughed with the others but forced no attentions upon him; these ladies of Corthia knew what no one else in the world knew—that this dark and indomitable adventurer, apparently so invulnerable at all points, yet had one extremely vulnerable spot, a veritable heel of Achilles. They took no chances on touching it inadvertently.

A RED FEAST IN CORTHIA

"Where's your music, Raymond?" demanded Alfonso suddenly, pushing back his chair. "If a feast like this is to be properly enjoyed, we must have a saraband between courses—Lady Biancha is going to dance it with me—"

"By all means," assented Raymond heartily. "And my Aglæ will dance for us, after your saraband—come, Donato—"

Angelo and his lady rose with the other two. At a sign from Raymond, a lute and viol among the fringe of trees swept into music, and the two couples swung into their stately saraband—which was not as stately as it should have been, thanks to the wine and a certain robust vigor on the part of Don Alfonso.

Neither Raymond nor his dark-eyed Greek shared in the dance. Midway of it, a figure came across the garden, his polished jack gleaming in the soft light, and Raymond turned quickly. It was the captain of the guard—the same ox-wit who had talked with O'Neill and let the latter escape. He came to Raymond's side and spoke, low-voiced, and brought a sealed parchment. Raymond tore at it and nodded.

"The envoy from Modena, aye—but what's that you said about a prisoner?"

"Someone who had attacked them on the way here,

they said, excellency." The soldier chuckled. "They seemed proud of having overcome him and want to hang on to him."

Raymond smiled. "Marucchi, eh? A soft-headed fool—yes, that would be his way. Bring them along here. And no word from Santinelli?"

"Not a word, excellency." The captain hesitated. "But here's a curious thing—that Mantuan archer of ours is at the gate, and he swears the horse this prisoner is riding is one that Rinserra rode off on! Rinserra went with Santinelli, you know, as guide. This archer was his crony and claims to know the horse."

Raymond's eyes became alert. "Eh? What's that? Who's this prisoner, this robber?"

The captain shrugged. "Who? Some scum, excellency—a slender dark man, he seems. Has a devilish odd ring on his finger I'd like to get—"

At this instant the music stopped. Donato and Don Alfonso came back to the table, and Angelo was just in time to catch the next words, which held him petrified.

"—a fine gold ring, too, set with a cross of Malta in some gray stone. A talisman—"

The captain jerked back a pace, for Raymond

came out of his chair as though on steel springs. From Angelo broke a sharp word.

"What's this? About the ring—"

"We'll soon see. Bring them in here, all of them! The envoy we expected from Modena, Angelo— bringing a prisoner who attacked him on the road. This prisoner has a ring—and rides one of my horses! If it's Donato, we have him now." Raymond turned on the three startled women and waved them off. "Clear out—clear out! Go on inside and await word from me."

"Eh? Then I'll go with 'em," said Don Alfonso, blustering. "I know how to treat a lady like Biancha—"

Raymond turned on him, showing teeth and temper at once.

"You swine of a camp-follower, do what I tell you!" he snarled. "Sit down! By the saints—to have a fool like you on my hands at such a minute! Sit down."

The prospective Duke of Ferrara lost his bluster and dropped into a chair, while the three women vanished hurriedly. Raymond's words were bitter, but more bitter and perilous were his eyes, blazing at them savagely. Angelo seated himself on the edge

of his chair with a nervous air, his uneasy eyes probing the shadowy depths of the garden, his left hand
fingering the poniard at his belt.

With an effort, Raymond fought back his impatience, composed himself, sat down and sipped at
his wine. He looked at Donato, read his disturbed
soul, and smiled.

"Calm down, Angelo," he said crisply. "Leave
your affairs in my hands, and I'll take care of them.
Get foolish—and you'll be sorry. Here we are,
now."

The captain of the guard approached, leading
three indistinct figures; at a gesture from Raymond,
he halted and strode away, melting into the farther
shadows. The three came on alone. One stepped
forward, saluted Raymond with a low bow, and
spoke.

"Your highness, I have come from Modena—"

"Wait," said Raymond, and rose, ignoring the
envoy. He, and the staring Angelo had eyes only
for the central figure of the three—Carlo Donato,
bare-headed, smiling a little, hands before him
wrapped in folds of rope. They looked neither at
the envoy nor at his tall, wide-shouldered companion
with uncouth black hair and sheltered face, who held

the ropes of the captive; it was Donato who held them both transfixed with his challenging and reckless gaze.

Raymond stepped forward to him, so the envoy had to move aside.

"You!" he exclaimed, his gaze biting into Donato with malignant emphasis. He did not note nor care that of the two messengers from Modena, the one was at his elbow and the other, in front of him, at his other elbow. "So you've come back, eh?"

"That was my intention when I left here," said Donato, and laughed a little. A dark tide of color swept into Raymond's face at the hint of mockery in this laughter—and O'Neill saw it. On the instant, he knew he had found the man's one vulnerable point.

"You're welcome," said Raymond acidly. "Where are your companions? Where's that one-eyed rascal?"

"At the Black Bull," said Donato. "He's come back too. So have others. The Irish girl you sold to a passing merchant—she's come back."

"Are you mad?" exclaimed Raymond. "That Irish girl?"

"Here," said Mary O'Neill, and one hand caught

Raymond's wrist, the other held a poniard swiftly to his neck. As he would have turned, O'Neill reached out, caught his other wrist in iron fingers, and whipped out a pistol.

Donato calmly took a step back and shook the loosely coiled rope from his wrists.

It was an instant of sheer paralysis for those who looked on. As for Raymond, his eyes drove at the girl, then at O'Neill; he felt the point at his neck, saw the cocked pistol at his breast, and comprehended his position without a word. The three stood motionless in the light of the massy candles, and the little stir and rustle among the trees fringing the garden showed that the guards hidden there realized their own helplessness. In this instant of silence, a fish leaped high in the pool beside them, and the splash sounded loud.

Then Angelo Donato cried out, and started to his feet. Carlo Donato, picking up the rope, came around the group of three and looked at him.

"Sit down, you!" he ordered, and Angelo obeyed, white and shaken. Don Alfonso did not move. Now O'Neill spoke, and a slight start from Raymond showed recognition of his voice, if not of his face.

A RED FEAST IN CORTHIA

"You remember my threat to you when I was here
before, Raymond? Should have warned you. Accept my orders, and you ride out of here with us,
freely, unhurt. Refuse, and before we can be killed,
you die. Not worth it, eh?"

"Agreed," said Raymond, promptly. "What do
you want?"

"No use bidding your guards withdraw; they
wouldn't! We'll kill you at the first move they
make—hence, tell them not to molest us, here or
outside."

Raymond turned his head, although the point of
the stiletto at his neck broke the skin. He called out,
and gave the order as O'Neill had commanded. A
word of comprehending assent came back from the
guards in the fringe of darkness.

"Send someone," said O'Neill, "for my sword—
the sword for which you murdered my brother at the
Black Bull."

"In fair fight!" said Raymond, proudly.

"As I shall murder you with that sword."

These words showed Raymond what his captors
intended, and before their eyes he took heart, gained
all his assured confidence, even smiled grimly. Well
he knew his own skill with a blade in hand. He gave

the order curtly, and again came an assent from the darkness.

"Cut the rope in two, Donato," said O'Neill.

Carlo Donato drew his sword and halved the rope which had formed his feigned bonds. At O'Neill's gesture, he came and drew the hands of Raymond together behind his back, and tied the wrists firmly. The girl drew a step away, but O'Neill kept Raymond covered with the pistol.

Again a fish leaped in the pool, and O'Neill glanced briefly at the marble-framed water, then looked at the table.

"Come here, you who call yourself Don Alfonso of Ferrara!" he said. "You hear? Come forward, unless you want to feel steel between your ribs— before the real Don Alfonso puts it there! Come, you dog!"

Don Alfonso, his protuberant eyes bulging, rose and approached, helplessly.

"What mean you by such words?" he attempted, blustering. "You low-born varlet—"

Donato struck him across the face with the length of rope still in his hand, and the man paused, put up an arm, whimpered in terror.

"Dog's too good a name for you," said O'Neill

304

sternly. "It speaks poorly for your scheme, Raymond, that you'd pick such a faint-hearted cur as this to take duke's rank! You'd have done better with your own scullion. Tie his hands, Donato."

Carlo Donato obeyed, the false Alfonso not resisting. Raymond perceived by all this how his whole plot was known to his captors. His dark eyes flashed from one to the other, came to rest upon O'Neill.

"So Santinelli failed!" he said slowly.

"He did," said O'Neill, with his grim smile. "But he hanged Gaspard for us, so he's earned his life. Should have had more men at the Black Bull, Raymond! By now, Don Camillo's at Pisa, and John Doria's posting hard for Genoa—aye, the Black Bull's gored! And the wound gave up powder. You've paid dear for killing a boy to take his sword, Raymond. But you're not through paying."

Raymond's face became pallid, and a dew of sweat broke out upon his brow and cheeks.

Here was more than the mere discovery of his plot —here was absolute ruin, with the secrets of the Black Bull known, his prisoners flown, and doubtless news of what he planned gone to all Italy! He

305

trembled slightly, though not with fear, and his eyes lashed out at O'Neill most venomously.

"Ah!" he said, and that was all, yet the word was pregnant with unuttered things.

O'Neill glanced at Mary, and motioned to Don Alfonso, from whose hands the rope hung.

"Take him out, tie him into the saddle, and wait for us at the gate—the town gate," he said. "Raymond, tell your guard-captain to escort these two to the outer gate and to have it opened, and left open. Also, warn him not to pursue or interfere with us, unless you want to be pistoled."

Raymond gathered himself together and called out his orders. O'Neill stepped a pace from him and put his lips to Mary's ear.

"We're all right now," he said softly. "But if anything should go wrong, make for the Black Bull and Carbajal—and get away."

"Don't be foolish, Brian," she said lightly, and turned to her captive. "Come along, lord duke of Ferrara! Come along."

She took the cord dangling from his wrists, pulled on it, and he followed mechanically. All the world of this petty adventurer had gone to pieces around him.

"There's your cousin, Carlo," said O'Neill to the Venetian. "D'you want to put a sword in his hands and settle matters?"

Carlo looked at the white-faced, staring Angelo, and laughed in scorn.

"Not I," he said in contempt, and turned his back. "That poor effeminate fop isn't worth staining a good sword with, comrade! But what about Beatrice? Where is she, Raymond?"

"She?" Raymond bared his teeth in a snarl. "In Rome. If I'd brought her, instead of these two piddling—oh, devil take such swine! Serves me right for meddling with their affairs. Don Brian, do you intend to fight me or murder me?"

"Fight you, unless you prefer the word execute," said O'Neill.

"Then I'll have them bring my own sword. Ho there, guards! One of you bring me the sword from my chamber—my own sword. And quick about it!"

"No hurry," said O'Neill grimly.

"Not a bit," and with a laugh, Donato went to the table, poured wine for himself, and emptied the goblet. He looked for a moment down at Angelo, and under his look the other became deadly pale.

Now from the shadows advanced a man, who

carried a sword. He brought it around the marble verge of the pool and halted at a word from O'Neill, who took the weapon. Without letting his pistol fall from Raymond's side, O'Neill motioned the man back and then held the sword up to the light, and his gray eyes gleamed as he looked upon it. Donato whirled, a soft exclamation on his lips.

Small wonder, indeed! Small wonder that Raymond, chancing to see this weapon, had brought down fate upon his head by murder of the boy who carried it! The scabbard was plain, but the hilt was of ruddy gold, studded with dull deep emeralds of Peru, and the pommel was an emerald carved in shape of a cross. One look at the hilt showed what a sword must be under the plain scabbard. Donato came forward and looked at it curiously.

"So this is it, comrade?"

"Aye," said O'Neill. "An ancient Toledo blade, remade into a rapier by Moors who had the old Toledo secrets. It came out of Spain into Ireland, and went back to Spain again—gold and emeralds of Peru, this hilt! And the blade's inset with gold, yet the steel's not harmed. I've seen it bent double—"

Donato turned back to the table and poured himself more wine, and lifted the cup to his lips.

308

A RED FEAST IN CORTHIA

Now happed the one thing expected by no one, least of all by Raymond. For Angelo Donato, sitting there cringed against the table, eyes darting from livid face, saw that O'Neill was looking at the sword, and saw Carlo Donato lifting the wine-cup to his lips two feet away. Like the flashing stroke of a viper, without warning, the stiletto swept forth in his hand, he flung himself forward, and buried the weapon in his cousin's side.

O'Neill caught Carlo Donato's gasp, let his sword fall, shoved his pistol against Raymond's breast. But Raymond did not move. He, too, was thunderstruck by this action, and for the instant could only stare. The cup fell from Carlo Donato's hand. Angelo wrenched at the poniard, drew it free, poised for another stroke—and then blenched and shrank away with a low cry. He turned his back on the man he had killed, and ran, blindly.

Carlo Donato jerked out his dagger, swung it up, flung it so that it flamed and glittered in the ruddy light. It struck Angelo as he scurried away, drove into him fair between the shoulders, sent him sprawling down in a headlong dive at the edge of the outspread carpets. He moved convulsively, and then lay quiet, face down, dead.

"Carlo!" cried out O'Neill. "You're not hurt—"

Carlo Donato put one hand against his side where the blood gushed, and for the last time his fine reckless laugh broke out.

"Not hurt, comrade, not hurt—cured!" he cried. Then a wild shout broke from him—a pealing shout that rose and lifted and echoed back from the gray walls. "Look out—ride for it, Monsieur—ride for it! Carbajal—"

The shout ended abruptly, as the Venetian pitched sideways and fell across the table.

With the shout, or perhaps because of it—so swift came these things, it were hard to say—Raymond's foot shot out, and his shoulder shoved forward. O'Neill, intent on Donato, was tripped and flung backward, with the push. He pulled trigger, and the pistol roared, but Raymond had dropped away from it. Then O'Neill went plunging into the marble pool, and the water closed above him.

Fighting desperately, frantically, for breath and balance, O'Neill found bottom under his feet; the pool was only four feet deep. He emerged, shook the water out of his eyes, and saw at a glance that all was lost. Men were running, Raymond was out of his sight, Donato lay dead across the table.

A RED FEAST IN CORTHIA

"Ride, Mary, ride for Carbajal!" he shouted, as he clawed for the smooth edge of the pool. "Ride!"

A crossbow clanged, and the bolt slithered from the water at his side. Another crashed and shattered at the marble edge. Shouts were lifting, men were darting about, a pistol banged away vainly—and drag himself from the water O'Neill could not, for the smoothness of the marble. He tried to lift himself, then heard the voice of Raymond in a shrill yell.

"No shooting! Take him alive—alive, curse you! At him, you fools—"

They began to come from all sides, hurling themselves into the shallow pool, sending the water up in spurting showers. O'Neill saw himself lost—and there, a foot away, saw the shimmering hilt of his own sword. He reached for it, jerked it to him, whipped the blade from the sheath; and, as the men came at him, turned on them. Arms clear, at least—

They had short joy of it, those who crowded and shoved at him the first, for the blade licked here and there like a living thing, now up at those above, now forward at those around, and threw glints of light in the air as it flamed. Caught, hemmed in, men striking at him with arbalests and hands, O'Neill worked away from the edge of the pool toward the center; hat gone, disguise gone, his yellow hair shone out ruddy in the light, but less ruddy than the sword in his hand.

He drove them before him, and as he moved, men shrieked and floundered, and the water was all shot with crimson. A dying man swept against his legs and threw him off balance; he went down, came up again, eyes blazing, sword darting in and out. They were upon him from all sides, surging about him in the center of the pool. Reach him they could not, and madness seized upon them all as the sword bit at them, until a tumult of shouts and curses and hoarse voices filled the air.

Little cared any of them now for Raymond's order —they came at him with steel out. Only the Milan links saved him as the blades from behind sent him staggering. He turned, and men died there as the water reddened more deeply. Then one, craftier than the others, dove under the water and gripped him about the knees.

This man bubbled up air and life as the sword drove down into him; but as his body twisted away, it wrenched the sword out of O'Neill's hand, and the others were already surging in. For a time they

312

swirled about him, steel striking, hands gripping, the yellow hair and blazing eyes high above them all. Weaponless, O'Neill fought with his fists, a strange warfare to these Italians, and still his yellow hair rose above the wildly surging mass of men as he beat them away, crushed them down, trampled them.

Raymond's voice rose shrill from the edge of the pool and a silver plate hurtled at O'Neill, struck another man and dropped him under the mass into the yeasty foam of blood and water. Goblets, bottles, platters came showering around him as he fought. A silver flagon caught him above the ear, and after that, the towering figure was gone, the yellow hair lost to sight.

Still there was a mad flurry of bodies, a slow and terrible convulsion among those massed figures; the water was sent frothing redly for a little and then, very slowly, it quieted. And the candles gleamed on cursing drenched shapes crawling forth of the pool.

CHAPTER XV

BEATEN down by sheer weight of men, dragged under water, trampled, half strangled and nearly drowned, O'Neill had yet escaped serious hurt, thanks to his mail-coat.

It was some little time before he was brought fully to himself. He had dim visions of terrible things around—dead and hurt men, wounds being dressed, limp dripping things dragged from the pool. Then, presently, the taste of wine in his mouth brought him around, and he could comprehend more clearly. His utter exhaustion, too, passed away. He lifted his head and looked about, after draining the wine-cup a man held to his lips.

He was sitting in one of the chairs, tied down to it. Everything was in mad confusion—the table overturned, half-hiding the body of Carlo Donato, the soft rugs littered with food and dishes and dark with blood. Before him stood Raymond, and sight of the

314

man jerked O'Neill fully to himself. Mary had got clean away, then, with her prisoner! This much at least was good, Carbajal would look after her.

"You must be the devil in person, Don Brian," said Raymond, struggling for self-control, eyeing his captive with bitter hatred. He fell to striding up and down, biting at his nails. To one side O'Neill saw his naked sword. Raymond paused to kick at it. "What a cursed price I'm paying for this blade! You were right about it."

O'Neill said nothing, relaxed, drew air into his lungs. After a moment Raymond swung on him.

"Well, Carlo Donato's out of the way—so is Angelo! You've let Doria and Don Camillo loose—that cursed one-eyed Alfonso is at the Black Bull—he's probably told half Rome that he's alive—everything gone to smash! And all I can do is kill you—"

Raymond talked, half to himself, and a slow smile grew on O'Neill's lips as he comprehended the man's raging impotence. In this moment Raymond beheld his whole carefully built-up fabric smashed beyond repair, the plotting of months and years gone to ruin. Nothing could now retrieve his hopes, for all secrecy had been ripped away from them.

The guard-captain appeared and saluted, with

word that the men were mounted and ready. Raymond, who now wore a sword at his belt, nodded and darted a gloomy look at O'Neill.

"At least," he said, "I'll have that one-eyed rogue back here, and the girl too—and I'll have her torn apart on the rack before your eyes!"

"If you get them alive." O'Neill broke into sudden sharp laughter—and saw he had not been wrong in his surmise. This jeering mirth brought the red into Raymond's face. The one thing to which the man was vulnerable was ridicule. "Oh, wise captain! One man and a woman holding the Black Bull—and you riding against them at the head of your troops! You, who might have been riding to seize Rome itself! Well, either they're gone or you'll not get them alive, be sure of that much."

A passionate fury seized on Raymond. He whipped out a dagger and darted forward—to be checked by a sudden noise of shouting from outside. He turned, poniard in hand, and a cry broke from the captain of the guard, to one side.

"Santinelli, your highness!"

And it was indeed Santinelli who came forward, panting, and then halted with something of his old swagger as he saluted the duke.

316

"Ah, nobilissimo! I've a message for you from that one-eyed devil at the inn. Ha! You've caught this Spaniard, eh?" and he waved his hand at O'Neill. "Well met, señor don! At least I was given liberty and a horse, as you had promised—"

"Name of the devil, are you talking to me or not?" snarled out Raymond, and jerked up the poniard in his hand. "Speak you ruffling fool! What's your message?"

Santinelli was still somewhat drunk, and staggered as he made another bow.

"An invitation, most noble! The one-eyed devil said to tell you that he'd render himself to you in exchange for this yellow-haired man—they think the Venetian's dead, for Monsieur said death was in his voice when he shouted out. I don't know who the one-eyed rascal is, but he said to bear you the message—give up this man unharmed, and he'd surrender to you. Otherwise, come and take him—and it would mean a fight. Ha! He's ready enough for fight, I can tell you—muskets and pistols laid out and loaded, too—"

"Silence, you drunken fool," snapped Raymond, and reflected.

Watching, O'Neill perceived what the answer must

be, for with Carbajal in his hands, no doubt Raymond might hope still to gather some scattered ends of plotting together. O'Neill had no intention of leting Carbajal die for him, but bided his time. Then Santinelli broke in in aggrievedly maudlin tones.

"Don't be threatening me with that poniard, excellency—you know I'm a faithful man. And you'd better let me speak, for I can tell you something, me—"

"Speak, then." Raymond regarded him attentively. "Eh?"

"No use in all this bargaining and exchanging," said Santinelli. "See here, now, I can show you—they've got into the caverns, but the inner door is smashed and they don't suspect anyone could get at 'em that way—understand? They've got the outer door wide open, that's the point. You send the men up to that hillside farm, and have 'em come down through the caverns—they'll jump out in the courtyard and finish the thing in a jiffy—"

A sharp exclamation broke from Raymond. But O'Neill, sitting there tied in the chair, felt the cold sweat start on his face, even under the drip of water from his lank hair. He burst into a sharp mocking laugh.

FAIR EXCHANGE NO ROBBERY

"Aye, there's the way for you, Raymond!" he exclaimed. "Always afraid of me—always talking of what you can do with a sword, yet never standing up to me! Slide behind a curtain when you face me— Raymond, the coward of Corthia!"

He ended with another laugh, and Raymond swung about suddenly, eyes afire.

"Fool—think you can prod me? Well, have it your own way! Devil take me, but I'll exchange you for this Carbajal—I'll finish the thing myself—"

"Ha!" broke out Santinelli. "I forgot to say— you must bring only two men—"

"Go to the devil!" Raymond screamed at him. "Better, get out there and mount, and guide the men to the hillside farm, and show them into the cavern— you know about it. Move, or I'll have you flayed, blast you! Here, captain, get horses ready for us— you and one other man will ride with us. Carry this sword. Quick about it, now! Send off the men— you head them, Santinelli, all of them!"

Raymond was like a madman, and Santinelli paused not to argue, but turned and ran. The captain followed. Raymond darted to the table, seized bottle and goblet, and put down a draught of wine, excitedly.

"Coward, eh?" he cried, shaking his fist at O'Neill. "You accursed outlander, I'll send you back to your father the devil! Aye, you and the girl too—all of you! Nothing matters now, anyway—"

He was gone on the word, running off into the shadows, hurling orders at one of his domestics.

O'Neill sat there, wondering, heard the sharp trampling of hooves outside in the piazza, knew the mounted men were off on their errand. Yet wonder held him above all else—even though he knew that Carbajal and Mary were now caught and done for beyond escape. Himself as well—that was a matter of course.

"To think of it—that a laugh could reach into that man so shrewdly!" he reflected. "If I'd dreamed it before—well, no use thinking of that! Ridicule. A jeer to him is as a slap in the face to any other man; everyone's been afraid of him, the world has stood off from him a long while—Raymond the Terrible! All the time, something in him has been afraid of ridicule, shrinking from it, driving him to cruelty—and now, when he needs it most, driving him to lose his cool and crafty head! Unless, of course, he changes his mind—"

Raymond had not changed—nor had he quite lost

320

his craft either. After a little he came back into the circle of light, kicked aside a wounded man who was groaning, and O'Neill saw the guard-captain and another man following him.

"So you don't like to be laughed at, Raymond?" called out O'Neill. "You're a rather ridiculous figure, after all—full of loud talk, afraid to stand up to the man you've injured—ah, listen to that! Listen!"

Raymond swung around, and the two men behind him turned and peered here and there, for a voice stole out upon them from the darkness of the fringing trees.

"Poor Raymond!" it said, with a thin little laugh. "Poor Raymond! He murdered a boy for a sword, and he's afraid to stand before that sword now! Poor Raymond—might ha' been lord of Rome—"

There was nothing of the fool in Raymond of Corthia. He shot a glance at O'Neill, remembered that voice in the Leghorn garden, and a sudden oath of comprehension burst from his lips.

"Put the gag on him!" he cried furiously to his two men, who were staring and sighing themselves at this voice from the trees. "The gag, fools!"

They obeyed, lumbering forward hastily, the guard-captain holding a gag of leather that was cruel on the mouth of a man yet efficient to keep clear-cut words from his tongue. They clapped it in place, drew it tight, and Raymond stood laughing at his captive, though his flaming eyes took the mirth out of his laugh.

"Montebank!" he jeered at O'Neill. "So that was your game, eh? Well, your game's played out now. Listen, you two!" He swung on his two men. "We ride to the Black Bull. There, we'll find the two companions of this man awaiting us. Understand? Leave the talking to me, do nothing, keep silent and quiet. I'm going to kill this man. When I do it, or before, Santinelli and his men will appear —then seize the other two."

The captain stared. "They'll appear?" he said. "But highness—"

"Devil take you, obey orders!" foamed Raymond in a spasm of sudden fury. "You don't need to understand now—you will soon enough! Free that man, tie his hands behind him, bring that naked sword, and come along! And keep your mouths shut."

He turned and strode toward the entrance. O'Neill,

freed, let his hands be tied behind his back, then followed with his two guards.

The gag had suddenly let down his desperate hoping against hope; after all, Raymond was too clever for him! No way to warn Carbajal now, of those men-at-arms coming through the caverns; no chance, no barest shred of hope—except in what might turn up. That way, one might always manage something.

Out of the garden and palace, the four swung into the saddle of waiting horses, rode across the plaza to the torch-lit gateway, and the men there saluted Raymond as he rode out of Corthia with the others following.

Breathing in the crisp night air, relaxing as he jogged along, letting strength creep back unhindered into his tired nerves and muscles, O'Neill put his brain at work. After all, there might still be a slim, desperate chance! That hillside farm must be somewhere very near the Black Bull, for the underground passages could not go on forever; and the men-at-arms under Santinelli must proceed cautiously along the cavern ways. Thus, being impatient and fired with nervous eagerness, Raymond might well over-reach himself a little in his confidence. If Santinelli's men were slow to appear—well, it would depend on how things fell out, that was all! The gag had changed everything. Remained the one astonishing factor of a jest making Raymond fling himself into the work, despite peril.

O'Neill made sounds in his throat as he rode, so that Raymond turned in the darkness and halted.

"Loosen the gag," he ordered the captain curtly. "Speak, then. What is it?"

"Would you accept my parole not to warn Carbajal that—"

Raymond uttered a harsh laugh. "You think I'm a fool?"

"At least, leave off the gag until we near the Black Bull."

"Leave it off," said Raymond. "But one word of your mountebank work—and it goes on."

They rode forward through the night, silent. Here in the hollows of the hills, away from Corthia, it was cold enough and penetrating. O'Neill, soaked to the skin, clothes all soggy with blood and water, sagged in his saddle and shivered. At length Raymond came to a halt, for he knew every inch of this ground.

"You'll have your fight," he said to O'Neill, and

laughed softly. He was quite himself again. "That is, if you still want it when you get there! Put on the gag."

They put it on again, and Raymond headed them forward.

Five minutes later, a glimmer of ruddy light showed ahead of them—a torch, set outside the gates of the Black Bull. The four rode on, and Raymond halted his men with a word, and then proceeded alone. They could see him ride up under the torch-light, and he lifted his voice in a sharp call.

"Within, there! Open!"

There was a moment of silence. O'Neill could fancy Mary at a window, peering out, Carbajal waiting at the gates. Then these swung open a little, and Carbajal's voice came clearly.

"Ha, Raymond! Bring up Don Brian and your two men. You get a musket-ball if all's not right—"

"Come!" said Raymond, turning and swinging an arm at his men. The three rode forward, and the gates opened a little wider. Carbajal stood there, a pistol in each hand.

"What's this?" he cried out. "Bound?"

"Aye, bound," said Raymond, and looked down at the one-eyed man and laughed. "So, Alfonso of

Ferrara—you'd like to put a bullet into me, eh? Well, don't do it. I'm not accepting your offer of exchange, just yet. Your Don Brian wanted to fight with me, and still wants it. With your permission, we'll enter—and fight. Do you say yes to it?"

Now Carbajal was joined by the figure of Mary O'Neill, and they stared out at the clump of horsemen.

"Why is he gagged?" cried out Mary suddenly. "Treachery here, Carbajal—"

"No treachery—prudence!" said Raymond, and laughed. "If it were treachery, would I be sitting here under your pistols? No, no! But Don Brian fights me gagged or not at all. Ask him if he accepts—ask him if we're here alone! No others follow. Ask him!"

Carbajal spoke out, his eye glittering darkly in the torchlight.

"Is this the truth, Brian? Will he fight with you? Will you fight gagged?"

Raymond turned and looked at O'Neill, who nodded.

"And if I won't have it?" snapped Carbajal suddenly. "Ah Raymond, you crafty devil—some of your tricks here! If I won't have it—"

"Then my men pistol him here and now," said Raymond. "And if you think I'm afraid of your bullets, let fly! Take your choice, my one-eyed duke, take your choice! Let us in, and all's well. Or else your friend stays here in the road."

There was little choice here for Carbajal to make. He stood licking his lips, knowing in his heart that Raymond was somehow tricking him, and yet unable to pierce the stratagem. Through the half-open gates O'Neill and the others could see into the courtyard where the door of the caverns stood open, and the sight of it sickened O'Neill a little. Hopeless, after all! If only Carbajal had thought to swing the outer door shut, and barricade it—yet why should he?

Then, against the great oak tree, showed a dark and grisly thing—the shape of a man leaning against the tree, yet not leaning either. A man, holding in his hand a sword, point to ground—and driven through his throat, driven full into the oak, holding him there, a sword. Raymond caught sight of it, and straightened up.

"What's that!" he demanded, pointing. "One of my men?"

"Aye," said Carbajal with gloomy satisfaction.

"One of your poor dupes, Raymond—your false Alfonso. Tried to fight, he did, but that was the best he could do. Well, then, come in, come in! And if you've more men behind you then you'll be the first to catch a bullet! Back, Monsieur—then watch here at the gates. Some trick about it all—"

He swung the gates open a little wider, so that a horse could pass. Raymond sent his mount forward and rode into the courtyard, and dismounted. Other horses, saddled, stood to one side. Raymond glanced around, looked at the oak tree, shrugged and turned. "Come along," he said pleasantly to his two men. "Bring him in and cut him loose. Don Brian, leave the gag alone—or you know what will happen!"

O'Neill knew well enough, had been weighing the chances of this very act for the past two minutes.

If he took advantage of his freed hands, tried to loosen the gag, tried to warn Carbajal and Mary, the odds were even that he would accomplish nothing. Both of Raymond's men held pistols, and would use them swiftly, swiftly—and on him. It would be wasted effort. Before he could speak, he would be past speaking, despite Carbajal and Mary.

On the other hand, if he acquiesced in Raymond's plan, he had one slim and slender chance of killing

FAIR EXCHANGE NO ROBBERY

Raymond before Santinelli arrived, before the men-at-arms came flooding out of that open door in the hillside. He perceived with what diabolical precision Raymond read his thoughts and counted on just this swing of the balance. Raymond, of course, deemed that no man could stand against him, and perhaps it was the truth; but O'Neill was willing to risk it. Yes, it was well worth assenting, playing the game, staking everything on his own skill and sword-work —and on the element of time!

He saw Carbajal and Mary looking at him, as he dismounted, and he nodded to them. Over his half-open mouth, his gray eyes blazed out strong and sure. Carbajal read the look aright and drew back toward the oak tree, where muskets and pistols waited. Mary O'Neill shut the gates, and Raymond gave her a sardonic smile as she did so—cutting off her own escape. She then joined Carbajal, swiftly. Raymond's two men let O'Neill free and stepped back.

"Give him the sword," said Raymond to his guard-captain, and the man obeyed, putting the naked blade into O'Neill's hand and then hastily retiring.

CHAPTER XVI

SOME MEN CANNOT BE KILLED

O'NEILL, leaning the sword-hilt against his thigh, stood rubbing his hands and looking about. He now, for the first time, realized why Raymond had left him there in the gardens and had run into the palace. For Raymond was wearing another doublet than the one he had worn at dinner.

He chuckled to himself, as he looked at the seamed, anxious face of Carbajal and the wide eyes of Mary O'Neill, and nodded to them. Crafty Raymond! If soggy garments had been left him, the mail-shirt had been left him also—but Raymond had run in, donned a steel shirt himself, donned a velvet doublet above it, and would meet him on even ground. He was not supposed to know it, of course. He would think himself in the advantage—

With a grimace that should have been a laugh, O'Neill rid himself of torn, ripped cloak and doublet, stood with the steel shirt glimmering in the torch-

330

light, his arms bare half to the shoulder. Raymond had tossed aside his cloak, and stood sword in hand, smiling a little, eyes on O'Neill, waiting. Carbajal and Mary, pistols ready and matches alight, were near the oak tree and the terrible figure pinned to it; the guard-captain and his comrade stood at the other side, wheel-lock pistols in hand, watching O'Neill narrowly.

O'Neill put the sword-point on the ground, placed his two hands against the emerald tipped cross-guard, and wrenched. He laughed to himself, despite the gag in his mouth, at the angry surprise in Raymond's face—for the great golden hilt, too heavy for delicate sword-play, came away in two halves, leaving the plain cord-wound handle of the sword. O'Neill tossed the two fragments of gold to Carbajal, made a gesture toward the two soldiers, seized the sword and strode at Raymond, who came to meet him with a snarl and a lunge.

The blades crossed.

Light came from a long torch set in a holder against the rear wall of the courtyard, close to the open door of the hillside. Looking past Raymond, O'Neill saw Carbajal and Mary move aside, withdrawing around the oak tree—then Carbajal had understood his gesture! With this, he put everything else from his mind and attacked Raymond savagely.

On the instant, he perceived he was dealing with a master of the Italian style—yet three years in the Imperial army, three years of practical sword-work against Swedes, French, Poles and Germans, were worth a dozen years of rapier-play in Italy. Grimmest of all masters was war, and the best teacher. After the first two minutes, O'Neill had no doubt of the issue, but he held himself well in check.

Raymond, on his part, had wakened to abrupt caution. If the flicker and clang of the blades, the feel of O'Neill's wrist, told him he had no mean antagonist here, they also warned him to be slow about it. Craft returned to him. Well he had known that no man could long handle the gold-hilted sword, which lacked all balance; now the golden hilt was gone, he saw himself tricked, and played only to wear O'Neill down, tire him out, take full advantage of his water-heavy garments and previous efforts.

Too, Raymond needed time here. He wanted Carbajal alive, not dead, and his consuming hatred of O'Neill would find scant satisfaction in ending matters with one sword-thrust! He must delay everything until Santinelli's men came pouring forth off

332

the hillside—then some would die, but he would have what he wanted. And Raymond, who was no coward, was willing enough to risk himself in the midst of affrays.

So, after the first savage exchange, he felt out O'Neill, played cautiously, throwing out trick after trick of fence, risking nothing. The gates were shut —he had his prey now, no matter what happened! A thin smile played about his lips as he let O'Neill drive in to the attack, and gave ground before it, retreated gradually, let his blade play before him like a shimmering wall of steel.

O'Neill pressed in just hard enough to keep Raymond on the retreat, perfectly comprehending the man's thoughts, content for the instant to run the risk of that open doorway in the hillside. O'Neill was countering craft for craft, now—playing a desperate enough game, but sure at last what he was doing. Now he had driven Raymond away from the tree, out into the center of the court, away from the two soldiers at the gate; back and farther back he pressed him, yet saving his strength for what must come rapidly.

Now, suddenly, swiftly O'Neill threw up his left hand to the gag behind his head, wrenched at the leathern straps, loosened them. Raymond changed countenance; a cry broke from the two watching soldiers, their pistols lifted. Beside the tree, under the dark shadow where the grisly dead shape of Don Alfonso hung, a musket roared out upon the night— and another. The two men by the gate pitched forward, their pistols unfired. Carbajal's wild yell shrilled up.

From Raymond burst a hoarse cry, a wild volley of oaths—he hurled himself forward at O'Neill in a savage and desperate attack, evidently hoping to finish matters before O'Neill could speak. The gag fell away, hung about O'Neill's neck, but for the moment the latter could not speak. Nor had he any chance—Raymond's attack was a very whirlwind of deadly steel driving in. Hoarse panted oaths, stamp of feet on the stones, click and ring of crossing steel —anything, tricks foul or fair, anything to plunge home the dark lean rapier before O'Neill could find voice!

Yet for all his savage skill, Raymond could not get past the glittering circle of the Toledo point, could not get within the firm unswerving wrist behind it; tricks parried, lunges and ripostes futile, sweat springing on his dark face, the man began to perceive he had met his master. Then O'Neill's voice lifted.

"Carbajal! Open the gates—they're coming through the passage—block the door—the gates first! Horses ready—ah! Now for you, Raymond— now!"

With this, for the first time O'Neill really attacked —attacked for the firm olive throat above the black velvet.

"Might have been riding for Rome, poor Raymond!" he exclaimed. "Rome's slipped from your hand now—here's the blade cost you Rome—this blade reaching for you—ha! Close there, Raymond —mark the pool of blood behind you—Alfonso's blood—"

Raymond said nothing, but fought, and fought well, like the master he was. The blades clung, drove in and out, clashed ringingly; the two men behind them were now up, now down, forward and back, sweating, panting steel-tipped men on springs it seemed. More savage grew the dark face of Raymond, more blazing the gray eyes fronting him—for all his skill, O'Neill could not reach home with the thrust he needed.

He was aware that the gates had come open, that

Carbajal and Mary were trying to get the heavy outer door of the cavern closed—then a new light in Raymond's face, a new gleam in the dark eyes, and a queer pouring noise of men shouting and a reverberation of feet. Carbajal yelled something inarticulate.

Raymond drove in madly—O'Neill could not take eyes from that dark and savage glare, could not tell what was passing behind him. The blades clanged, and clanged again. A thrust drove home, and O'Neill staggered, but once more the mail-shirt had saved him. Then, desperate, hearing a sharp cry from Mary, drowned in the roaring explosion of a musket, O'Neill took one wild chance to end it all, knowing the Milan links would save him—he stepped forward, disengaged, let Raymond thrust directly for him, took the lunge full above the heart.

Too late, Raymond tried to shift it upward, and failed; the rapier drove home, bent double as O'Neill deliberately stepped into the thrust. And above it, the Toledo steel glittered, drove out in a lightning lunge. Raymond leaped, but faster than he was the leap of the Spanish blade. His rapier fell on the stones. He stood staring an instant at O'Neill, a dark patch growing on his throat, eyes suddenly

336

bulging. He opened his lips, but blood came instead of words. Then he coughed, and abruptly fell forward on his face.

A crash of muskets and pistols, a spreading plume of whitish powder-smoke, filled the courtyard with sound and fumes.

O'Neill turned, but for the moment he could not move—his own fight was ended, another was forward beside the oak tree, and the utter exhaustion of the reaction held him helpless to move, breathless, spent. Through the smoke clouding the hillside portal he saw the figure of Santinelli plunging headlong, saw Carbajal and Mary emptying musket and pistol into the doorway, saw men falling and heard wild shouts and shrieks vomiting from the caverns. Through the mass of men filling the passage the bullets tore, and more bullets, fast as Carbajal could pick up fresh weapons.

Then fell sudden silence, as the men, unable to face this deadly riddling hail, left the foremost piled at the entrance and shoved back out of danger. Carbajal reached for another musket, then threw up his arm at O'Neill with a shout.

"To horse! Off—both of you—I follow—"

O'Neill found Mary running to him, and with

337

an effort forced himself into action. The gates were open, the startled horses tethered there, Carbajal was busy with his muskets. As Mary came to him and caught his hand in hers, O'Neill shouted once.

"Come—now's the time!"

"Go on, go on!" shouted Carbajal. "Get mounted —I'll fire the train and be with you—"

Ah, the train! O'Neill had forgotten this. He could see the dark scattered mass of powder there, just to one side the piled bodies at the entrance— well, perhaps the train would fire, perhaps it had been scattered in the passage. No matter now, Raymond being dead—all was finished, and the fate of the Black Bull was of no import—better to get away living than bring down destruction and perish in it!

Carbajal emptied another musket, crammed with bullets, into the yawning mouth of the cavern, and a faint yell made answer. Now O'Neill, sword still in hand, had gained the horses with Mary, dragged loose the reins, helped her into the saddle.

"Off with you—make the Pisa highway and wait for us!" he cried, and clapped the horse on the rump. Then he scrambled into the saddle of the second horse, holding the reins of the third. But, as Mary's

338

frightened beast scurried out of the gates, he heard a cry from her, saw her pointing—

He whirled in the saddle, reining in his horse. Too late! He had thought Raymond dead—but that black figure staggering at Carbajal was Raymond in the flesh, holding poniard to strike— striking!

Too late came O'Neill's shout. He saw Carbajal reel sideways, saw Raymond go plunging in at the open door of the cavern, and vanish there. Then, like a flash, Carbajal leaped at the torch, tore it from its socket and brandished it at O'Neill, with a shower of sparks.

"Go, comrade!" he screamed, face contorted, blood pouring from his left side. "Go quickly—'"

And, a wild laugh breaking on his lips, he hurled the torch into the open doorway, past the bodies there. Up flashed a billow of white smoke—and wrenching around his horse, O'Neill drove in his heels and let the maddened animal leap from the gateway. As he went, he heard a faint, shrill screaming of men.

Then the earth shook and thundered.

339

CHAPTER XVII

THE GATE OF LUCCA

THE dusty coach, which had left Pisa that morning, whirled along toward the Strangers' Gate of Lucca—the one gate whereby all strangers could enter or leave this tiny republic, which guarded its liberty so jealously. Then the horses slowed to a walk, for it was seen that a small crowd was about the entrance, blocking it. One of the two cavaliers riding beside the coach went ahead to discover the cause. Presently he came back, reined in beside the open window, and laughed.

"An argument," he exclaimed. "Two travelers who have no *bulletino* want to go through the city, and the guards won't let them—ah! There they are now."

The crowd opened out to give the coach passage. To one side, in obviously hopeless argument with the captain of the guard, were the travelers in question —a slim cloaked cavalier, and another who rode

340

bare-headed, yellow shaggy hair glinting in the sunlight, a naked sword slung at his belt and the rough
peasant's cloak about his shoulders not hiding the
shirt of mail beneath it. At sight of them, a harsh
and dominant voice rang out from the coach.

"Stop! Stop, I say!"

The coach was already stopping, to permit the
cavaliers beside it to show their papers. O'Neill,
furious but helpless, saw the head of Christina of
Sweden thrust from the coach window, and saw her
hand beckon him.

"Here, knight errant—what the devil is your
name? Come here! What's all this fuss?"

He pricked his horse toward the coach, and smiled
a little as he bowed in the saddle. The Swede queen,
of all people!

"Good morning, Your Majesty," he said lightly,
though his face showed somewhat of what he had
passed through lately. "So we meet once more, as
we met first—"

"On the highway," she broke in, with a laugh.
"Do you know you were damned discourteous to me
there in Rome? But so was I to you, and I'm sorry
for it. D'you mean to say these fools won't let you
pass?"

"Not without a bill of health—and I'd have a job getting one," said O'Neill, with an answering laugh.

"Eh? Where'd you come from, then?" demanded Christina. "You weren't in Pisa yesterday or last night—I've been there a whole day! Who's this gallant with you—tut! A woman, or I'm a fool! A woman! Out with it, sir don! Where are you from now?"

"From killing Raymond of Corthia," said O'Neill bluntly, almost desperately.

Christina regarded him attentively for a moment, her eyes startled. She looked him over from head to foot, and her eyes blazed a little at sight of the sword at his thigh. Then she looked at Mary O'Neill, and suddenly put out her hand.

"I'm going to Paris," she said abruptly, "to get some money out of Mazarin. Get in here with me, you! What's your name? Who are you? Why are you with this man?"

Mary O'Neill laughed a little, despite her weariness.

"Why not?" she said. "I hope to be with him all my life."

"There's an answer for you!" cried Christina. "Out of the saddle with you—get in here and ride

342

with me! Don Brian, I'm in your debt. Ride with
me as far as you will, tell me what you've been doing
—killing Raymond, indeed! Come along into town
with me, forgive me what's past, tell me your story—
here! You're a soldier, take my hand and cry quits!"

And leaning out of the door, which she had flung
open, Christina held out her hand to O'Neill. He
leaned over in the saddle and gripped it. Just then
the captain of the guards came up, uncovered,
bowed low.

"Ah, Your Majesty, we did not know you were
coming," he said. "I am sorry I can't allow these
others to enter the city—I have strict orders—"

Christina's eyes blazed. She directed upon the
head of the unhappy officer such curses as he had
doubtless never heard before; English, French, German, Italian, fell from her lips in a stream of liquid
fire.

"Send to the Duke, you fool!" she continued.
"I'll have your head for this—so my friends can't
come with me, eh? What do my papers call for,
imbecile? Either they pass with me, or I stay here
until your Duke and Senate come to beg my pardon
—"

"Your Majesty," broke in the officer, bowing

again, "for the love of the saints, say no more! They may pass."

"Get in," said Christina, and held open the door for Mary O'Neill.

THE END

www.ingramcontent.com/pod-product-compliance
Lightning Source LLC
Chambersburg PA
CBHW032234010726
47494CB00002B/492